John O'Donnell grew up in the small town of Gort Co. Galway in the west of Ireland. He graduated from Mary Immaculate College in 2017 and has worked as a primary school teacher since. A lover of all things that have to do with fantasy since he was young, John has always aspired to be an author. If he isn't spending time with his family and friends, he can often be found reading, writing, or drawing. He has always loved to immerse himself into new worlds where the possibilities are endless. He wrote his debut novel 'Wolf-Blessed' over the lockdown in 2020.

Wolf-Blessed

John O'Donnell

Wolf-Blessed

Vanguard Press

A CIP catalogue record for this title is
available from the British Library.

ISBN 978-80016-541-0

*Vanguard Press is an imprint of
Pegasus Elliot Mackenzie Publishers Ltd.*
www.pegasuspublishers.com

First Published in 2024

**Vanguard Press
Sheraton House Castle Park
Cambridge England**

Printed & Bound in Great Britain

I would like to dedicate this book to two people. Firstly, to my sister, Claire, who has always stood by me in whatever endeavour I take part in. Secondly, to my fiancé, Ross, who inspires me and pushes me to pursue my dreams even when I doubt myself. Thank you both for everything, and always being my biggest fans.

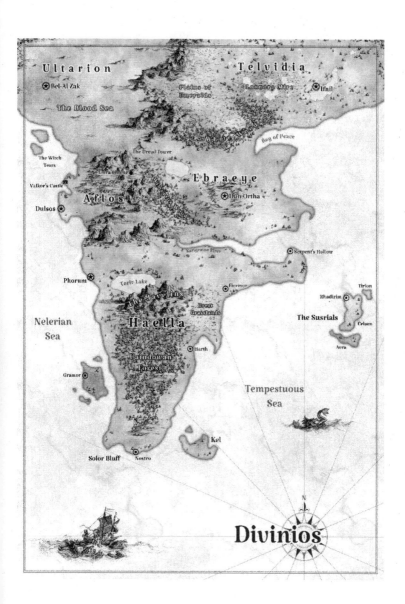

Chapter 1

The leaves had begun to transition from the emerald tones of summer into the warm autumnal shades of red, orange and gold. There was still a warmth in the air, keeping the creatures of the Uaindowan Forest stirring. The prints of their hooves and paws covered the earth, adding a clue to the presence of life within the forest. From the edge of the trees you might think that there was nothing alive within its density, but the rare snap of a branch or flapping of wings alerted those nearby to their existence. Mothers searched the deep forest for food while their young tread curiously alongside them. A lone fox lurked in the brush, his golden eyes alert to his surroundings. Birds of all kinds darted between the soil and high branches, carrying worms and beetles to eat in peace. This was their home, here they felt safe.

It was near the edge of the slow-moving river that most of these animals lived. The water was clear and cool, a vital resource for those living there. It meandered like a serpent along the length of the forest, being fed from Torir Lake to the north. It drew them to it to quench their thirst, but also allowed them to hunt. The predators stalked their prey unbeknownst to them among the undergrowth which bordered the river. The bushes allowed them to creep closer and closer until they could pounce on the unknowing beast. The final squeal or grunt were often heard along the riverbank as teeth and claws sank into flesh.

But it wasn't only the animals that were hunting. The forest gave cover to another hunter — man. Crouched near the ground, using the foliage to hide her was the hunter. Slung across her back was a cylindrical iron quiver housing the arrows that were intended for the heart of some creature, deer, she hoped. It was a fine art to be silent in a place where everywhere you stepped was a twig to snap, a leaf to crunch or a stone to kick. Careful and surefooted, she made her way through the forest scanning her surroundings in search of her next target. But the forest was like her second home. Each step along the path she knew for she had walked it a hundred times. Her boots had met the earth beneath them many times. They guided her further and further into its depth where she knew the best prey roamed.

The wet mud on the riverbank proved to be an ally as she made out the prints of animal hooves, they were fresh. Their marks had not yet been washed away or trampled by something else. This animal was close and going south. Not the direction she had hoped for; the further south you go the less cover there was as the wooded landscape slowly turned to open grassland that any deer could outrun a human. Today, the hunter decided to leave her horse behind where she had entered the forest, she preferred the art of a silent kill rather than the chase. A slight feeling of regret came over her but was quickly extinguished as her pace increased. She made her way down river looking for any other signs of the animal, antler markings on the trees, hair caught on a briar but nothing. The ground, blanketed by fallen leaves, covered up any more prints from the animals' hooves. A curse quietly was released from her lips. Returning home empty handed was not on her list of things she enjoyed, she could just hear the mocking's of her two oldest brothers. Even though she had come home triumphant many times with game or fish, they still enjoyed mocking her when she did not. Their little sister Arica who tried so hard to be big and strong. The thought placed a grimace on her face. She did not try, she was. She would return and slam the animal on their beds in pride or perhaps indignation. Determination fuelled her, there was no way she was going to go home and endure their taunts.

Out of the corner of her right eye there was a reddish flash of something amongst the trees. Within a second she had pulled out a white fletched arrow and had it ready to imbed into the animal's hide. Her eyes focused, *where are you?* Remembering the lessons from her father, she held her breath to help keep the bow still. The bow rested in her hand, her arm straight. The drawstring was pulled back taut, her elbow pointing sideways. A snap directly in front of her guided her body and she let the arrow fly in that direction. The sharp whistle of the arrow ended in a blunt thud and a cry. A hit. What started as a jog towards the kill, suddenly became a sprint as the animal with an arrow protruding from its hind leg jumped up and began bounding away. With a grunt of frustration, Arica ran as fast as she could after it while reaching behind her for another arrow. The deer was bigger than she expected, not a doe but lacked the large antlers of a fully developed male. She was in pursuit of a young buck. The ground shook from the stomping of hooves and feet running for life and kill, respectively.

The thickness of the forest allowed her to keep up with the deer as he had to keep twisting and turning to avoid crashing into large rocks or tree trunks. Her smaller size made it easier to manoeuvre amongst the obstacles. She jumped over a fallen tree and onto another firing another arrow at the frantic buck. Her foot slipped and this time the arrow did not find its target. She hit her fist against the tree as a shout of disappointment burst out of her. *You are not getting away*. The chase continued through the forest, suddenly much more alive than earlier. The breaking of branches, splashing of water and cries of other smaller animals fleeing created a symphony of noise. The adrenaline pushed her on. She would succeed.

This method was not going to work, however. It was clear that a human could not keep up with a deer forever, she needed to think of something. Her eyes dashed from side to side, looking for anything that could become an advantage for her. She had already tried standing on a fallen trunk, but perhaps that was not high enough. If she attempted to climb any of the trees that would waste far too much time. By the time she reached the branches and notched an arrow, there would be nothing to hit. Then she saw it; up ahead at the base of a hill were three rocks varying in size. When looked at from the right direction they resembled steps. This was the answer. She kicked the earth beneath her boots behind her as she ran. Her bow swinging at her side as she quickened her pace, her chest beginning to hurt. With an effort she launched herself for the first rock and landed on it, less than gracefully, but landed, nonetheless. She pulled herself up onto the second rock and looked for the deer. She could still see him bounding parallel to her. She still had time. Quickly, she jumped up and grabbed the edge of the final rock and hoisted herself up. Once standing, her arm automatically grasped another arrow, and she took careful aim. Her arm drew back the string until it was tight. Her lungs filled with air, steadying her. *Fly true.* She loosed the arrow. A final shriek.

Standing over her kill, she was filled with pride and shortly after, exhaustion. She chastised herself about her initial arrow. *You could have saved yourself a LOT of trouble if you just aimed properly.* Now the distance home was much further. Had she been closer, she would have skinned and butchered the animal then and there, but she was not going to carry it all the way back. The hunter raised two fingers to her lips and blew long and hard. That signal would be hugely helpful right now if it was heard. She removed her two arrows, wiped them on her sleeve and placed them back into the quiver. There was no point in wasting materials, too expensive. Her father always told her the importance of cleaning your blade and arrows. They would rust and be nothing more than a blunt stick. It was almost a ritual to her at this point, always making time for the maintenance. She decided to sit down and wait to see if her call would be answered. She twiddled with her hunting blade as she waited, tossing it into the air and catching it. Knives and arrows were always her go to when it came to hunting. Her brothers all used arrows too but preferred throwing axes or spears instead of blades.

'You'll never kill an animal with those tiny knives,' her oldest brother, Garo, would say.

We'll see about that, she always said to herself.

Twenty minutes or so passed and just as she was beginning to lose hope, she heard the sound she was hoping for. The rhythmic thumping of hooves was a welcome noise. Through the dense forest, she began to see glints of gold and white. The beautiful colours seemed starker amongst the dark brown of the tree trunks. Now standing, the hunter whistled again to show her location. The thumping quickened and soon the hunter was greeted by her horse, a beautiful palomino stallion. A gift from her father for her twelfth birthday. He was the envy of her brothers as they had not received something nearly as magnificent as their own horse. It was a favourite hobby of hers to ride passed her brothers and smile down at them from the saddle. Her mother also had not been happy upon his arrival as she did not think they could afford him. Her father claimed he was a workhorse to help with deliveries or to pull the cart on long journeys. But she had yet to see her horse do either. They greeted each other as they always did, she hugging his muzzle and him whinnying. His golden coat shimmered as it caught the sunlight appearing in the cracks of the canopy layer. She admired his white stockings that somehow still remained a brilliant white. She laughed. Sometimes she thought the horse must take a bath in the sea or river to ensure he was always so clean.

'Good, Sundancer,' she smiled.

The stallion nickered and nudged her gently with his head. Arica petted him from forehead to muzzle before getting to work. In a few short minutes the deer was strapped across Sundancer's croup. After pulling on the straps to ensure it was tied down properly, she placed a foot in a stirrup, threw her leg over Sundancer and was sitting in the saddle. She gently tapped her foot against him, and they began the journey home.

Chapter 2

The return journey was not a great distance from the forest. She enjoyed this part of hunting as she got to see the beautiful scenery that surrounded her home. The forest was to the west of the town that she grew up in. It bordered the Nelerian Sea, one of two seas that lay either side of the landmass of Haella. The Tempestuous Sea was to the east, which separated her country from the three islands known collectively as the Susrials. She'd heard stories about them when she was young; her grandmother loved to entertain her for hours telling stories and talking about the myths of their land. It was said, she told her, that the Susrials were the birthplace of the legendary Queen Lyneer who reigned during the Enlightened Age. These were her favourite stories, where Queen Lyneer, alongside her trusted companion and lover Irielle, defeated hordes of monstrous beasts that crawled out of fissures that appeared all across their world. The queen wielded not just a sword but also something amazing - magic. She fought with Irielle and slayed beast after beast using steel and sorcery. As a girl, the hunter was enamoured by these stories, but now as she entered her seventeenth year, she knew they were just that, stories.

Just then her home appeared on the horizon. She could make out the tall, grey watchtower that marked the entrance to the town. Her middle brother, Kal, worked as a guard there. He thought himself to be a real man when he was assigned that position after the Trial. *Only real men get chosen to protect their homes* was what he said to their family that night. Garo scoffed at him saying that he was no more of a man than he was. He worked in the centre of town as a tailor. Both good and respectable jobs but that was the hubris of boys who deemed themselves to be men before they really were. When their incessant bragging began, that was the time that her youngest brother, Malin, would take her hand or give a look with his eyes that meant it was time to escape. He was not one for their bickering either. He was the only one of her brothers that did not partake in the mocking or boasting. The two of them were quite close and could often be found whispering in the attic of their house that was also her bedroom. They would tell each other all about their day and any news or gossip they came across. He worked in the local tavern, so he usually had a lot more stories to tell than her, but he liked talking so that was never an issue between them.

She rode her horse through the gate of the town waving two fingers at the guards on duty. They saluted her back and nodded at her bounty strapped to Sundancer. She felt a sense of accomplishment as she glanced back at the buck. Her foot gently tapped the horse's flank, urging him on down the main street of the

19

town towards her family's home. The street was full of people making their way to work and running errands. People made their way from shop to shop with their baskets full of goods. Children ran across the streets shouting and laughing as they played together. Others walked to and from their work assignments. For a small town it seemed to be bustling. She turned down a side street and stopped in front of a large wooden door. After dismounting from Sundancer, she unlocked the door and slid it open to reveal a small stable with two stalls - one empty and the other that housed Primrose, the family's brown cow. Without wasting any time, she took the buck off her horse and left it on a table next to his stall. She slowly led her horse into the stall, removed the saddle from his back and the bit from his mouth. He nickered quietly and licked his lips. She grabbed his blanket from the shelf and spread it across him.

'Good boy,' she said lovingly, hugging his muzzle.

She walked towards the door also giving the cow a rub on her forehead. She always had an affinity for animals. Her mother told her that when she was a toddler, she would play with the street dogs before even looking at another child. Sometimes she would still rather spend her time with those dogs than the other young people in town. They had not always been the kindest to her while growing up. The girls shunned her for acting too much like a boy, so she tended to spend her time with the boys. But as they grew older, they began to prefer the attention of the other girls rather than hers. As a result, she often found herself alone.

As she stepped into her house, the smell of cooking hit her. A fusion of spices filled the air with beautiful aromas that made her imagine faraway places. She guessed that today's meal would be chicken stew. Her mouth began to salivate at the thought of dinner. Her assumption was proved correct as she turned the corner into the kitchen. Her mother stood next to the fire, stirring a pot. She had her usual tan apron wrapped around her waist and tied in a tidy bow behind her back. Her auburn hair was pulled back into a bun to keep the hair out of her face while she was working. This was a scene that filled her with joy, she loved seeing her mother like this because she was always so happy when cooking.

'Are you just going to watch me or help with the vegetables?' her mother teased.

She laughed and made her way to the knives, grabbed the sharpest one and began chopping the carrots and parsnips. She sliced them into thick chunks, the way her father liked them. Once she had finished, she brought the chopping board to the pot and dumped them in. She wiped the knife clean before placing it back into the drawer. The next job was to set the table, she began doing it before her mother had the chance to give the order. Taking out enough cutlery for her family, she walked to the table and laid them out.

After about an hour, the food was ready and steaming on the table ready to be devoured by her family of seven. Her father sat at the head of the table, her mother at the opposite end. She sat in her usual spot, to her father's left. Malin flanked her, with their grandmother to his left. Her two other brothers sat at the other side of the table. This was their usual dinner routine on the days that Kal's guard duty did not clash. Everyone started to dig into the food. The chicken was beautifully seasoned and tasted amazing. She told her mother so, much to her delight.

'I'll teach you the recipe whenever you like, Arica.'

That was her mother's dream, for her to be a homemaker like her, but she didn't want that life. It was too mundane for her. She would rather be outside with the wind blowing across her face, rain splashing her cheeks or the sun tanning her skin. Nothing made her feel more alive than when she had her bow and riding Sundancer.

'Maybe you can teach Malin, he loves to cook,' Arica said, 'and he's much better than me anyway.'

'Yes, I'd love to learn, Mother,' he chimed from beside her.

Their mother nodded as she took a bite of her food. The offer was always there for Arica but whenever Malin's interest came up it was met with silence. As a man he was expected to go out and earn a living; being a homemaker was not an option as far as their mother was concerned.

After dinner, Arica made her way up the two flights of stairs to her bedroom in the attic. Being the only girl in the family had its privileges. Her three brothers shared a room downstairs, next to her parents' room. Their grandmother had her own room on the ground floor of the house. The best part of her bedroom was the large bay window that she perched on looking at the rooftops of the neighbouring buildings. It was up high enough that she could see beyond the town walls. The rolling plains that surrounded the town's northern side went on forever. Arica had never been beyond the horizon line in that direction, only as far as the forest to the west and sea to the south when her father made a rare trip to Haella's most southerly town, Nostro. Sometimes when she was younger, her father would bring her and her brothers with him and allowed them to play along the beach while he conducted business.

There was a knock, and she turned her head to see Malin's head poking up from the stairs up to the room. She waved him over to her. He strolled over and sat down next to her. They simply stared at each other for the first few minutes. Arica knew why Malin had come up to see her this evening. The nervous feeling in her stomach started to bubble. *Just come out and say it,* she said to herself.

'How do you feel?' he said quietly.

'Like the entire contents of my stomach is going to end up on the floor.'

'If you wouldn't mind facing the other direction then,' he said laughing.

Arica managed to push out a short chuckle.

Her brother had a gift for making her relax, even if it was just a little bit.

'Honestly, I don't know,' she admitted. 'On the one hand I'm terrified but— I'm also excited?'

'I understand, I was too.'

He had gone through the same ordeal as her two years previous. Garo and Kal, three and five years respectively before that. Each of them had prepared for the ordeal that everyone in their town dealt with once they had reached the age of seventeen. That was her age now, which meant that tomorrow's Trial would include her. The Trial had been a tradition in her town for over a hundred years and everyone participated in it because if not they would be exiled. It was almost blasphemous to even consider not taking part. But she did not have that problem, she wanted to be a Trialist more than anything.

The Trial consisted of three parts, each more difficult than the last. During the Trial everything would be tested, strength, speed, instincts, and sometimes survival. It would determine who the apex members of the town were; if you can't complete the Trialthen you are eliminated. The aim of it all was to decide where you belonged in their small society. If you cannot make it through the first test, you go back home and are assigned to a job that suits your skills or just where you are needed at the time. That was how Malin ended up working in the tavern. He hated the noise and antics that came along with tavern work. He longed to be reassigned but that rarely happened.

If you get passed the second Trial it means you'll be conscripted into the town guard. Kal had wanted to complete the entire Trial but a loose rock sent him tumbling into the river during the final test, thus ending his dream. He claimed that he was delighted to be a town guard and that he could not wish for a better profession. Only that was not his attitude the day before the Trial.

The third trial however could mean something brilliant. The passing of this test meant that you would become a part of something bigger, a part of the imperial army of the King of Haella. That was her dream. She would make it happen in any way she could. Arica had been training for it for as long as she could remember. When the other girls were playing with dolls, she was practicing sword fighting by using a stick. She rode her horse almost every day, always trying to perfect her balance. She helped her father lift heavy items onto the cart despite her mother's protests that girls need not do so. It meant everything to her to become a part of the army. The Trial was an annual event but they were different in some way, year after year. Last year it was water themed. All of the tests took place in or around Torir Lake or the sea her town was built beside. She wondered where her Trial might take place; she hoped for the forest, she would pass any test thrown at her while in there. It would be the perfect location as she already knew every section of it. All she could do was pray to the gods that wherever the Trial may be, that she would succeed.

Before Arica knew it, the sun had set and her room was pitch black. Malin told her goodnight and said he would see her in the morning. As his footsteps sound grew less and less loud, she climbed into her bed and rested her head against the pillow. Tomorrow was the beginning of a new chapter in her life. Tomorrow would be the start of a future she had been dreaming about for years. Her eyes slowly closed; her mind full of possibilities of what was to come.

Chapter 3

Arica left her house early the next morning. The excitement and nervousness kept her tossing and turning for most of the night. She tumbled out of her bed at the first sign of sunshine. The light creeped in through the crack of the thin curtains pulled across the bay window. All she wanted to do was get in some practice before having to make her way to the site of the Trial. The shipping dock seemed like a good location to do some training, there wouldn't be anyone working today. Trial Day was a national day where no one was expected to work, they were meant to spectate. She was outfitted with her bow, quiver and knife — her usual companions. She said a silent prayer to her favourite of the gods, Merenia, goddess of the hunt. Every village, town and city in Haella had a temple that worshipped one or more of the gods. While not everyone still participated in the old traditions, they were still present in Haella and across the entire of Divinios. In Harth, her home, they had an affinity for the gods of the sea and trade. But she had always looked up to Merenia. A beautiful, flaxen haired woman who wielded a bow made of white oak with the ability to hit anything she aimed for. A great white wolf at her side in every depiction. She was the epitome of strength and grace; everything Arica wanted to have and be. It was the reason she took up archery. The goddess was a strong and beautiful female that was respected by women and men alike. Arica wanted to be treated the same. Someday, a little girl would want to be a soldier and Arica would be her role model.

Standing at the dock, she looked around for some potential targets. Wooden crates and barrels were spread all around the area. *No, they won't do*. She needed something that would pose some challenge, a stationary target would not suffice. A rat was scuttling across the ground close to a granary, she thought about it momentarily but decided against it. Her eyes scoured all around her. Then she noticed high above was the pulley used to lift crates off the ships that docked in the harbour. The breeze was blowing it from side to side, the hook shifted and turned slowly. They were going to be as good as anything. She drew an arrow, running the feathers through her fingers. The arrow was notched, a deep inhale, and it was let loose.

The screaming of the crowd made it seem like the ground was shaking. The vibrations of their voices filled the air. Now, the sick feeling in her stomach was beginning to return. She started to breathe slowly and deeply, trying to calm her nerves. Malin, Garo and her parents were standing next to her, wishing her luck. Kal was on duty, he was to stand next to the leader of their town, Lord Valkor. It was among the many

28

responsibilities of the lord to preside over the Trial each year. He sat atop a large chair, not grand enough to be called a throne but certainly not the type that Arica would find in her house. The audience sat along tiered seating set up specifically for the Trial. A loud drum was beat once, twice, a third time; this signified that they were set to start. Her parents kissed her cheeks.

'Good luck, my love,' her mother said brushing an auburn hair out of Arica's face.

'Take this, for good luck,' her father said, handing her something small.

She looked down and saw a small circular, brass pin. There was a wolf with a rose under its paw carved into it. It was beautiful. She recognised it, she had seen it in her house.

'Your grandmother asked me to give it to you, she's sorry she can't be here,' he told her.

Arica kissed the pin and attached it to her tunic.

'Do us proud, Ari,' Garo said to her with a smile.

Malin was the last to wish her luck. He had a tear in his eye. As he wrapped his arms around her, she also found her eyes beginning to well up. She had been waiting for this day for so long, and Malin knew that better than anyone.

'Remember, you have been training for this since you could run, and can conquer anything you put your mind to,' Malin said, assuring her.

They broke their hug and he walked away to the stands with the rest of his family, leaving his sister behind among the rest of the trialists.

Lord Valkor stood up tall, making himself look bigger than he was. His moderately broad body appeared to increase in size when he straightened himself up and pushed out his chest. He had a reputation for acting princely despite only being a named lord of the kingdom. He was an ordinary man from the town, no richer or more important than the average person, so it was suspicious when he was announced to be the new Lord. The people thought he must have blackmailed someone or had some tie to the king's inner circle. Whatever it was, it was something behind closed doors. Arica didn't trust him; the way his mouth was in a permanent frown unsettled her. His eyes were the worst part, so cold and icy that they could pierce your soul from miles away. He cleared his voice and began his speech.

'People of Harth, welcome to the great and wondrous event that we Harthians and people of Divinios have celebrated for over a century. It is a great tradition in which we honour our heritage by taking part in tests that will determine our strengths, our weaknesses—, our truth. Our young demonstrate their bravery and their intelligence. Anyone can be a part of the Trial, but not everyone can be champions. According to Haellan law, and under the rule of His Imperial Highness, King Solomir the Glorious, the first five to complete the Trial will be bestowed a special gift. A gift that is worth more than a tonne of gold. The privilege and glory of entering into the imperial army. To become an Amber Lion is a blessing that not even the gods could bestow.'

At this, people started to mutter in disbelief. The once reverent power of the gods had waned over the years but there was still a substantial portion of people who believed in them. Even if you did not believe, you were still respectful. She was one of them that still believed. Her whole family did. The temple in Harth that paid respect to many of the gods was still used and visited each day by many families. Another reason for Arica to distrust him. A leader should respect all the beliefs of the people, not just his own. But then, she did not think of Lord Valkor as much of a leader. She quickly realised something else, what did he mean by the first five?

He cleared his throat. He made a look at Kal and the other guard who then lifted their spears and banged them against the wooden floor. The spectators quickly quietened down, one thing you didn't want to do was make Lord Valkor angry. He had a habit of making those who disagreed with him end up in the cells beneath his manor or just disappear.

'Now, we may begin,' he announced. 'Welcome to all of our courageous trialists today who come here to display their skills and abilities. I now invite you all to come forward and state your name.'

The trialists began to step forward and call out their names in loud, strong voices to make them appear bigger. She watched twenty other young people from Harth introduce themselves to the masses and finally it was her turn.

'Arica Preandre, daughter of Garvin and Ramira.'

She stood back as the final few entrants introduced themselves. She found her eyes drifting to the stand to get a final look at her parents and brothers. They knew how much she had looked forward to this day. She had bragged how she would pass every test without so much as lifting her finger, but now that the day had finally arrived, she was not so sure. She looked around at the others, she had known them her whole life. They had been schooled together, grew up alongside each other, and now she had to beat them. If she wanted her wish to come true, no one was going to grant it for her. She had to claim it for herself.

Once the last person had stepped forward and called out their name, Lord Valkor continued his speech. He started to explain that this year, there was going to be a special Trial. This year there would not be the usual three tests, but only one great one. He explained that over the previous few years the talents of the trialists had dwindled and that was because of indolence.

'For years this, once sacred, event has become a mockery,' he bellowed. 'We embarrass ourselves in the eyes of our glorious sovereign by sending weaker and weaker people—. Now we will only send five.'

The gasps could have been heard for miles. These were soon followed by shouts of disagreement and anger. Arica could feel the outrage, the burning emotions of her fellow competitors seemed to spread over the crowd. Lord Valkor continued his speech over their voices.

'You will have five hours, one for each of the possible winners, to successfully track and kill one of the black deer found in the Javelins. They are a symbol of Haella. To catch one would show your prowess and prove your worth.'

Arica had seen these mountains before while in the forest, they were like giant spears jutting out from the earth. The uneven and jagged stones gave the treacherous mountains their name. The deer lived high above the treetops that grew along the base of the mountains. Five hours would be cutting it close. She could not waste any time.

As soon as he finished explaining the task, he directed everyone's attention towards a podium to his left. Something was beneath a black shroud. He snapped his fingers, and his guard pulled it off to reveal an hourglass filled with white sand. This was our official timer. We had to get there and back within five hours. Time was everything in this challenge. It was going to take a miracle. With a final look at the trialists, Lord Valkor grasped the hourglass and flipped it over.

Chapter 4

She held on tightly to his mane as they barrelled towards the foot of the mountains. The sound of Sundancer's hooves thundering against the hard earth filled her ears. The sands were falling in that hourglass, and she had to beat it. Lucky for her, she had a horse of her own; some of the other trialists did not. As she called for her horse, she watched as others flailed about shouting at the crowd begging to borrow one. She scolded herself that she did not ride to the starting line, that decision set her back a few minutes. She knew she should have been more prepared and had saddled him before she left. Now there was nothing but a blanket between herself and Sundancer's body. Her legs would be weak after riding to the mountain and back. She decided to cut through the forest rather than go around it. It would save valuable time. Sundancer flew through the thick density as he had run here many times before. All of the days she spent in the forest had paid off. Other trialists tried the same, some got lost and a screech alerted her that one even rode into a branch and was knocked off their horse. The first fall of the competition. The sick feeling of urgency bubbled in her stomach. She did not think this would be a feeling that would come over her during this. Worry. Lethargy. Even fear. But now all of these combined with the exigencies of the challenge had changed things. Before, you just had to worry about finishing, now, it was a race.

As she reached the mountain, she scanned to see what would be the quickest way up. The mountain appeared to be the least steep where the river flowed into the forest. She nudged Sundancer in that direction and they cantered towards it. Arica turned her horse up the mountain, following the snake-like curves of the river. She could see other trialists making their way up in other locations. All of their heads darting around to watch for incoming competition. No one had taken the same route as her, whether that was good or bad she had not decided. She praised Sundancer and patted his thick, strong neck as he brought them further and further towards the peaks of the Javelins. The trees of the forest were like veins on the mountains, curling around them. She imagined they would seem like they were throbbing from the sky because of the breeze.

The ground began to get more uneven the higher they climbed. Sundancer's front hooves slipped on the gravel; he let out a shriek of panic.

'I guess that means it's time to part,' Arica said as she climbed down off him.

She left him next to a tree where there was a patch of grass that he could graze on as he waited. After hugging his muzzle, she turned away and began the ascent. She pushed forward while keeping a steady

35

pace. It would not serve her well to slip and break a leg. Half of the mountain still lay between her current location and the summit. Still no sign of the black deer.

Following another twenty minutes of climbing, her legs were beginning to tire from the constant incline. The slope appeared to never have an ending, it kept going as she did. Even when her head was pointing straight up, she could still not see the top. A halo of clouds swirled around the peak. *Please let me come across one cursed deer before having to get up there.* The ground was not soft enough to leave any tracks so she would have to rely on less beautiful clues. Arica made her way into a thicker section of trees where there would be some cover. The ground here was lain with twigs and leaves. Crouching, she inspected a nearby bush; tiny red berries dotted the foliage. Her first indication that her target could be nearby. Out of the corner of her eye she noticed something thin and dark stuck to a leaf. Carefully, she picked up a loose black hair. Finally, a sign. The deer had to have come this way.

She went towards the eastern side of the mountain. Her footsteps quiet against the ground, trying to approach without being heard. The trees were becoming sparser as she progressed. She kept herself to the shade, concealment was critical. She held her head up high as she heard a snap behind her. Whipping her head to the left she saw a glimpse of what she was searching for. Running through the trees and around her, the deer bounded up the mountain. She had no choice now; running was her only course of action. With a grunt, Arica kicked her feet against the ground trying to keep up with the deer. A feat she knew that would not be possible for long. It was clear why these deer were sacred animals, its beautiful black hair shined as the sunlight hit it making it almost appear a midnight purple. The deer was flying into the air by bouncing off its powerful hind legs. *How am I going to catch this beast?* Her training had prepared her for the chase but not the terrain, she had never run long-distance on a mountain. She hoped none of her opponents had either. The deer weaved between the tall pine trees, trying to shake its assailant. Determination was fuelling Arica, she could taste victory. She reached her hand behind her and pulled out an arrow. She notched it and let loose. The arrow sailed through the air towards the deer. It flew above the deer's head, and she let out a curse.

Her footing went from under her against the loose gravel, resulting in her tumbling down the mountainside. Arica let out a scream as she clung to the ground to stop her from going any further. She grunted as she pushed herself up. A new cut marked her forearm, not too deep but would need to be bandaged. As she stood up, she searched for the deer, it was gone. She let out an exasperated sigh. *How much time has gone? It must be over an hour*. Time was speeding past her and all she had done was waste an arrow and injure herself. She set off again in the direction that she had last seen the deer. It had sprinted around a bend in the mountain and was now out of sight. Her boots flicked stones behind her as she hurried after the animal. She clambered her way around the bend, making sure not to fall again. When she arrived at the other side, she could not believe her eyes. This part of the Javelins did not suit its name. Where the rest of the mountain ended in spear like peaks, this part was a plateau. The plateau was covered in grass, with yellow wildflowers. A few more pines dotted the ground, casting long, thin shadows across it. A small pool of water sat to the western edge of the plateau. Underneath a pine on the opposite side, right in plain sight was the black deer she had been searching for. It was almost too easy. She took out another arrow and set it against her bow. She said a silent prayer to Merenia that her shot would be true. The goddess of the hunt would guide her arrow to its mark. She sucked in a sharp breath and closed one eye as she took aim. *One... two...*

The next thing she knew she was flat against the ground. There was a throbbing pain in her back. The wind had been knocked out of her chest. She shrugged her shoulders and propped herself up on her elbows. Standing next to her were a pair of dusty, black boots. She raised her head up to see the familiar face of Ronin Bryt. A boy she had grown up with, went to school with. His wavy brown hair was flicking against his forehead in the wind. But what unsettled her was the look in his eye, almost happy. She stood up and brushed the dirt off her.

'What was that for?'

'You're my competition, and you got in my way,' he said slyly at her.

He started to run towards the deer, his feet thudding against the ground rhythmically. He had not run ten steps when he was stopped by a tackle from another trialist, Ivon. They both tumbled to the ground, punching at each other. Ronin crashed his knuckles against his attacker's jaw. Ivon clasped his hands around Ronin's neck and rolled on top of him. She could see Ronin's face start to go purple from the lack of air. She screamed at them to stop. This did not happen in the Trial. Yes, it was a competition, sometimes a fight, but not to the death. Ronin pushed his hands up and dug his thumbs into Ivon's eyes.

Arica couldn't take her eyes off the brawling animals on the ground. Suddenly, two shapes appeared climbing onto the plateau from opposite sides. Another boy and a girl ran onto the grass, their eyes searching for a target. The deer was not even there any more; somewhere between her being tackled and the brutal fighting on the ground it must have bolted away. She watched the new trialists run at each other. The boy slammed his shoulder into the girl's, and she crumpled to the ground like an autumn leaf. *What is going on? They're acting like they're possessed.* The boy's eyes were on her now and he was running straight for her.

She quickly rolled to her right to avoid contact. Before he could retaliate, he let out a roar of pain. At first, she was confused, but then saw another trialist standing behind him. Selaena Bilgard had a look of hate in her eyes, and a knife with another's blood on it. The wounded trialist clutched his thigh as he swung his leg around and kicked Selaena's ankle. She fell down, dropping her knife.

Before Arica knew it, there were ten trialists fighting viciously atop the plateau. Some of them had weapons and had managed to leave gashes on their targets. Wherever she looked there were boots meeting stomachs and fists hitting chins. She rolled out of the way as Ivon swung his elbow at her face. She jumped over a leg that was heading for her ankle. She took a few steps back and watched the chaos in front of her. These were not the people she knew from growing up. This new altered Trial had birthed something evil in them. The Trial was never meant to be a competition, it had always been a display of a person's individual skills. But now, it was giving an excuse to people to give way to their darker impulses. Arica wanted to win but not at this cost. She wondered where the other trialists were. Had some of her fellow competitor's used their weapons on them before they climbed the mountain? Or before they had even reached it at all? Becoming an Amber Lion meant everything to these people, and they were all willing to kill for it.

Arica's thoughts were proven right when she found herself in the middle of all the fighting. Their slams into each other pushed them closer and closer to her until in an instant she was standing in the centre of it all. Their fists, kicks, and shouts were creating a savage cacophony that made her think her ears would bleed. Her head was starting to hurt. She put her palm against her forehead, sweat awash. She quickly managed to push away Ronin's fist as he tried to smash her nose. A kick to the stomach knocked him further back. The kick came from fiery-eyed Selaena. Her fury turned its attention to Arica.

'I'm going to be a Lion and you can't stop me!' Selaena screamed with a ferocity that Arica had never seen.

She launched at Arica with both hands, digging her nails into her shoulders. They tossed on the ground. Arica felt a claw across her neck, and she let out a howl of pain. She thrust her knee into Selaena's ribs and swiftly crawled away, finding her footing once again. The pain in her head began to flare again, stronger, and more intense than before. The arrows had all fallen out of her quiver and she had lost her bow somewhere amongst the madness. She had no weapon and soon she would tire from the running and defending. *What am I going to do?* This was not going to end well for anyone here. Even if someone succeeded in the fight, by the time they managed to find a deer the time would be up. They would never be able to return to Harth in time.

Then they would have to deal with the retribution of the families whose children were left behind on the Javelins broken or possibly dead. She clutched her head with both hands as it felt it might burst. She could see someone heading right for her; her vision was too blurry to be sure. The pain burned behind her eyes, like a raging fire that would not extinguish. Her ears began to ring. It was all becoming too much, she felt like she was going to faint. The pain made her drop to her knees and her back bent backwards so her face was to the sky. The sky was so clear, the opposite to her head. The burning was white hot, like someone stuck a searing-hot fire prod through her temples. She sucked in a deep breath and finally released an almighty scream. When she came to, the burning was gone. The fire had been unleashed.

Chapter 5

The air was thick with dust. The sun and sky looked like a cloak of dirt spread across it. There was a smell of smoke and burning filling the air. Groaning through the pain, she sat up and saw the horrific scene that befell her eyes. The once evergreen pine trees were now charred trunks, black and brittle. The grass on the ground was now completely erased, leaving only the scorched earth. Small wisps of smoke were rising up from the ground, which was once abundant with plant life. The pool of the water was now completely empty. The plateau was a barren wasteland. It was not even one piece of land any more. Down the centre was a huge fissure in the shape of a bolt of lightning that had split the surface like an axe to a log. *What happened?* Arica slowly stood up and looked around her. This was utter destruction. She did not understand how it happened or what caused it. All she knew was that there had been ten trialists there before she had passed out, and now, she was the only living thing among scattered bones and burnt corpses.

She covered her mouth with her hands as the realisation hit her. They were dead. These people that had grown up with her, they were all still children. The burnt carcasses were strewn in unnatural poses, twisted in pain. Some of them seemed to have been cowering and were solidified in ash. Their anguish ridden faces frozen in perpetual horror forever. She stepped towards them. *Is this real? Yes, it has to be… that's Selaena's knife in that hand. Selaena's hand.*

Arica had to get away. This place was dangerous, whatever did this could come back and destroy her this time. She ran to the edge of the plateau and hurried down the side of the mountain. Her feet shuffled against the rocks as she tried to keep her balance. Her mind was racing, filled with so many confused thoughts. An image of fire flashed in her head. The orange flames licked the earth like demonic tongues tasting the whole world. She shook her head, that fire could not light again. The burning pain was excruciating. Her heart was pounding as she ran between the trees, using them to keep her upright. They were acting as a crutch to keep her tumbling to the ground and cutting herself again. Her descent was quick and clumsy, every few steps she stumbled. Her speed was making it more difficult, but she had to escape from that scene.

The splashes of the river as she ran through it jolted her awake and snapped her back to reality. Her thoughts went straight to her horse. She put her middle and index fingers together, placed them in her mouth and blew a sharp whistle. It was not long before she heard the familiar clopping of hooves. Sundancer appeared from out of the trees, his white mane flicking behind him. She rushed over to him and hugged his muzzle and let a single tear stream down her face. It all seemed like a bad dream, but she knew it was true. She grabbed hold of him, pushed off the ground and threw her leg over. Once she had settled on top of the stallion, she signalled him to run. Sundancer's hooves kicked against the ground, launching them forward. He went faster and faster, as if he was sensing Arica's distress. Before long, they had reached the foot of the mountain and also flat ground. Arica leaned over to his ear and pleaded with him to go faster than ever before. As if they spoke the same language, Sundancer responded just as she wanted and stormed ahead.

They galloped through the gates of the town and towards the starting line of the Trial. Civilians jumped out of the way and screamed to avoid getting crushed by Sundancer. She felt his strong muscles tighten and release as they rushed through the streets. Dropped baskets left scattered goods rolling around on the ground. They jumped over a barrel that had fallen into their way. Then she saw it, the starting line. The stands were still filled with people. Their shouts began to fill the air as she approached. There was Lord Valkor too, sitting on his make shift throne. When she reached him, she pulled Sundancer to a stop and she jumped off him. She could now see that there were two other trialists here, their kills lying at their feet. She couldn't believe they had actually managed to hunt the deer, catch them, and get them back here. How had they avoided the bloodshed? She was glad that they had not been on the plateau. She didn't recognise them, they hadn't gone to school together. They must be from the fishing village outside the town walls. One was a hulking sized boy with short blonde hair. He had a quiver slung across his broad back. The other trialist was a girl with dark skin and black hair pulled into a braid that hung to the small of her back. She had a twin set of knives hanging on either side of her belt. They looked like two hired mercenaries, not seventeen-year-olds.

'Welcome back, trialist,' Lord Valkor said, 'but it appears you have forgotten your task.'

'I didn't forget!' she called back.

'Oh?' he said, raising an eyebrow, 'I don't see a black deer strapped to your lovely steed.'

'No, i-it's— something happened.'

'Something more important than becoming an Amber Lion? Something more than dedicating yourself to Haella?' he said raising his voice.

She was starting to feel warm again. He was getting angry.

'The mountain, it cracked— like an egg,' she started nervously, 'the fire, it burned e-everything.'

'What is this you speak of? Mountains falling and firestorms! Nonsense!' he bellowed as he stood up.

Arica took a step back. She could almost feel his outrage at her words. She did not know why but a sick feeling in her stomach was developing. The bubbling was making her nauseous. Lord Valkor stood at the edge of the podium looking straight into her eyes.

'Tell us what happened! Enough of your fabrications.'

'I'm not lying. The mountain— it was wide open like a gaping mouth,' she began, 'when I woke up, everything was gone.'

Once she said that, the shouting from the stands began. There were questions about the other trialists, about what she meant by the mountain was cracked, what fire? There were worried cries and pleas for their children. People were getting louder and louder, wishing for their voices to be heard. But it all just became an angry mix of wailing that was giving her a headache. The pain in her head was becoming fiercer and the burning sensation was returning. She thought she might vomit. The taste of bile was starting to fill her mouth, burning her throat. The crowd was getting angrier by the minute, and it was all becoming too much. Arica felt like pulling her own hair out in the hopes that it would alleviate the pain in her head. But it would not work and like a volcano erupted inside of her. The ground started rumbling beneath their feet. Nearby trees were being split down the middle like some giant invisible hands were peeling them. Lord Valkor who had started to approach her was flung back with such force he broke through the benches he hit. He started writhing in pain, clutching his face in his gloved hands. Arica's skin was hot, and she could feel the sweat rolling down her arms and face. She needed to do something before anything bad happened. Again. She knew now that it had been her fault for what had happened in the Javelins. It was her rage that had killed all of those people.

She needed to extinguish this feeling before the fire came again. Closing her eyes, she started to inhale and exhale deeply and slowly. She tried blocking out the distress of the people around her. *Calm down, just calm down.* But it was not working; every time she tried to push the fire down inside of her, she just felt it flare up. Her fingertips were starting to spark, like the embers in a fireplace. She squeezed her hands tightly to try and hold the fire within. Her palms started sizzling and she had to let go and in doing so the fire burned free. The flames burst from her hands like two explosives after being detonated. She could see the looks of confusion on everyone's faces, but the worst part were the looks of terror. The viewers started screaming louder and ran towards the town away from her. People were falling over the benches and on to the ground. The fire was spreading around her like a ring. She did not understand what was happening to her. It was like something out of a story her grandmother would have told her when she was a child.

Something grasped her wrists from behind her and she could hear a voice.

'It's all right, everything will be all right. Just stop.'

That voice. One she knew so well. It made her glad to hear it. But the heat was still there. The voice had distracted her for a moment, but it still remained.

'Please, Arica— before it's too late,' Malin pleaded.

She listened to her brother's voice. She wanted to do as he said. So, she listened only to his voice as he continued to speak to her. She thought about their childhood and the things they used to do. It was always Malin and herself that would sneak off and play together as their brothers thought themselves too grown to play with children. On one occasion, they were playing next to the sea whose waves met the shore of Harth. They were skipping pebbles across its surface, trying to see who could get the most hops. Before long, another child from the town came down, but he was no friend of the Preandre children. He was a foot taller than either of the siblings and twice the width of Arica. He took it upon himself to kick the pile of pebbles they had gathered and laugh. Arica was so mad that she marched up to him and shoved him in the chest. He was about to get his own back, but Malin stepped in between them and took the push. He held his sister back and said it was not worth her hurting her fist. He could always do that; make her see the right decisions. Now, she prayed that he would this time too. She listened to him comforting her and reassuring her of her safety. He stepped around her and put his forehead against hers. Their breathing became synchronised and a sense of peace spread over her. The burning lessened to a tingling and finally, to nothing. Her temperature returned to normal. Her headache waned. She felt like herself again.

She opened her eyes and saw her brother's face. He was wearing a smile; how? She did not know. He was still holding her hands. She turned her head from side to side. Her eyes widened as she saw the devastation she had wrought. The ground around her had vein-like cracks along the surface, some with uprooted trees half fallen in. The scorched earth spread around her. The stands where the townspeople once stood were black and in disrepair. The canopies that hung over them for shade were all but destroyed, save for some torn pieces of fabric. Smoke rose from many different places, the smell filling her nose.

'What is happening to me?' she said, her voice breaking.

'I don't know,' he answered. 'Whatever it is, we will get through it— together.'

Chapter 6

Tears streamed down Arica's face as they rode back to their family's home. Malin had pulled her onto Sundancer and insisted they rushed away. The town was no longer going to be an amiable place for his sister he knew for sure. There was a sense of panic in his voice as he ushered on the horse. He made certain to lead them down backstreets where the least amount of people would see them. The images of torches and pitchforks in the hands of furious townspeople filled his mind and he feared for his sister. Her future was uncertain right now. There had been no recordings of magic in Haella or anywhere on the continent of Divinios in hundreds of years. At that, people thought they must have been myths, stories fabricated by storytellers and bards to make the histories more interesting and epic. But now... he had seen it with his own eyes. His sister had conjured fire, split the earth, and blew over trees like some celestial being. After the destruction of the mountain and now all those people seeing her power first-hand her life as she knew it, was changed forever.

After putting Sundancer into his stall the siblings rushed inside their house and into the kitchen. They found an empty room with nothing on the stove. No smell of cooking, a highly unusual occurrence in their home at this time. Arica looked at Malin with a raised eyebrow. Then they heard a throat being cleared. They followed the sound into the room next to the kitchen; Garvin, Ramira, Garo, and her grandmother all sitting and staring at them. Arica felt like shrinking and wanted the world to swallow her whole. Fear was swelling in her stomach. All of their faces looked so confused. *Just say something*. Silence filled the room for the next few minutes which seemed like hours to her. Finally, it was broken.

'Can either of you explain to us what happened today?' her mother whispered.

Arica and Malin looked at each other. He put a hand on her shoulder and gave a smile of reassurance. With a deep breath she relayed the story to her family. She explained to them what had happened since the beginning of the Trial. She told them about riding up the mountain, searching for the deer, hunting the deer and finally the big brawl atop the plateau that resulted in the inhuman explosion wrought by her hands. Tears were pouring down her cheeks as she the words poured out of her mouth, 'I killed them, it's my fault.'

Her mother's hands were covering her mouth, while her father and brother stared at her blankly. The silence was deafening. Garvin stood up and began pacing along the back wall of the room. It appeared as though he had something to say but did not know how to put into words. Finally, it was not either of her parents who spoke but Garo.

'I saw everything that happened at the starting line, the destruction, screaming,' he started slowly, 'but none of it was your fault, Arica.'

She lifted her head to meet his eyes. There was a deep sadness in them.

'You did not mean for any of it to happen, you were pushed by Valkor and the crowd.'

'I tried to stop it, it was too powerful,' Arica said with a crack in her voice.

At this, her father stopped his pacing when he was in front of his daughter. He stared at her for a moment and gently put his hand against her cheek. Their gaze held for what seemed like forever. She saw herself in her father's green eyes, a picture of despair. This was not how she wanted her life to turn out; to be this being with no control over themselves.

'You are still our daughter, and we will love and protect you until our last breath,' her father announced.

'Nothing will ever change that,' her grandmother said with a seriousness that Arica recognised as pure love.

Garo walked over to her too, placing a hand on her shoulder. He smiled at her. This was all she needed.

She looked up to see her mother was now standing. Their eyes met and she knew her mother was not as convinced as the other members of the family. The look in her eyes was one that Arica had never seen in her mother before, but she recognised it. Fear.

'Mother?' she said, holding out a hand.

Ramira looked at the hand. Her daughter's plea of acceptance. The same hand that she held as a child, the same hand she kissed when her daughter was upset.

'I don't know what to think, I-I need a moment,' she decided and left the room.

Her family watched in unified silence as their wife, daughter-in-law, and mother hurried out of the room, leaving them feeling abandoned.

The silence was deafening. Her brother, grandmother, and father had left upon her request. She wanted to be alone. The quiet was all that accompanied her. That, and of course, her thoughts.

What is going on? How did this happen to me? Why me? Why now?

Her mind was awash in worries and images of the past and future. She imagined what was to become of her now that she was the town witch. They had watched her burn and tear open the earth around her. They would never see her as the Arica Preandre of Harth ever again. The innocent child of a humble shopkeeper was gone. It was bewildering how quick the perception of a person could be irrevocably changed in a swift instant. She was something else now, something mysterious... something dangerous.

Arica was utterly lost in her thoughts that she did not notice the door next to the stairs creak as it was opened. Her grandmother entered the room and took the usual place of her rocking chair next to the crackling fire. Arica did not know what to say to her. She did not know if she wanted to speak. What was there to say? *I'm sorry your granddaughter is an unholy beast.* But no words left her grandmother's lips. Arica waited for her to speak, but nothing came.

'Grandmother?'

'Yes, my love?' her grandmother said to her.

Arica sat up straight and held her hands together, resting them on her knees.

'Is there something on your mind?' she asked her granddaughter.

Arica did not know what to say. She had not expected her to know anything about what happened, she was not at the starting line. She did not see, but she was there when she entered the house. Sitting alongside her parents and brothers. Everyone in Harth must know by now she realised. They would all be running from house to house, dying to tell the next person about the monster in their home.

'Everything is ruined, grandmother— I don't know what I am.'

'You are who you have always been,' she said, 'you are the same little girl who brought me a fresh flower every day for a whole summer because I said how happy flowers make me.'

'I just wish it never happened,' Arica said, her head hanging.

'This is not something that can be changed, love, but something that makes you special.'

'I do not want to be special; I want to be ordinary!'

'Why be ordinary? There is enough ordinary in this world that we could choke on it,' her grandmother said smiling. On an ordinary day Arica would have laughed.

Her grandmother was not one to sit about and mumble. If she had a story to tell or a point to be made, she said it without delay or apology. It was a point of contention between her mother and grandmother.

'They will fear me,' Arica said sadly.

'The unknown is always feared, Arica. We humans are weak creatures who hate difference before we understand it,' her grandmother told her, reaching across to hold her hand.

'But it does not mean that we all must accept that,' she continued. 'You are a light in my life and always shall be. Others may take some time to appreciate your new gifts, but you must remain strong until then, or you won't survive.'

Her grandmother's words would stay in her mind forever. She knew things were not going to be easy but with her family's support she believed she could get through it.

An hour passed, allowing Arica to bathe and remove the dirt and dried blood from her body. She patted herself dry with a towel and stared at herself in the oval-shaped mirror. She ran her fingers through her hair before tying it into a high ponytail. Her eyes were still slightly red from all the crying. She splashed some more water onto her face hoping it would do something. She dried her face again and went to her dresser. She slipped on a white tunic over brown trousers, a dark green jacket and her black boots. Not wanting to be alone with her thoughts, she returned to the living area and sat with her grandmother, talking about idle things. It was a good distraction from what happened earlier. She did not know how much longer she had before her next outburst would happen. They seemed to happen without much warning, other than a boiling heat spreading over her entire body. The heat was something extraordinary, it was as if the very sun was radiating from within. She shook her head to stop herself. It would not do her any good to dwell on the future. Arica stood up to head to her bedroom to rest, but before she could reach the stairs, she heard a crash. Her grandmother made a yelp from the shock of the slam. Heavy footsteps approached from the kitchen and Kal appeared. He was panting and had a look of distress in his eyes.

'Run!' he pleaded with his sister, grasping her shoulders.

Arica was confused. A gruelling feeling of anxiety slithered inside her. She wanted to demand an explanation but before she could her father entered the room holding a rucksack.

'You need to go, now,' he said holding the bag before her.

Before anything else could be explained to her she was ushered out of the room and towards the stable where Malin had already saddled Sundancer and was waiting with his own rucksack. Sundancer was not alone, there was another horse next to him. A beautiful grey mare with a dark mane was saddled beside him with a small bag slung over her back.

'What's wrong?' Arica asked, looking into her father's eyes. His own worry stared back at her. A deep sadness resided in his brown eyes.

'It's Valkor. He's coming,' he said.

Arica could not believe her ears. He was coming for her. To take her or imprison her. Or worse, execute her.

'They're coming down through the main street, straight from the Lord's manor. I heard the order myself at the change of the guard,' Kal informed her, 'I ran home as fast as I could. You must leave now.'

'Go? Where?' Arica asked, alarmed.

'We'll ride east, towards Fiermor,' Malin told her. 'Aunt Khea lives there and will hide us.'

Arica looked at her brother in disbelief. Was he really telling her that they had to run and leave their town, their home, and their family behind? For how long she did not know. Her grandmother, face pale with worry, stood at the threshold of the house. It made Arica sick to her stomach to see her like that.

'I don't want to leave you,' Arica said to her.

'And I do not want them to take you,' her grandmother told her, 'you must go.'

Her grandmother placed something into her hand. Arica looked down and saw the pin she wore during the Trial.

'I found it on the table, keep it, and whenever you feel lonely, I want you to look at it and remember I am always thinking of you. I wish there was more time, so much to be explained. Now— go!'

'We have to ride out of the stable, they'll come through the front door,' Malin said, grabbing her hand.

'But what can be explained?' Arica asked, pulling against her brother's grip.

Her grandmother held her face in both hands. 'If only there were time, my love. Remember, you are much stronger than you think you are. Now, run.'

Arica looked at her grandmother, at her father, at Kal, and then at Malin.

'All right, let's go.'

Malin quickly got up on the mare's back and ushered his sister to do the same. Arica put her foot in the stirrup, threw her leg over and after a glance at her family, she cracked the reins sending Sundancer bolting out of the stable, towards the town gates and her uncertain future.

Chapter 7

The journey took them three days. They rode out of Harth's gates and did not look back. They made it quickly across the grasslands, to their surprise. They were convinced that Valkor would come barrelling after them, looking to put Arica's head on a spike, or strap her to a pyre in the town square. The fear kept them going like an invisible rider whipping them to go faster and faster. Their horses moved like lightning, relentless along their path. Their hooves kicked up dirt behind them, creating a cloud of dust. They decided they would go off-road and ride along the western edge of the grasslands where the Uaindowen Forest bordered it. The trees gave them some cover and would allow them to evade any pursuers. Each day, as they moved further and further away from their home, they watched the sun rise in front of them and set behind them. They would make camp only when it had turned too dark to see in front of them. The first night they camped within the forest, amongst the trees that shielded them from view of the road. Still, it seemed too open for them, like someone would jump on them at any second. That night her grandmother's words played in her mind over and over. *Stronger than I think I am?* She wished only for a moment to have her words explained, but life had a different thought on it.

The next night, they came upon an old, dilapidated barn in an unused field. They tied their horses up in the remnants of stalls, which still had troughs for water. Thankfully it had rained sometime earlier, and the troughs were brimming with fresh water for their steeds. They used old burlap sacks for bedding and Arica started a fire. Malin had remembered to bring a quiver and bow with him, which Arica used to catch a pair of lop-eared rabbits. Malin prepared them with some wild onions and mushrooms. They ate them like half-starved wolves, it was the first meal either had had in two days. They slept well that night, bellies full and a roof over their heads.

Fiermor was a different type of town to Harth. Harth, being a coastal town, smelled of sea salt and the screeches of gulls filled the air. Sailors and fishermen made up a great part of their town. Many men and women of Harth lived half of their life at sea. Fiermor was inland and therefore, had a different draw to it. The town had gained renown for its livestock trade. The town was surrounded on every side by paddocks with cattle, sheep, and pigs. The smell here was something less than desired. The road into the town was long and they saw many people working hard in the fields. They saw men and women covered in dirt as they cleaned out barns, filled troughs and moved large square bales of hay. They arrived in the town and looked around for a tavern called 'The Black Rose'. This was the tavern that their father's sister, their aunt, owned and ran. They had visited it when they were younger, but it had been some time since they had travelled this far north. They trotted down different streets looking for a sign with the matching symbol of a black rose. They passed by merchants selling their wares clothing, pottery, woven baskets, amongst other things. Their voices fought to rise above the others, trying to attract customers. Arica marvelled at a stand with beautiful pendants of all colours and shapes; gold and silver, ruby and sapphire, she had never seen so many opulent things in one place. Opulent things which she could only dream of. Things of such extravagance did not find their way into the hands of a common girl. The only jewellery that would pass through her fingers was that of her mother's and grandmother's wedding bands. Simple, golden rings sat on their fingers every day no matter what task they were undertaking. How they never lost it, Arica could never understand. If she was to wear one, she did not think it would last the first day as it would surely slip off while she ran through the forest. No, she did not think to trust herself with some piece of finery. If she ever did marry there would have to be some other solution than wearing it on her finger. Perhaps around her neck on a chain, she thought to herself.

Suddenly a tantalising smell hit them. Both Malin and Arica took a deep breath, inhaling the glorious smell of meat cooking. The smell was so strong in the air it was like they could see it. They trusted their guts and followed the scent down a narrow side street that reminded them of the one that ran behind their home in Harth. The path was wet beneath their boots. Malin suggested that it may have rained the night before. It had rained before they arrived at the old barn, so it could have earlier today too. An old door swung open, and a homely woman garbed in a stained apron appeared and dumped a bucket of water out, narrowly missing the brother and sister. Before they could shout in protest or annoyance, the door slammed shut. Malin's face shrivelled up.

'I really hope that is not what I fear it is.'

His sister grimaced herself and they rushed down the alley and arrived at a square. In the centre of the square were a variety of stalls. While the shops they passed earlier boasted things like clothes and pottery, these were food stalls. The many different smells mixed in the air, creating a concoction that would make even the person with the fullest belly's mouth water. Their proprietors called from each of them, trying to sell whatever they had. Some took the kind approach and complimented the passers-by to entice their interest. Others opted for a more aggressive way of grasping their attention by shouting. Some even took it as far as blocking the way of the people as if to corral them to their stall. Arica made sure to avoid those people and veered around them. Malin sniffed the air and smiled. They were in the right place. Arica followed her brother as he guided them into the thick of it. Stall owners battled for their attention, but they would not let themselves be distracted. Malin had his eye on a particular stall with a red awning above it. The wooden table at the front of the stall was draped with a white cloth. Sitting on the cloth were a multitude of the most beautiful foods either had seen. Jam tarts. Sticky buns. Iced cakes. Warm bread. Hundreds of biscuits.

'Hungry?' a voice said.

They lifted their eyes from the sweets to a smiling man standing behind the table. He was carrying a fresh tray of rolls. He set them gently on the table and turned to Arica and Malin.

'What can I get you?' he said, clasping his hands together.

Arica turned to her brother. He shrugged his shoulders and pulled out the empty pockets of his trousers.

'No thank you, we're not hungry,' Arica said, taking her brother's hand to walk away.

'I know hungry eyes when I see them,' the man said. They turned back to face him. 'Can hear hungry stomachs too!'

The man held out one of his warm rolls for each of them.

'But we have no way of paying you.'

'Hungry people are a terrible sight— please,' he said, his eyes going between them and the rolls.

Arica and Malin reached forward and took the rolls. It did not take them long before they sank their teeth into them. They made a satisfied sound. These were not like any roll they had tasted before. They could taste tomato and garlic. Delicious. They took another big bite.

'Thank you!' Arica said with her mouth full.

'It's wonderful,' Malin added.

'I'm glad you like it, it was my mother's recipe.'

The siblings finished their rolls and thanked the baker again. He sent them off with a smile and jam tart each. He pointed them in the direction of their aunt's tavern after they asked. They were to leave the square by walking under the arch near the fruit stalls. They waved and thanked him once more as they walked away. Both of them had smiles on their faces as they weaved through the people and found the arch. Stalls full with fruit of all colours lay on either side of it. They had both finished their tarts before they arrived. Malin stated that they were the best jam tarts he had ever seen and tasted in his life. His sister agreed with him.

They turned another corner and finally they saw it, the Black Rose. It was smaller than they remembered but a good size. A large stained-glass window that depicted a field of black roses with a woman clad in ruby-red armour in the centre of them was the main feature. It was an amazing piece of work that must have cost their aunt a small fortune. It reminded Arica of the goddess, Dorcoga, Lady of War and Keeper of the Night. She could see the sword at her hip, but her famed spear was missing from her hand. They tied up their horses in the patron's stable around the back of the tavern and went inside.

The tavern was busy with people drinking and eating. There were two men singing drunkenly in the corner waving their tankards in the air and spilling half of their contents on themselves. Two barmaids were serving the people, their trays heavy with food and drink. Arica and Malin walked to the bar and asked the brunette girl pulling pints if their aunt was here. The girl pointed them in the direction of a large wooden door next to the staircase. The pair found their way to it and Malin knocked three times. A few seconds of waiting ended with the door being opened by a woman with rosy cheeks and dark curly hair.

'Malin? Arica?'

'Yes, Auntie,' Malin said.

'What are you doing here?' she asked, 'come in, come in!'

They hurried inside and their aunt sat them in front of her fire that was flickering in the corner. She offered them warm cups of tea which they both accepted gratefully. They were thankful for the warm fire and a place to rest their weary bodies after the three days of riding. She asked them about the purpose of their visit and Arica told her the strange story.

Aunt Khea felt great sadness for her niece. She understood why they feared for their lives and ran when they did. She agreed to hide them here, they would be safe here she assured them. They would be disguised as workers here in the tavern. No one would know they were kin, to protect their identities. Arica would serve the food and drink, while Malin would work in the kitchen. Their aunt apologised that they would have to share a room as she was short on space. They thanked their aunt and said they would be more than grateful for her hospitality. By the time they had finished speaking, the sun was setting, and the town lanterns had been lit. Khea brought them upstairs and into the room in which they would be staying. It was a modest room, two beds on either side with a small table in between them. A chest lay at the foot of one of the beds and a round mirror hung on the wall. Their aunt kissed them both on the forehead and wished them goodnight, leaving them on their own. They settled into their beds, lit only by a candle on the table. Arica silently thanked the gods for this bed and the down-filled pillow.

'How do you feel?' her brother asked.

'Exhausted.'

'Praise be to the gods we got here safely, I feared the worst, sister.'

Arica could hear the fear in her brother's voice. He had done well in Harth. He was so sure of himself and strong. It was not in Malin's nature to be commanding. It was a different side to him than his sister had ever seen.

'I cannot believe we made it here— I wonder what happened at home,' Arica said worriedly.

'I don't know, they will have deterred Valkor I'm sure.'

'Our brothers, our parents— Grandmother. They will be imprisoned for helping us escape.'

'They would die for us, Arica. You know this.'

'I do. It does not mean I will delight in it,' she said mournfully.

'We will go back for them,' he told her, 'one day, when we are ready. When it is safe.'

Arica lay her head against the pillow. If it was safety they were waiting for they would never go back. There would be no place for her in Harth any more. But she would return one day. She would see her family again. She would free them from whatever cell Valkor deemed horrible enough. Her eyes began to close slowly, the tiredness washing over her like a hungry wave at the shoreline. The last thing she saw was Malin blowing out the candle, leaving them in the dark.

Chapter 8

It had been four days since their arrival in Fiermor. The siblings had been working hard in the tavern. Arica had spent her time going back and forth between tables, the bar, and the kitchen. She cleaned tables after the people had finished and sometimes pulled the pints herself. It did not take her long to learn which customers to avoid and how to handle them. *A swift slap to the jaw*, one of the other barmaids had suggested. Malin spent his time in the kitchen preparing the food. It gave him great joy to chop vegetables, stir the pots and season the meat. He loved cooking and now he finally was doing it, and for other people too. He wondered what his mother would think of that. It was a busy way of life, but they enjoyed it. Malin was doing what he had always wanted to do. For Arica it was the bliss of not having time to be alone with her thoughts. It was the idle hours of the night before bed when her mind would race, filled with the images from atop the Javelins. Her sleep was filled with terrors, replaying the events. Sometimes it was a fiery explosion, leaving nothing but ash behind. Other times she watched as flame melted the flesh off the bones of the other competitors. Their wails rang in her ear each morning. She would rush to get ready and start to work to cloud her thoughts. Anything was better than being alone thinking about it.

Today, the tavern was busier than usual. It was market day so there was an influx of people from neighbouring towns and villages who had come to sell their produce. On his way from the butcher that morning, Malin spied a woman from Harth who was selling fish. He knew her as he attended school with her daughter. He made sure to avoid being seen by her. He told his sister about this, and they agreed not to leave the tavern for the rest of the day. Arica's job was to clean the tavern floors, windows, and the bar itself. She lugged the heavy bucket of water around with her as she mopped every inch of the floor. The water was black when she was finished. She made a face of disgust as she poured the water out into the alley behind the tavern. She quickly learned to wipe the windows in straight lines from top to bottom to avoid streaking them. After she finished washing the windows she went to the bar and wiped it down until it shone. Pleased with her work, she joined the other serving girls who were already busy passing around foaming tankards of mead.

The day went by quickly and soon the bright blue sky had begun to turn to its dusky orange hue once more. Arica and Malin had both been working since dawn so their aunt said they could take the evening off. A gift they both appreciated. They quickly returned to their chambers where they changed out of their clothes and into clean ones. The market had finished and the merchants would be well on their way home to make use of the setting sun as much as possible. Malin suggested they go for a stroll along the river to get some fresh air.

'We could visit the baker in the square?'

They had been cooped up all day, so Arica agreed. Her mouth started to water at the thoughts of his jam tarts. It had been strawberry filled one she received but she longed to try the blackberry. Two silver coins clinked against each other in her pocket, more than enough for a tart or two. Her hard work had already started to pay off. They threw on hooded cloaks in case the sky decided to open and left the tavern. They shortly arrived at the slow flowing river that meandered through the town. The merchants would often use small boats to transport their goods to the town gates rather than cart. A few rowboats were moored along its edge with nothing but an oar or two inside. Arica looped her arm around the crook of her brother's arm as they walked. They spoke of idle things. Both of them appreciating the reprieve from speaking about their worries and fears. Arica was so tired of discussing the sadness they had experienced over the last week that she relished the topic of the stars, or the light breeze. Her brother pointed out his favourite constellation. The Great Hound. She always laughed when he did this, it was the *only* constellation he knew she was certain. Their steps were guided by the shape of the river, going straight when it was straight and turning on its bends. As they passed the mill, Arica thought that the sound of the water wheel was almost soothing. The splashing of water was a sound that brought happiness to her as she had always loved swimming in the sea near Harth. She still found it strange living in a place where the sea did not touch. The familiar smell of salt was replaced by animal feed and manure. She wondered if perhaps this was where the baker bought the flour that he used to make his delicious treats. They would visit him this evening, but first she wanted to go elsewhere.

The siblings arrived at one of the town wells where they would fetch water for their aunt. People would bring their own buckets, hang them on the hook, and lower them into the well to fetch fresh drinking water. They stopped to rest here as it also happened to be the location of the twin temples of Fiermor. This was her first destination of the evening. Two identical temples sculpted from white stone stood tall and beautiful amongst the ordinary buildings which encircled them. Here the people of Fiermor honoured the gods Deregoth and Rhialdir. Deregoth was the god of craftsmanship, while Rhialdir blessed animals. It made sense to Arica why they would favour them in Fiermor, being that their entire economy depended on both. The statues outside towered over the well. Deregoth was depicted the same way as always, broad with huge hands, a hammer clasped in one. Rhialdir held his staff in one hand, an owl perched on top of it, and a fox seated by his feet. As a child, Arica always imagined that Rhialdir would have fought with Merenia as she favoured those who would hunt his beloved beasts. She wondered if he would dislike her too as she prayed to the goddess daily. Both temples had candles lit outside, welcoming any to enter at any time. She decided that it would be best to stay in the Lord of Beasts' favour, so she would say a prayer to him. Malin said he would honour Deregoth while his sister prayed to Rhialdir. The inside of the temple was as lavish as she imagined. Carvings of all sorts of animals adorned the walls. Blankets and pillows were laid out for the worshippers to rest on. Tall, white candles cast a warm and inviting light around the temple. The altar at the top of the temple was covered in gifts to the great god. Bowls of fruit, coins, flowers and much more showed that the god was greatly loved within the town. Arica knelt down before the altar and bowed her head. She placed her two fits gently against one another and began her prayer.

O Lord of Beasts, I thank you for filling this world with creatures of all sorts. I admire and worship each one as a living work of art. May they flourish always. I ask that you bless my horse, Sundancer, with long life. He is strong and worthy of your name.

Arica knelt in silence for a few moments. She inhaled deep and long as the smell of the burning incense filled her nostrils. It was a spicy smell, not one she had smelled before. Perhaps the acolytes of this temple burned their own kind. She bowed once more and left the temple. She began to walk down the steps when she felt a shift in the air. She did not understand how she felt it but it was like a cold wind settled into her bones. She stopped in her tracks and looked up. It was not their black garb and masks that surprised her most, but her brother with one of the masked people's arms around his throat. They were approaching slowly in unison.

'Malin!' she exclaimed. 'Who are you? What do you want?'

'We came here for you,' the masked figure in the middle said.

'You're not taking her!' Malin shouted, throwing his elbow back into the stomach of his captor allowing him to get away.

The masked figures launched at them with such speed that it took them both by surprise. The first of the attackers reached them and threw a punch at Malin's face which he blocked just in time. But before he could counter, he was knocked to the ground by a sweeping kick. Arica jumped out of the way as another assailant tried to land a kick into her ribcage. She retaliated with a swing of her arm which resulted in her elbow cracking against a jaw of another of the masked ones. Malin had found his feet again and was battling against two of the attackers, sending punches and kicks towards them with a relentless force. Arica was surrounded by the other three and they were inching closer to her. She thought about attempting to summon the power inside her to defend them but quickly decided against it. The power was too unstable, and she did not know if she could control it. A stray flame would burn Fiermor to the ground. The first masked figure jumped into the air with a leg headed for Arica's stomach, but she leapt over it and brought her elbow down on his head. He crumpled to the ground as another tried to grab her. She dodged his arms and kicked him in the back, knocking him forward against the wall of Deregoth's temple. The final masked figure edged nearer, keeping its eyes fixed on Arica. Arica ran, intending to break the nose of her aggressor. But she was stopped in her tracks as she heard the muffled shouts of Malin. She saw that he was tied and gagged on the ground, struggling to break free. She moved to help him, but was quickly stopped by being knocked to the ground herself. The last thing she saw was a blindfold being tied around her eyes and then felt a pinch and blacked out.

Chapter 9

The world was hazy when she came to. Wincing as her eyes became accustomed to the bright sunlight. The light was coming in through cracks in a timber roof above. There were no birds chirping outside but she could hear the whinnying of horses outside and other voices so there must be people nearby too. *What happened?* Her head tingled like someone had hit her with a log. Then she started to remember. The temples. Being attacked. Malin. *Where is he?* She looked around the room. The room was less than that, it must have been a makeshift building. The walls were made from logs standing up straight and went around her in a circle. There was no sign of Malin here, not even another bed. If you could call it that. Arica was sitting up on the bed of straw; she made a face as she removed a strand from her hair. She stood up and noticed a part of the wall that had a gap covered by a piece of fabric. She pushed it forward and the fresh air hit her.

The sky was clear of any clouds. Judging from the sun's position it was late afternoon. She could not believe how long she had been unconscious. She was standing in the midst of a busy campsite. There were men and women in all locations doing an assortment of activities. Some were moving materials, others loading crates onto carriages attached to large draft horses, but what really caught her attention were those practising fighting. There were many people duelling with swords, throwing spears, and also shooting arrows at tree trunks. She walked towards the archery range only to be stopped in her tracks by something else. Something that she did not believe she would see. On a patch of grass lined by oak trees were a trio of people thrusting their arms at targets. They were not throwing spears or knives, but what appeared to be arrows fashioned from the air around them. Arica watched the man closest to her swirl his hand, spin the air in front of him and pull it into an arrow. He flicked his wrist, and it whistled through the air, stabbed the target, and disappeared on impact. Her eyes widened as the woman next to him did the same but with two wind arrows at once.

'Arica!'

She spun around and saw a familiar face running to her.

'Malin, you're all right!' she hugged her brother when he reached her. 'What happened? Where are we?'

'About half a day's ride east of Fiermor,' he answered.

'Half a day's ride? Aunt Khea is going to be fraught with worry!'

'Relax, Arica,' he said, taking her hands in his. 'I've written a note and it is on its way to her as we speak.'

'A note? Why bother with a note, we have to escape!'

'No, Arica. It isn't like that. They want to help.' She could tell by the look on his face that he meant it. But she could not understand why he would feel this way. The people in masks had attacked them. They knocked her out. Her mind went to her aunt. She would not believe that we would just leave without saying a word.

'Who is *they*? It was those masked animals, wasn't it?'

'No, no — well, yes it was. But it is not what you think,' Malin said shaking his head.

'Tell me what is going on.'

'I could, but I do not think I am the right person to,' he said, holding out his hand.

'Wait. What about Sundancer?' she asked. The thought of her horse being left behind made her sick. He would think that she abandoned him.

'He is with the other horses, grazing next to camp,' he explained, 'they got him after us.'

Malin brought his sister through the camp. They passed the central fire where the person cooking had a large pot suspended over it. There was a mouth-watering smell of spices rising out of it. Her stomach growled and realised that she had not eaten in nearly a day. They had intended on visiting the baker, but that plan was interrupted. They stopped in front of a large green tent with a canopy held up by wooden poles at the front. It was larger than the other tents around it. It seemed almost grand in appearance. Malin nudged his head towards the flapped entrance of the tent. He smiled and told her there was nothing to worry about. The two of them walked into the tent where there were two other people. A tall, barrel-chested man stood to the right of a large oak desk. He had a stern face that was scarred on the right side from forehead to jawline. It was pink in colour and looked as if something with very long claws had done the damage. Arica's eyes were drawn to the large axe that he had strapped to his back. Next to him and behind the desk was one of the most striking women she had ever seen. Her dark skin was free of any mark or blemish. Her braided hair hung behind her and fell to her elbows. She looked up from the papers on the desk, her brown eyes staring at them. She sat up straight and put her hands together.

'Hello, Arica. It is a pleasure to meet you.'

'Who are you?'

'My name is Jyneera,' she said, 'I am the Grand Chancellor of Ebraeye.'

Ebraeye lay beyond the Great Karigraine River to the north of Haellan peninsula. She had heard it described as being so wide it was almost like a narrow sea. It had so many twists and turns that it had been nicknamed the Serpent. It was home to a barbaric people that took part in blood rituals. Some of the older children had told her that they sacrifice the oldest daughter of their families to appease the gods. Since she was the one and only daughter in her family this had petrified her as a child. Beyond that she did not know too much about the place. Haella had become somewhat of an excluded country since King Solomir's father's reign began. Information, or indeed people, did not pass easily into or out of its borders. It had not always been like that. Her father had told her about the days when his grandfather was young, and his own father would take him and his brothers on journeys to many different places all across Divinios in his carriage to sell his wares. He had been a carpenter and would sell furniture and toys he crafted in, what is now, the stable in their home. But once Solomir's family sat on the throne they ordered closed borders around Haella and there was no more trading or travelling between countries. It was all she had ever known but she knew that the older people of the country thought it strange. But now it was commonly accepted amongst the people, for if you did not accept it, some terrible misfortune would fall upon you.

'Why would someone from Ebraeye be here?' Arica asked, confused.

'Well, you would be that reason.'

'Me? What could you possibly want from me?'

'You are special. You have great power,' she said standing up. Arica almost froze. She could not fathom how a woman from Ebraeye could possibly know about her. About what had happened a week ago.

'I do not have power, I am an uncontrollable destructive force,' Arica blurted out.

'Arica, it's all right. They are here to help,' Malin said as he placed a hand on her shoulder.

'How? How can you, or her, or the giant help me?' she asked angrily.

The large man grunted and walked out of the tent. Jyneera slowly walked around the table, her hands still clasped together.

'You cannot do anything for me. I am alone in this,' Arica said weakly.

'But that is it, Arica. You are not alone. You are a part of something much greater than you have ever imagined,' Jyneera claimed.

'What are you talking about?'

'This power within— it is not an uncontrollable destructive force. Your true self has awakened,' she told her with a strength in her voice.

Arica looked at Malin. The look on his face told her that he believed everything Jyneera was saying.

'My true self— and who exactly is that?'

'A caster— a wielder of magic.'

Arica's jaw dropped. *A caster?* She could not believe the words she had heard. Casters were merely something found in children's stories like unicorns and mermaids. These things do not exist. Her mind immediately went back in time to when she would sit on the ground in front of the fire in her grandmother's room with her brothers. They would listen to her for hours as

81

she would tell them epic tales of heroes of the past. How they would slay great and terrible beasts with iron and incantations. Now, this mysterious woman was telling her that all of these stories may have been true and that she was a part of it.

'Magic? How can that be?' she whispered.

'Your people have long thought magic died with the dragons, or that it never existed at all. It was not long ago our people crossed paths, but the Haellans have chosen to forget. Magic is more alive than any of us, it is in everything and everyone. It is a part of the world that will never disappear, and you are its newest addition.'

'In Ebraeye, magic is respected and there are many casters,' Malin said from beside her, 'I know it sounds deranged, but you saw it yourself outside. Those men and women were using the air around them as arrows.'

'We heard about what happened to you in the Javelins, news of magic that powerful travels far and wide. We had to get to you before someone else did,' Jyneera said as she leaned on the table.

'Who would come for me?' Arica asked.

'The Amber Lions— Solomir hunts down casters to use them for his own sick schemes to enslave us all,' she grimaced.

'The king knows about magic too? Then why do the Haellan people not know?'

'He would rather keep you in the dark to enable him to spin his webs of deceit right in front of your eyes,'

Jyneera told her with a bitterness, 'he uses casters like you to corrupt the minds of others and make them bow to him.'

'This world is much more intricate than I thought it was a week ago,' Arica uttered as she sat down in a chair next to the desk.

'Take some time to process this, explore the camp, perhaps speak to some of the other casters— but find some time to rest too, we leave in the morning,' Jyneera informed her, sitting back in her seat.

'Where are we going?' Arica and Malin asked together.

'Dun Ortha, the city of magic.'

Arica could not believe what she had been told. Upon leaving the tent, she hurried to a large tree and rested against its trunk. Her body slid down without a thought and she stared at nothing. *Magic… it cannot be true. How could it? And me, a* caster*? I am nothing more than a plain girl from a fishing town. This Jyneera must have made a mistake.*

But Arica knew it was not a mistake. Deep in her stomach, she knew she was right. The fire. The earth cracking before her as easily as an egg. Nothing else would make sense. Her eyes landed on the man from earlier. The caster who turned the air into arrows. He looked ordinary. Brown hair and a broad nose. No scars or tattoos. No extra eye or wings. Nothing that made him look any different. This is what casters looked like, like her. Like normal people. She pushed out a breath and looked up at the intertwining branches above her. Some had already gone bare.

'Anything up there?'

'I thought I had lost my mind and it might be there.'

'Oh, you lost that a while ago,' Malin joked as he squatted next to her. He smiled. He was trying to soothe his sister who he knew was lost in her thoughts. This was how she reacted to big news. He knew her inside out.

'I know it appears daunting now, but in time it will just be another part of you like your green eyes.'

'Green eyes are real.'

'As is magic.'

Chapter 10

The road to Dun Ortha was long and twisted like a raging river. The carts bounced as they were pulled over holes in the road. She was relieved to see that when they were attaching the carts to horses that her own horse was at the camp. Malin had convinced Jyneera that having Sundancer with Arica would make her cooperation much more likely. He was right. Sundancer was now pulling the cart along with another horse. He was used to this work from the odd job Arica's father would task him with. The road was rough. It was a beaten track that many people had walked over the years. No plants grew along it as the footsteps of those walking on it stomped out any chance of life. The tracks of carts and carriages marked the ground like two twin serpents. There were brown puddles dotting the path, as it had rained the past two days. The wheels of the carts splashed along the track. The grasslands of Haella slowly transitioned to a wooded area. The trees separated the grasslands from the Karigraine River, except for a gap wide enough for the carts to pass through. The branches of the trees twisted and turned in all directions. The trees cast shadows across the ground, making shapes like a map of an unknown world.

Time was passing slowly for the Preandres from the back of their cart which they shared with four other people. Two soldiers with swords at their hips, a cook that reminded Arica of a bear with his beard and chest hair emerging from his collar, and a caster with tattoos lining his arms from fingertip to shoulder. Arica had spent her time in the cart asking questions about Ebraeye and its connection to magic. She wondered how the caster's magic awakened and was it as explosive as her own. She asked if everyone's magic was the same and could everyone do the same things. The caster answered her questions with not much enthusiasm but answered them, nonetheless. He explained how everyone's magic awakens at different stages, usually during childhood but can take longer, sometimes not until adulthood. He said that hers was a particularly volatile awakening, but it was not uncommon for the magic to manifest in this way. The caster also explained that not everyone could use magic in the same way; his own magic lay in the water. He was able to control the rivers and seas, turning them into liquid snakes with so much as a snap of a finger. He explained that his magic had developed over time, and he could change the form of water into ice and steam. He spoke of earth casters who could shake the ground and cause devastating earthquakes that crumbled entire cities. He gave details on air casters who could tear forests apart with their typhoons. She marvelled at the stories of fire casters who could cause volcanoes to erupt and encase everything around them in lava. Tales of magic that she never thought possible, if only her grandmother could hear them too.

Arica was wide awake as everyone next to her was breathing heavily or snoring. Night had fallen and the rain had begun once again. The sounds of the drops hitting the earth were like tiny feet tapping against the soil. The sounds were calming, the rhythm giving her something to focus on other than the thoughts in her head. She tried to think about things she deemed meaningless but when she saw her brother's peaceful face, she could not help but think of her other family members. *How are they? What happened after I left?* She knew that Valkor was wicked and would not hesitate to hurt them or imprison them. Her poor grandmother would not do well in those conditions; it made her sick to her stomach to think about it. Her brothers would protect the family with their last breath. They were always like that, no one could insult them without one of them retaliating. It made her angry as a young child but deep down she loved them for it because it was their way of showing they cared about her. She would give anything to be back at home, sitting in front of the fire with everyone around her and discussing their days. This was something which she knew in her heart would not happen for a very long time, if ever again.

Once night fell, the orders were to go off road and camp hidden amongst trees or a cave if luck was on their side. Over the days travelling, they only had one such night. The Ebraeyens had discovered a cave underneath a hill that was not big enough for the entire group, so Jyneera enlisted the earth casters to make it so. Arica helped them do it as her earth casting ability had improved over the previous days. The tattooed caster, Ryger Alfarion, had somewhat taken her under his wing. He was a water caster, but all casting came from the same place. He described it as living lightning within them that they can channel. He would take her to a secluded spot away from camp when they set up for the night and run drills. It surprised her that after just a few sessions she had gone from her magic uncontrollably exploding out of her, to being able to summon it at her own will. He had shown her how to use her magic to defend and to attack. It was important to learn how to do both because not every fight can be won with violence. Arica, for the first time since it all began, was beginning to like her magic.

The next day, the group packed up their carts and continued to their destination. Hours passed by quickly as the carts were pulled towards Ebraeye. Apart from where she used to practice her hunting skills, she had not seen any other forests. She had not seen much of anything else. Since that day on the mountain, she had seen so many places and met so many people. The world was a bigger place now. They set up camp along the southern bank, the Haellan side of the river. Arica had heard about the width of it but its sheer size was immense. When standing on the bank, she could just about see the dots of trees on the far side, Ebraeye's side. She wondered what Ebraeye would be like. Jyneera had told her that they were waiting on a ferry to carry them across the river, but they had arrived earlier than expected so they would have to make camp. She decided that she would take the opportunity to talk to some more of the casters. Malin had become friendly with the cook they travelled with and went to help him make the food for later. It made Arica so happy to see her brother do what he loved to do. Malin loved to cook and use fresh ingredients. He almost skipped to the cooking area when they had finished setting up their tent.

Arica walked for about ten minutes down the shore where a trio of casters were waving their arms, manipulating the elements around them. The casters tended to move far enough away from camp to avoid disrupting the other people. There were two girls with jet-black hair, about her age, with identical faces. The only difference between them was one had hair down to the small of her back while the other had cropped hair with the left side above her ear shaved to expose her scalp. They were accompanied by the tattooed caster that rode with her in the cart. She admired the intricate lines that coated his fingers and arms. They highlighted the muscles that rippled beneath his skin. He was barefoot and the water was lapping against his ankles. His arms and hands waved in the air like a breeze was moving through him. Threads of water were flowing out of the river like a pit of dancing snakes. He was using them to whip earthen projectiles being hurled at him by the striking twins. Arica did not notice at first that she was smiling but soon caught herself and stopped before anyone noticed.

'Are you going to come practice or keep staring at us?' The tattooed caster smiled, looking over his shoulder.

Arica felt the blood flow into her cheeks. She made her way over to them and they welcomed her into their group. They explained that the girls, Alys and Tamar Olfaris, were practising their attack while Ryger defended. Before she could decide which side she would be on, he held her by the wrist and asked would she help him.

'You already know what your offensive magic is capable of, why not test your defensive skills— if you can keep up,' he said, still flashing his teeth.

'I'll do my best,' Arica replied.

He started to walk backwards and ended up tumbling into the water. He looked dazed and noticed a piece of rock abnormally sticking out of the ground. His gaze met Arica who, in turn, was smiling back at him.

The four casters practiced their attacks and defence with great focus and intensity. The twins were firing balls of rock at them trying to knock them out but Arica and Ryger's blocks were impenetrable. Ryger used the river like a wall, causing the rocks to turn to mud on impact. Arica pulled a slab of earth up and was using it as a shield to repel their attacks. They began to launch their own attacks that Alys and Tamar were quick to defend against. The casters moved like dancers all to the same beat, their arms waved, and their magic reacted. The earth and water sprang to life and did as their masters told. Arica had not felt so alive in a long time, her whole body was tingling with energy. It made her feel like lightning had struck her body and was running on it. Arica raised up her right arm and was about to flick her wrist to send a wave of earth to knock the twins over but ended up on the ground herself. She looked around for whatever invisible force hit her.

'What was that?' she shouted at her sparring partners.

Out of the edge of the trees that lined the shore a group of soldiers ran out. They were wielding swords and had them drawn. Arica recognised the sigil that was engraved into their armour. It was the head of a roaring lion. The same sigil that hung in the Lord of Harth's manor and flew over the walls and castle in the city of Phorum, that King Solomir resided. The Amber Lions. Haella's imperial army. They were here and ready to fight, and maybe kill. Arica clambered to her feet and stood close to Ryger and the twins. The four of them stood back-to-back as the Lions prowled closer and closer. The casters locked eyes with the Lions. Arica could sense the fury within them. One of the Lions ran at them, sword brandished. Alys stamped on the ground, jutting a pillar of limestone out of it, and sending the attacker flying into the Serpent. Four more Lions ran directly at them with their swords high in the air, ready to strike. Each of the casters used their magic to defend themselves creating a spiral of earth and water that knocked the Lions' weapons to the ground. Tamar laughed and spat a taunt at them. She moved forward to finish them off when an olive-skinned Lion thrust both palms forward and crashed a gust of air into her. Tamar tumbled to the ground. *Magic? They're casters too! That's how I fell.* Ryger acted quickly and forced a wave out of the river and with another surge of magic froze it, forming a barrier around them.

'What are we going to do?' Alys asked.

'They have an air caster, and god knows what else!' Tamar grunted as she got back up with help from her sister.

'There are seven of them and four of us, it is hardly a fair fight,' Ryger smirked.

Having set themselves up in formation, Ryger clenched his fists, cracking the barrier. He then pushed them out to fly at the Lions. The ice was razor sharp and left gashes on their enemies. The same air caster twirled his arm and blew Alys over onto her knees. The wind was persistent, he was trying to force her into the river. Tamar and Ryger were preoccupied battling against the other soldiers, so Arica was facing the air caster alone. He, on the other hand, had help. A swordsman armed with a broadsword came at her, looking to land it into her shoulder. She swung herself in time to dodge the blow and kicked him in the ribs. He turned and punched her in the stomach. She buckled over and hardly had time to react when another punch cracked against her shoulder. She looked to her right and saw Alys at the water's edge, gripping the earth. She was going to be thrown into the water. The swordsman was looming over Arica and had the sword held high like an executioner. Arica felt the surge of energy within her again; the fire was coming. As the swordsman chopped down his sword, her hand rose up to meet it. She grabbed it in her searing hot hand, the metal glowing white from the touch. The Lion's eyes widened, and he stumbled back. Arica stood up, pushing him back as she melted the sword into drops of iron. With a burst of energy, she sent forward orange flames that encased the swordsman. The last thing he did was scream.

As she watched the Lion crumble to the ground, Arica turned to face the air caster. He was waving his arms faster now, pushing Alys closer to the river. Arica shouted at him and sent a ball of fire roaring at him. He deflected it with his wind, but it also distracted him from Alys. She did not miss her chance and with two fists pummelled the ground, causing a wave of earth higher than any man to come crashing down on him. Arica quickly ran to her side and helped her off her knees.

'Are you all right?'

'Yes, thanks to you.'

They started towards Tamar and Ryger who were still fighting the last Lion. They had disarmed the others, two of which had run into the undergrowth of the forest and the third had been flung into the Karigraine. The fourth and final Lion had a cruel look in his viper-eyes while he flourished a long and razor-sharp sword that curled at the top into a hook. He moved quickly for someone of his size. His sword swung ferociously at the two casters as they dodged and deflected his attacks with their magic. Tamar was using her rock-shield to block him and also to push against him. This gave Ryger the chance to make the water at the lion's ankles to climb up his legs and freeze him in place. He was struggling to get out, shouting at them. Arica rose up a rock into the air and shot it at his sword arm, making his sword clatter against the ground. Tamar was about to send another rock to slam against his head, but Ryger held up his own arm in protest.

'Wait! He's coming back with us.'

Chapter 11

They were all standing in the largest tent in camp along with Jyneera and her loyal bodyguard, Hamir. The captured Lion was now restrained with rope around his wrists and ankles while he was forced onto a stool. The twin earth casters stood at either side of him to ensure he did not try anything. Arica and Ryger were next to Jyneera's desk after having informed her of the attack. They were still in shock about the air caster helping the Lions. Jyneera had mentioned that the Haellan army had started to put casters into their ranks, but it still distressed Arica to see it. Magic did not exist in Haella and yet, there was one marked with the sigil she had dreamed of wearing since she was a child. It sent feelings of both anger and sickness through her, it was strange, but her world was strange now.

'Let us begin with what you were doing in that forest?' Jyneera said in a sweet voice.

The Lion stared at her defiantly.

'Perhaps I did not make it clear to you,' she said stepping closer to him, 'after I ask you something you will answer or Hamir here will force you.'

Hamir took a step closer. His hulking size seemed to shrink the man. He had a cold look in his eyes, sending an icy chill down the Lion's spine. Even Arica knew she would not like to be on the receiving end of that look.

'Again, what were you doing?' Jyneera questioned.

'Even if I wanted to tell you anything, I could not,' he replied flatly.

'Talk. Or lose your tongue and be unable to for the rest of your miserable life,' Hamir growled.

The Lion groaned and spat out. 'I shall try—but allow me to keep my tongue.'

'If the information you give is good enough, then you just might,' Tamar said curtly.

The Lion began to tell his secret of what he and the other Amber Lions were doing in the forest. He said that the lords of the land had each been sent regiments from the imperial army. Every lord had strict orders from the king that what they were doing was to remain invisible to the public. He admitted that he did not know what they had been doing but that they were instructed to go into all kinds of places and search for something. Something that he knew had to hold some sort of power because whenever it was mentioned the lords' eyes would light up. It was almost as if they hungered, yearned for it. They had spent the last few months scouring the Haellan side of the Karigraine searching for it.

'Searching for what?' Jyneera asked, 'you must have some notion of what it is?'

'I do not— I swear it.'

'What lord were you assigned under?' Ryger asked.

'Lord Cothomir of Serpent's Hollow,' he responded.

'Serpent's Hollow is only about six hours south — east of us,' Alys informed them, stepping next to Arica.

'We could send a party to infiltrate and discover what this mystery relic is,' Ryger suggested, looking at Jyneera.

'It would be too dangerous, Ryger. I cannot risk losing anyone.'

'But this would be invaluable to us, we would finally know what it is Solomir is doing!' he exclaimed.

'Ryger Alfarion, remember your place and who it is you are speaking to,' Jyneera snapped viciously. Ryger's jaw clenched. Arica could tell he wanted to say something else but was biting his tongue.

'Perhaps he has a point, Chancellor,' Hamir said.

'Hamir?'

'It has been months of running around searching for regiments of the Amber Lions and snuffing them out or finding newly awakened casters— but, we do not have any idea what it is all about. We need to unearth their plan and put a stop to it once and for all.'

The room was silent for a few long moments. It was strange to hear Hamir speak more than five words. He was usually the silent giant that stood in the corner scowling.

'You may be right— it is agreed. Ryger, you will take a small party to Serpent's Hollow and use the cover of nightfall to sneak into the Lord's manor and find anything that tells of Solomir's plans,' Jyneera disclosed.

'Yes, Jyneera,' he uttered, 'we will do you proud.'

For the rest of the evening Arica sat on the beach staring up at the stars and across the water. The air was calm, not even a breeze was blowing. The water was like smooth glass without a ripple to be seen. There was something peaceful about the unmoving river. It had been flowing much faster during the day but now with the moon's rising it had become frozen in motion. The coarse sand felt good between her fingers as she dug her hands into it. Her chest rose and sank as she released a deep sigh. So much had happened today and her mind was spinning. Seeing the Lions come at them like that was not what she had expected. For years she had admired them, practically worshipped them. Whenever a group of them would ride through town on their huge horses and their armour glittering in the sunlight she would feel such happiness. That was all she wanted to be, a shining light for other children like her. Defending her country and people. It was a dream that was all but shattered now. The knights of Haella, the Amber Lions, were nothing but pawns for the king and his tyrannical regime. It was nothing but shock and disgust that swelled inside of her when she heard about the things they had done outside of Haella.

During their time in the carts, herself and Malin had listened to their companions' stories of the terrors they brought. The two swordsmen were from the same village just passed the spruce forests. They were a farming village that grew grain to sell to neighbouring towns and villages. One night when they had been twelve, they heard shouting and from their windows saw fire burning the crops. In between the rows of grain were Amber Lions on horseback throwing torches, not just on the crops, but the thatched roofs of the cottages too. It was because they were feeding the people of Dun Ortha they were told, as they watched their home turn to ash.

The bearded cook, Sandar, who Malin had been working with was not, in fact, from Ebraeye. He was from a smaller country to the north of Haella, beyond the Javelins, called Aflos. A region famous for their precious stone mines. While it was small in size, their riches made them large. In the capital city their buildings were gilded in gold and the royal palace was encrusted in jewels. Sandar said their rivers were like liquid sapphires. It sounded beautiful. But these riches had their flaw; they, like moths to a flame, attracted insects — Lions. They were invaded overnight; the Amber Lions swept through the city in a matter of hours killing many people but enslaving three times that number. They threw the royal family, including the young prince, to their deaths from a tower. Sandar explained that he avoided the same fate by hiding under his bed, while his brother covered the gap underneath with the bed clothes. It was the last thing he did before soldiers burst into the room. Sandar slipped out after they had left and moved further into the city and escaped by lying flat on a small boat and let it flow down the river.

The deep sadness in their eyes as they told their stories was heart-breaking. The sorrow in their voices was evident. Malin squeezed Sandar's hand and gave him a smile which he returned. Arica sympathised with them, commending them on their bravery and strength to have gotten through those situations. Arica and Malin could not believe they never knew anything about this. No one in Harth did as far as they understood. It seemed as though everyone had been affected by the Haellan forces. Even the Haellan people themselves. If you did anything that the Lions deemed wrong, you were punished. Arica thought it would not take much to warrant punishment under Solomir's rule after everything she had heard. Each and every person in this army had been directly affected or knew someone who had. The hurt on their faces and in their voices whenever the Amber Lions or their king was discussed proved that. This was made clear further when Ryger got up and jumped out of the cart the second they stopped. She listened to his footsteps as they stomped away quickly. She shared a confused and concerned look with her brother and promptly hopped out after him.

She found him in a grove of trees sitting on a rock. He had his knees bent and his hands clasped together over them. Slowly, she made her way over to him asking if she could sit with him. He nodded his head in silence. Arica did not know how long they sat there together. It was not until she noticed small orbs of light floating around the grass, fireflies. She watched them dance around like fallen stars. They were so delicate and beautiful; it brought a smile to her face. The tiny balls of yellow-green light danced amongst the blades of grass. She heard a sniff next to her and looked at Ryger to see a tear falling down his cheek. She did not know what to say, what could she say that would make him feel better? Arica inched her hand forward, resting it on top of his. For a moment, nothing was said, but then he turned his head and rested his forehead against hers.

'Thank you,' he said quietly as he held her hand in his.

Chapter 12

The setting sun's rays were spreading across the water in a myriad of colours from yellow to orange to pink. All of the different shades were making the cold waters of the Karigraine look almost warm, like a welcoming bath. Nothing blemished the glass-like river, not even a lonely branch. Everything was calm. Everything was quiet. There were no sounds of animals, wind or people. All was silent up the edge of the Serpent. Like lightning, the party sent from the camp were making their way towards the target at great speed. The hooves of their horses thumping against the earth as they swept further towards the mouth of the river. Here the river would meet the Tempestuous Sea known for the legend of the great sea serpent for which the river and town were named.

Arica remembered the story. It was one of the scary stories her brother, Garo, loved to tell his younger siblings when it was dark and stormy outside. The town of Serpent's Hollow had been ravaged for years by the monster. It would destroy any ship that attempted to dock in the town and swallow its contents, people included, whole. It was said that its mouth was home to three rows of razor-sharp teeth. Sometimes, it would lurk near the shore where, if you got close enough to the edge, it would snap its jaws shut around you. It was not until the people made a deal with it that the constant tyranny ended. Each year on the spring equinox, they would sacrifice ten people to the beast who would devour them, and it would leave the town alone for the remainder of the year. It was said that it even protected the town from raiding parties by smashing ships and swallowing their crews. These people would be flung from the cliff into the sea for the beast. Rumour has it that the townspeople still continue the age-old tradition to this day. Shivers went down her spine as she thought of plummeting into the deep, dark sea to be shredded apart by giant serpent fangs.

Kneeling behind the rocks, that sat on the beach looking up at the town, was the Ebraeyen party. Their heads tilted upwards at the town that stretched from the base of the cliff up to the very top. Their horses were tied amongst the trees behind them to avoid being seen. The town gates were shut tight with patrolmen walking along the walkway. They would have bows and arrows ready to take down any intruders approaching. Ryger was scanning the perimeter of the town, looking for a way in. After a minute, he turned to his partners and explained what the plan was. Once he had gone over the details with them, they all began their stealthy approach.

Luckily for them, the land below the cliff top town was littered with rocks and debris from ships who had run aground. Arica swallowed a lump in her throat as she thought of the serpentine story. They reached the docks where ships were moored waiting to be unloaded by workers. Night had fallen so there was no one on the ships. Small lanterns dotted the docks, lighting the planks in their way. The sentries along the walls would be able to see them if they did not do something about them. Arica nodded as her friends looked at her. She stepped out from behind the crate she was crouched behind. Focusing on the tiny burning lights she raised her hands up. Her breathing became slow and rhythmic, matching her heartbeat. She imagined flames in the palm of her hands; she could feel the heat. The warm sensation felt good, she liked it. She concentrated on the fire and carefully squeezed her hands shut. As her hands closed the flames grew smaller and smaller until they were quenched. All of the practice she had been doing with Ryger really did help her. It did not matter that his magic lay in the water, he could still help her. *Breathing and concentration*, were the virtues of casting that he sang to her during their training sessions. The four of them continued down the steps and onto the docks. They manouvered through the crates and goods piled on the wooden planks. They kept close to them to shroud their presence from any of the sentries' peering eyes. They reached the end of the dock, where, to their left was a large drainage pipe, big enough for a person to fit through. Ryger lifted his hand up and swished it from side to side, forming steps of solid ice up to it.

'Hold your noses,' Tamar scowled.

The grimy pipe twisted and turned until finally letting out in a courtyard. They climbed out carefully while ensuring no one was watching them. Alys kicked the muck from her boots and scoffed. Once again, Arica used her magic to put out the little fires in the lanterns hanging along the street. The cobblestones had gone dark and nothing but the shadows cast from the light of the moon were strewn across them. From the information the captured Lion had given, they appeared to be in the upper district of the town. The lord's manor would not be too far from here. They took off towards the manor, venturing downside streets rather than the much more conspicuous main one. They clambered over fences and dodged being seen by patrolling soldiers. Arica made a face of disgust as she saw the Amber Lion sigil engraved on their chests. She found herself holding back the urge to hurtle a boulder their way. Shaking her head, she pushed on up the hill. Soon, they came to a halt at the end of an alleyway. There in front of them was a huge house with a deeply pitched gable roof. The timber framing streaked along the walls like stripes on a cat. There were banners with embroidered crests hanging either side of the main entrance to the house, the crest of House Cothomir. A two-headed snake eating a ship. Another nod to the story with the new addition of a second head. The more time she spent in this town, the more she believed the legend.

'Here's where we split up. We meet back here in two hours; if anyone does not come back by then, we leave without them. Understood?' Ryger explained to the party.

Arica, Alys and Tamar nodded and agreed. They said their farewells and split into two groups — Alys and Tamar, and Ryger with Arica.

Arica watched as the twins rose a ladder fashioned from stone out of the ground and used it to climb up to a balcony above. They were tasked with searching the upper levels of the manor. They disappeared from sight and their ladder sank back into the earth. Now it was her turn to use her magic. They found the entrance to the storeroom around the back of the manor. It was padlocked as they had predicted. Arica knelt down next to it and grasped it. She closed her eyes and let the flames bubble up inside of her. She felt the heat pass from her chest, down her arms and finally to her palms. When she opened her eyes again all that was left behind were drops of molten metal on the ground.

'Well done,' Ryger told her, patting her shoulder.

She pulled open the doors and they stepped down into the dark space. The storeroom was in the cellar and it was utter blackness. The doors clattered behind them as Ryger pulled them closed. His shoulders tightened as he waited for shouts from the guards. After a moment, he relaxed and squinted to see. Arica conjured a ball of fire in her hand, casting light around the room. Nothing was in the room apart from them, dry food and bottles of wine. Ryger picked one up, wiped the dust off it and held it up.

'Quick cup?'

Arica let out a laugh and pushed his shoulder. He smiled as he put the bottle back onto the rack. It was clear that there was nothing of interest in this room. They reached for the door out and walked into the kitchen. No one was there. The cooks would have long since finished their duties and returned home. They sneaked out into the hallway, being as quiet as they could. Arica knew they were looking for an office of some sort, somewhere that Lord Cothomir would keep records of his doings or letters revealing his plans. But nothing. After looking in the pantry, they climbed the staircase which the servants would use. They searched the different rooms and found nothing but the parlour and the great hall. Walking into the foyer, there was still nothing to be seen. They were about to head up the curved oak staircase when they heard voices.

'Where is that servant girl? I might have died before she came back!'

Arica whipped her head towards Ryger. His eyes were wide. *That has to be Cothomir, who else would be shouting for a servant?* The voice was answered by another and they sounded like they were approaching. Arica's heart was racing, she knew they would descend the stairs and find them. They pushed up against the wall trying to find a quick escape route. They would be seen running back the way they came. Arica felt something prod her in the back and reached for it to readjust it. She pushed it and it moved into what felt like a slot. There was a click and suddenly they stumbled backwards down steps and into a dark room.

Arica and Ryger were sitting in a heap at the base of a stone staircase. They both ached from the impact. The room was pitch black. She felt around for something to hold on to. A rough slab to her left became her anchor which she used to stand. She reached her hand down and helped Ryger up. A strange smell hung in the air. It was different from anything she had smelled before. The stone wall was cold to the touch. A chill went up her spine. There was something about this place that unsettled her. Closing her eyes, she held out her hand and summoned the fire from within her. The light washed the room in a warm, orange glow. It revealed that they were in a long tunnel. The entrance they had fallen from had shut itself behind them. Ryger started walking down the tunnel with Arica close on his heels. *What is this place?*

The tunnel ended with a large door. They opened the door slowly, not knowing what may be behind it. The room they entered was also dark, but Arica quickly lit the candles with the fire in her hand, allowing her to extinguish the orb after. Wooden tables were spread around the room. Some were topped with glass vials and jars containing different coloured liquids. Upon looking closer, Arica noticed that the larger ones were filled with more sinister things. An eyeball floated in one, next to another jar containing what appeared to be a giant tongue. The back wall was covered in baleful looking metal tools — knives, tongs, pokers, amongst others.

'What do you think this is all for?' she questioned. She had an idea in her head from the terrible items that littered the room. She had to look away to stop herself from retching as she noticed what appeared to be a heart in a garish green liquid.

'Something unnatural has happened down here, I can feel it,' Ryger admitted.

'There's blood on this table,' Arica noticed. 'He is hurting people.'

'But who? And why?'

'I do not know— maybe there are notes around here somewhere,' she suggested. 'There are other doors to look behind.'

She stepped towards a door on the opposite side of the room. She attempted to twist the handle, but it was locked. A bang came from the other side of the door causing Arica to jump back in alarm. Looking at Ryger, she shrugged. A wrinkle creased her worried brow.

'Someone is in there.'

'We have to get them out,' Ryger said passionately.

Arica knew what to do. She placed her hand on the lock of the door and concentrated. The white-hot heat returned to her palm, and she felt the metal begin to melt away. Soon, there was a handprint shaped hole in the door. Ryger pushed it open, and they saw what was behind the door. In the corner of the room, on the straw covered floor was a girl huddled in a ball. She was tiny, from malnourishment based on the protruding bones. Her once-blonde hair was dirty and hanging over her face. Ryger stepped into the room.

'Hello, my name is Ryger. I am from the Ebraeyan army, we are here to help.'

He reached out his hand to help her up, but she did not take it. Instead, the girl made a gurgling sound. Her head twitched at an abnormal angle, and they were met by her stare. Her eyes were not the eyes of anyone Arica had ever seen; in the place of the usual round pupils were slits like a lizard. They were a sickly yellow colour. The girl pushed out her arms, one on the wall and the other on the floor. Her hands were scaled and ended in sharp black claws. A shrill shriek came out of her mouth, revealing fanged teeth. This was no human girl. She resembled a creature from a child's nightmare. Faster than a flying arrow, the girl threw herself forward, straight at Ryger. She knocked him over and the two of them grappled on the floor. The deranged girl thrashed and bared her fangs. Arica had to act quickly or Ryger would be mauled. The urge to hurtle fire at her came first, but she restrained herself as the fire could just as easily burn Ryger as the girl. She pulled her knife from her boot and plunged it into the girl's back. With a quivering last breath, she fell lifeless, on top of Ryger.

Arica pulled the body off of him and helped him up.

'Are you all right?' she asked, panicked. Her eyes scanned his body for injury.

'I will be,' he said panting, 'that was insane.'

'What was wrong with her?'

'I don't know, but she was not just a human,' he told her, brushing himself off.

'That was a lot of noise, they have to know someone is down here.'

Ryger agreed and the two of them went for the way out. In the distance, down the tunnel they could hear shouting. Someone was coming. Arica felt frantic. *If we are caught, they will torture us and then kill us. We have to get out.* They checked the other doors, all revealing other holding cells. These were all empty, thankfully. Footsteps were coming down the hall, fast. Arica's heart was racing. Soon they would be captured. She would never see Malin again, or her family. She grabbed hold of Ryger's hand and looked into his eyes. He squeezed it. The door into the torture chamber burst open.

'Oh, my Gods!' the sisters screamed, upon seeing Ryger and Arica.

'We need to leave, now!' Alys shouted, before either could have asked her a question.

Chapter 13

The night was calm and clear. A glowing yellow crescent moon was shining onto the water. The reflection was like a shining smile looking back up at the sky. All was quiet except for the crackling of orange flames dancing. The campfire was spreading a warmth around it, illuminating the people surrounding it. Their legs were hot from the heat. It was very welcome from the cold of the night. The horses were grazing amongst the trees behind the campfire, getting their well-deserved rest after galloping away from Serpent's Hollow. No one had followed them, thankfully. When the twins came rushing into the room of horrors it felt like the end. They found their way down to Arica and Ryger from a hidden door upstairs that revealed a ladder that led down here. A servant girl saw them as they began their descent and raised the alarm. They could not run the way they entered; they would be able to follow them easily. They had to find a new escape route. They all hurried into an empty cell with a clay wall at the back. The three women used their earth casting to break the earth apart and made a personal tunnel for them to run through. They clambered up and emerged into the fresh night air. Shouts were echoing up from the tunnel and as quick as they opened it, the earth casters avalanched it shut. The rumbling soil caving in ensured they could not be followed. Arica and her partners ran through the back streets of the town and kept to the shadows. They could not risk being caught now. They used the same pipe that they used to enter the town and sprinted over the docks. Ryger waved his hand in the air to create a thick mist and shrouded their movements. They fled Serpent's Hollow under the cover of fog.

Ryger caught their dinner in the river by casting the water up and forcing it to flow the fish to him. The river spat two fat carp onto the rocky shore. Arica made a fire, while the twins cooked the fish. They made a good team. Arica was happy she had met them; it was like it was meant to be. She thanked the gods for bringing them together. The four of them were enjoying the relaxation after their night of reconnaissance. They began to trade stories from their past, explaining how they got to where they were that day. Arica detailed her whole ordeal beginning with the Trialand ending with her and Malin's flight from Harth. Ryger knew the story from their travels, but the twins had yet to hear it. They were shocked that she had gone through her entire life without any indication or idea that she was a caster. They all laughed when Arica told them she did not even know that casters existed.

'Haella is a very strange place— so many secrets,' Tamar admitted.

This was something they could all agree on. Arica still found it hard to believe that there was this entire world outside of what she knew as reality. The stories of myth and legend, or what she *thought* were myth and legend, were in fact the truth. Magic was alive and flourishing in other parts of the world, and even in Haella hidden in plain sight. There were soldiers, members of the Amber Lions, who were casters. There may have been casters living in Harth with her for her entire life and she just never knew.

The Olfaris sisters, Alys and Tamar, told their story in sync. The two girls came from a lumber village in the southwestern corner of Ebraeye. Here, their father and brother worked in the forest cutting down large trees and brought them to the mills. In the mills, the women would heave the heavy logs onto the lines where the sawblades were. It was tiring and laborious work. The twins did not enjoy it. Alys dreamt of being a painter and would spend her spare time painting on the back of pieces of bark left over at the mill. Tamar, on the other hand, wanted to be a hunter. In the evenings, before sundown, she would venture into the forest and hunt animals for their meat and fur. They both had their own dreams, but the lifeblood of the town was the forestry. Their parents would not understand their desires. So, they decided that they would leave and move to Dun Ortha. They were gone for about a month when they heard that a huge forest fire had engulfed their home. Everything had been destroyed. After investigation by the Ebraeyan army, it was clear it was not a natural fire. Traces of a large force were found, hoofprints and in particular, a sword with a lion-shaped hilt. Alys and Tamar joined the army and vowed to avenge their family.

Arica expressed her sadness for the sisters. She told them they should not feel guilty about their leaving because if they had not, they would not be here. She promised that she would help them in their quest to take vengeance for their family. When she looked at Ryger, he was definitely upset. He was not going to share his story tonight. The three girls understood that it was not easy for everyone to talk about their past. They all shared a silent look of understanding; they were not going to push him on it. They all finished their meal and rolled out their sleeping mats under the trees next to their horses. Sundancer was lying down and Arica lay her head against his barrel-shaped stomach. His long face nestled on the grass next to his rider. The team said their goodnights and fell into a peaceful slumber.

The next day, they waited for the ferry that would carry them across the Karigraine River and onto Ebraeyan soil. The army had made their way across the day before while they journeyed to Serpent's Hollow. They were moving a day behind the others but would catch up to them in time. The ferry was a wooden vessel with plenty of room for them and their horses. Arica stood next to Sundancer, rubbing his muzzle and neck. He had never been on water before so she wanted to keep him calm. Every so often he would let out a whinny, reassuring Arica. The others were spread out around the boat staring into the distance as Haella grew further and further away. Arica closed her eyes and said a prayer to the goddess of the sea, Farrig, to protect them on their journey across the water. She had always liked the water, having lived beside it growing up. She liked the way it tossed back and forward as if waving at the person looking at it. As much as she did like it, she wanted it to be over. The excitement about seeing Ebraeye was all she could think about now. She was looking forward to seeing the nature, the people, and buildings. But most of all it was the city of Dun Ortha. The tall towers with roofs of green copper. The cobblestone bridges arching over their crystal-clear rivers. The glowing balls of fire that cast a radiant light along the streets at night. It sounded so beautiful and different from anywhere she had ever been before. Ryger had told her all about the city during their journeys in the back of the cart. He spoke about it with such nostalgia and often wore a smile. She could tell that it was a place that had been good to him.

They were back on the road shortly after the ferry docked on the far side of the Karigraine. Their horses cantered down the dirt track, leaving a trail of dust in the air behind them. They were rushing to try and catch up with Jyneera's party. They had important information to report back with. What they saw under Lord Cothomir's house was abnormal. That girl.

Something had been done to her. There was little humanity left in her from the way she reacted. More beast than man.

They were passing through the spruce forests that lined the Ebraeyan side of the river. The thick foliage of the trees made the path dark even though the sun was high in the sky. Arica kept to the back of the group as she did not know the way. Tamar rode at the front, encouraging her chestnut stallion to move faster with fierce determination. The others followed behind her like they were different parts of one being. They ran around the bends, avoiding the branches by ducking their heads. She was not sure how long they were on the track, but it seemed like a very long time. The trees were endless, the forest was very deep. *Is there going to be anything that breaks this up?* The evergreen needles of the trees were blocking much of the sun, so it was hard to tell what time of day it was. As if something was listening to her thoughts, she saw a light. Further down the path there was a red light, brighter than a star. They quickly pulled hard on the reins, their horses skidding to a halt.

'That is not good,' Alys said to the others.

'We have to be careful, Haellans can cross that river as easily as we can,' Ryger warned.

They steered their horses into the trees, off the track. The horses walked slowly towards the light, in a curved line to come at it from the side. There was no telling what it was. This light was a bright red-orange.

It unsettled Arica, she knew that colour all too well. As they moved closer they could hear voices. Some barking orders, while others were pleading. For what? Arica was afraid to see.

They left their horses a small way behind them. Standing amongst the bushes, they were hidden from where the voices came from. But it did not hide them from Arica and her companions' eyes. They were looking at what appeared to be an outpost. But there was not much standing. The wooden towers that were on either side of the path had been burnt and were smoking. Men and women clad in armour were looming over people who were either whimpering on the ground or begging for mercy on their knees. These men and women were bearing the sigil of the imperial army. *Not again. Why are they everywhere I go?* There were carts with large iron cages on the back of them. Some of them contained people that were bruised and weak. The Amber Lions were loading these poor people into the cages. They were taking them somewhere.

'We have to do something!' Arica said frantically.

'You're right, but we need to be smart— there could be other casters with them,' Ryger said.

'And not just one this time,' Alys added.

Arica looked around, trying to think of a plan. The carts were blocking the track. The soldiers were dotted around the area forcing people into the cages or beating them if they refused. What she noticed was just that, they were so busy looking at the people that they were not watching the burning outpost towers behind them. Arica looked at each of her friends and told them what they had to do. Once they were all in agreement, everyone moved into action.

Arica stepped out of the bushes, letting out a shout. The Lions looked at her and moved to attack. *If you like fire so much, here is some just for you.* Arica lifted arms at her sides and pulled them quickly back towards her and the fire answered. The flames flew out like arrows at the soldiers heading straight for her. Their howls of pain shook the trees. As they writhed on the ground Tamar ran in from the right, striking the earth with a fist, causing a crack to snake towards other soldiers. Two of the Lions fell into the crack and soon their screams stopped. Alys and Ryger ran from the left together. Ryger uncapped his flask on his hip and guided the water out. He used the moisture in the air to expand the water and caused it to come crashing down on other enemies. Alys lifted her arm to send rocks hurtling at some others, but her arm was stopped by an icy arm. She let out a gasp and then was thrown backwards into a tree trunk, winding her. Her body was still on the ground. Tamar screamed and ran towards the smirking water caster. Before she had time to react, Arica was knocked to the ground by a wave of earth. She rolled to the side as a foot stomped the ground where she was. She pulled her knife from her boot and stabbed it into her attacker's leg. With a shriek, the earth caster opened the ground under Arica. Arica fell down into the pit.

Think fast. She held out her hands and flicked them into action. A net of rock formed and caught her like a fly. The air in her lungs was knocked out. She winced as the pain travelled over her body. The shouts from above echoed down into the pit. Arica stood up and pulled steps of rock out of the walls around her and ran up.

When she emerged from the ground, she saw that Ryger was now on the ground too. He was bleeding from his forehead. Four unconscious Lions were scattered around him. *You did your best.* She saw Tamar was mid battle with the water caster and two swordsmen. There were three more Lions making their way towards her. Arica sent a wall of rock crashing up in front of them to block their path. They turned to her and two of them sent rocks right at her. Arica dived to the right as the rocks crashed past her. Arica summoned a fireball and threw it at the third Lion, ending in him clutching his face in pain. The earth casters sent more rocks towards her, one of them hit her shoulder. She groaned and grabbed the shoulder. She could see Tamar was starting to falter; the water caster was too strong. The two earth casters and the other Lion rushed at Arica. She let out a shrill cry and thrust her arms out. The lions flew backwards into the wall she created, and they crumpled to the ground. *What did I just do? Was that wind?* She did not have time to question it. She ran towards Tamar, pulling a sword off a knocked-out soldier. She pierced it through a gap in one of the swordsman's armour and he fell. She let it go and grabbed either side of the other swordsman's helmet and commanded the fire within to flow out. The metal of the helmet melted inwards, crushing, and burning the soldier. The water caster turned and lifted her hand to strike. This was the opportunity Tamar had been waiting for. She used her magic to pull apart the rock wall and used both sides to crush the caster between them like an insect. Tamar and Arica looked at each other, their shoulders rising and falling with deep breaths. Arica wiped the sweat from her forehead. *Ryger!* She ran to him and knelt on the ground.

'Ryger! Can you hear me?' she said holding his face.

His eyes remained closed.

'Please, Ryger! You are going to be all right, just nod or move a finger. Anything to show you can hear me!' Arica pleaded.

Tamar was soon at her side, with her arm around her, now conscious, sister.

'Alys, you're awake,' Arica said, thanking the gods.

'Let me help,' she said, reaching for her own flask.

She twisted off the cap and poured the water directly onto Ryger's face. His eyes flashed open and he coughed as the water went up his nose. His eyes darted from side to side, looking at the girls.

'Is it raining?' he asked groggily.

Full of relief, they laughed.

Chapter 14

The outpost's fire was extinguished and dull smoke rose up towards the sky. The charred remains were like a dark skeleton on the world's surface. Seventeen men and women were rescued from an unknown fate. They were now salvaging what they could from the ruined outpost and buildings around it. The Haellan army had attacked without warning, for what, they did not know. Arica thought it must be whatever Haellan lords were looking for. It was clear that they were not there for money or blood as they killed no one. They disarmed them and then started loading them into the cages on the back of the carts. One managed to get away before Arica and the others reached them. Four people, three men and a woman. Taken to someplace far away for a reason unknown. The head guard of the outpost explained to them that this was becoming a regular occurrence. People being snatched from their homes and carried away. Never to return. No one knew why.

After they had helped the people of the outpost, they continued their journey along the path. They piled the Lions and casters, that were still breathing, into their own carts bound at the wrists and ankles. Here they would wait until guards from the city came to deliver them to the dungeons. They had to reach Dun Ortha and report back to Jyneera. She needed to know that this was happening, and so close to the city. They were less than half a day's ride from it. There would be no stopping them now. They urged their steeds to run faster than they had before. Their movements were relentless. The dirt beneath them thundered like a ferocious storm. They burst from the forest with one thought in mind — get to Dun Ortha. Arica encouraged Sundancer to keep going. She rubbed his neck and praised him. He had never had to run like this before. She knew he would be exhausted but he needed to keep going. The sweat was pouring out of him. His smooth neck was glistening. Ryger and Alys' horses flanked her while Tamar took the lead again. Their small group entered the Taifor Valley. A stretch of grass covered land with huge hills either side. A narrow river flowed through the centre of it. Alys had told her about this place, she described it as the passageway to Dun Ortha. At the other end of the valley would be the city. Her destination after what seemed like forever. Soon, she would see it. Soon, she would see Malin again. Soon, her journey would be over.

The earthen path along the ground suddenly became a masoned limestone path. The smooth stone allowed for carts and carriages to roll along them with great ease. Here they were beginning to meet other people, travellers coming from afar with goods to sell. Ryger told her how to recognise the different peoples of the world. The Aflosi wore bright colours with golden jewellery, the Ultariac tribes of the deserts to the north clad themselves in loose fitting robes with headwraps, while the marshland people from Telvidia all had white hair styled into intricate braids with metal hoops and beads adorning them. All so different. Arica could not help but smile at the diversity all around her. Harth was not like this. She presumed that everyone and everywhere was like Harth and Haella, but she knew it was not now. She was glad of it. There was something beautiful about all these unique people mixing together in one place. The world appeared more colourful now.

A huge archway was the entrance to the city of Dun Ortha. Two round towers with parapets near the top were the guardians of the city. Soldiers patrolled them and the wall, keeping a watchful eye over the city and its people. Arica leaned into Sundancer's ear and praised him for getting here so fast.

'There is a bucket of oats and a warm stable waiting for you,' she smiled.

They entered the city and Arica quickly saw why everyone spoke so highly of it. The streets were bustling with people, but they were not overcrowded. All of the shop fronts were decorated with individual signs with windows displaying their wares. Looking up, she saw the green coloured caps of the towers that Tamar explained happens to copper after it gets wet. The city was divided into different districts with rivers separating them. Each district was like its own island, bridges connecting them like veins to the artery. Their reflections looked up at them like dreamy mirages from the crystalline rivers running under the bridges. Arica followed her friends as they weaved through the streets. Their horses' hooves clopped against the stone paths beneath them. The flag of Ebraeye, a rearing black horse in front of an orange sun, hung from poles dotted around the city and flapped in the breeze. As they trotted over the final bridge, Ryger told her they had entered the Cerulean District. Each district was colour coded, blue being the colour of the governing buildings, including the Chancellor's home. It was known as the Azure House due to the sparkling blue tiles on its roof. Here, the men and women that ran the city lived and worked. It was here that they would give their report on what they saw in Serpent's Hollow and also at the outpost in the forest. It was news that Arica knew was vital to get to Jyneera. She did not understand it but she felt it in her bones that it must be told.

The Chancellor's home was a great house with smooth-faced rustication along the walls. Tall windows on the building were embellished with sculptures of animals and flowers. A large statue of Malfor, the god of justice, stood in front of the door at the top of the white marble steps gazing down at them. His book of law nestled in the crook of his elbow as always. Arica stared at his stern eyes that were staring back at her. There was something about them that made her think he was alive. Her father always spoke about doing the right thing; *what would make Malfor smile?* he would ask her and her brothers. This was his way of ensuring they never told a lie to him or her mother. *Mother.* Arica could not help but feel sorrow at the thought of her mother. The look of fear in her eyes the last time she saw her. That was not how any child ever wanted their parents to look at them. All she wanted was for her mother to hug her or smile at her. But all she got was terror in the eyes of the woman who bore her.

Four soldiers, two on either side of the door, stood still as stone guarding the entrance. Each had a sword nestled in a scabbard on their hip. Arica had seen enough swords for a while. She longed for a day where she would not have to see one. To think, this is what she had wanted not but a month ago. To be training with sword and shield, with bow and arrow, for the rest of her days. Now, she could think of nothing worse. One of the soldiers opened the door for them. They walked in and Arica's head began to turn in all directions to take it all in. She stood at the entrance of a huge foyer, a greeting area for the Chancellor's guests. The room had a marble floor, like the steps outside. It gleamed with the light of a hundred stars. The walls were adorned with the Ebraeyen flag and paintings. The most beautiful paintings she had seen. Past chancellors of Ebraeye, Ryger whispered in her ear when he noticed her looking. Long curtains, the colour of burnt orange draped the long windows in the foyer. As she walked further in, Arica noticed a huge sigil was set in the marble floor. The same black horse rearing on an orange sun was under her feet. The symbol of Ebraeye. The symbol of liberation.

Suddenly, a door to their right swung open and a man she recognised strode out. The long, pink scar that ran the length of his face on the right still made her wince. He did not say a word, he merely cocked his head. An order to follow him. His silence did not surprise Arica, she had grown accustomed to it. They followed him dutifully down a long corridor, finally stopping in front of a pair of double doors. The sigil of Ebraeye carved into the stone about it, like a crown. Two lamps, lit by glowing orbs of light, hung on the walls next to it. Hamir knocked twice. They waited for a few seconds until they heard one word, *enter*. Arica walked into the chancery of Jyneera. There she sat at the top of the room in a padded chair waiting for them. She welcomed them and offered them a seat on one of the many chairs in the room. They gladly accepted the offer. Hamir, however, took his usual stance next to Jyneera.

'Well, I am sure you have much to tell me.'

'That we do, Chancellor,' Tamar said looking between Jyneera and her friends.

They relayed the story to them. They told them of their mission in Serpent's Hollow and the strange findings beneath the lord's manor. Jyneera's face twisted in a fusion of disgust and sadness upon hearing about the girl being held in the cell. They continued telling them about their escape and journey across the

Serpent. Their faces dropped when they heard about the attack on the outpost so close to Dun Ortha. They could not believe that the Haellans would dare strike so close to the capital. After hearing about the people captured and taken to an unknown location, she had heard enough. Jyneera thanked them for their service and said she had much to think about. She informed them that she would speak to her advisors and decide what the next move was. They, for the moment, were to rest. They had travelled a long way and encountered many troubling things. Jyneera rang a small silver bell on her desk and a short, plump man scurried into the room as if out of nowhere. He was ordered to show them to their rooms, they were going to stay here as she would require their services again shortly. The man nodded his head and beckoned Arica and the others to follow him. He brought them up a marble staircase with a metal banister. The smooth metal felt cool against her fingers. It led them up two levels and onto another corridor. The short man stopped between four doors and told them that these would be their quarters.

'Dinner will be brought to you shortly, and jugs of hot water for your baths,' he announced. Then, just as quickly as he appeared, he disappeared down the corridor again.

The twins took the first two rooms, saying they were each going to sleep awhile. Leaving Arica and Ryger alone in the hallway.

'What a day,' Ryger said with a sigh.

'It has been a long one for certain,' Arica agreed.

'We should rest then,' Ryger said.

'Yes, I suppose we should— until tomorrow then.'

She wanted to invite him to her room. It had been a long journey and she longed to spend some time alone with him. It was strange to her to have grown to feel such closeness between them in the short time of knowing one another. She wanted to be together, if not only to sit together in silence. They did not need to speak. His presence would have been more than enough. But alas, she did not make the request.

'Until tomorrow.'

Arica stepped into her room and closed the door behind her. She stood with her back against it for a moment, listening to Ryger still in the corridor. She heard him sigh again as he went into his own room. With the sound of the door clicking shut, she seemed to deflate. The hope that he would call her back or knock on the door flashed through her mind. But she knew that he would not come back. He did not have the same hope as she did. She released a deep breath and continued into the room. It was a fine room. A fireplace with a lounge chair capped the southern side. Double doors led onto a balcony overlooking the gardens. It was dusk now, the sun slowly creeping below the horizon. Arica could see the glowing orbs had started to illuminate the city. They were so beautiful, like thousands of fireflies fluttering in the streets. But the piece of furniture she most admired in the room was the four-poster bed. She threw herself onto it, laying her tired body against the soft mattress. The down-filled pillows felt like clouds beneath her head.

Laying there, looking up at the ceiling, she noticed the mural. A beautiful painting of the gods. Rhialgir accompanied by his owl and fox. Farrig, the sea goddess, wielding her net and orb that held the power of control over all water. The twin goddesses of peace and war, Sgealneas and Dorcoga, opposite sides of all battles stared down at her. All these mythical men and women watching over her had always been a part of her life. Deities to pray to. Great protectors of the race of men. She always believed in them, but now they felt closer to her somehow. All of a sudden, a knock rattled against the door. Her heart almost skipped a beat. Arica leapt from the bed and pulled open the door. She was greeted by a pair of green eyes and a mop of curly dark hair she knew very well. Her brother smiled at her and stepped into the room, closing the door behind him.

'Had to come see you once I heard you were here.'

'I'm glad you did, I missed you.'

They sat on the bed together, cross-legged. Malin filled her in on what she had missed while on her mission to Serpent's Hollow. And she did the same for him. She knew that what they saw on the mission was not meant to be spread around but this was her brother. He was always the person she told everything to, and that would never change. They spoke for what seemed like hours. Dinner had arrived and been wolfed down in the time he was there. Day turned to night before too long. She did not feel tired at first, but as if a spell had been cast, she found her eyes beginning to shut. Malin was already sleeping at her side. Bit by bit, her eyes closed until she saw nothing but black.

Chapter 15

The weeks that followed were weeks that Arica enjoyed. She would begin her days by breaking her fast in the Chancellor's dining room, along with her friends and Malin. Following that, she would train with both casters and *ordinary folk*, as she learned those without magical abilities were called. In the training ground, her skill with both blade and arrow were to be honed. The quartermaster ensured that she was outfitted with a sword and bow immediately.

'It will not do for you to rely only on your casting—iron is always reliable,' he told her as he brought her through the armoury.

Her new quiver was leather-bound with an imprint of the Ebraeyen crest; orange-tipped arrows filled it. Hanging on her hip was a similarly designed scabbard, metal encased in leather. The gleaming hilt of her sword sitting neatly on top. She always saw the necessity for a bow and arrow to provide for her family. The dream of being a soldier with her own sword was something that played in her mind for years, but now having become one, she no longer knew how she felt. Powerful? Dangerous? Or perhaps, just terrified.

After working on her swordsmanship and archery skills, she would go to where the casters were housed. The casters trained in a special place they called the Ring. This was a large circular building without a roof, specifically designed for them to develop their magic. There was a section for each of the elements. The earth casters were surrounded by earthen mounds and boulders. A pool of water surrounding a small island was where the water casters practiced. Pits dug into the ground were smoking and burning to allow the fire casters to train without having to worry about conjuring the flames themselves. Arica had never had any problem with doing so but apparently that was not common. The wind casters were perched atop an elevated structure so they would be surrounded by the open air. She spent her time here going between the groups. This was not just uncommon, but completely unheard of. Casters had power over one element, she however, had shown an affinity for three. Arica worked with the wind casters first as this had been the newest addition to her arsenal. She received no warning when it emerged at the outpost. Thrusting herself forward had caused a surge of air to blast past her, toppling her enemy. While she felt strong, she could not help but notice the piercing stares from the others around her. She was something different. Something that could do things that had not been done in an age. These types of things often awoke misunderstandings in people, and from those misunderstandings, fear.

The element that she felt most powerful using was fire. When it started to come alive inside her, she never felt more herself. It was as if this was the way she was always meant to be. A being charged with fire. But it was without a doubt her least favourite training session. This was because of a slender woman with black hair usually left to hang loose. Bretta, the prodigy fire caster. Alys told Arica about her over dinner after she asked. She was one of the most gifted fire casters in the nation in years, or so Alys said. From a young age, Bretta was able to conjure fire at will and control it effortlessly. She was a formidable warrior and was respected amongst the other fire casters. Unfortunately for Arica, Bretta decided Arica was less than worthy. During the training, Bretta would *accidentally* knock into her or blatantly whisper about her to the other casters. Arica felt like a lonely schoolgirl again.

'You make her uncomfortable,' Tamar announced at the dinner table.

'But *why*?'

'Isn't it obvious?' she asked flatly, 'she has been the *wondrous and awe-inspiring* fire caster for years and now you, an unknown girl from Haella, possess more power in a single strand of hair than she does in her entire body.'

'I did not ask for this,' Arica said angrily.

'So, you did not,' Tamar agreed, 'but do not let some envious little girl with her schoolyard trickery unnerve you.'

'Show her that you are not one to be trifled with,' Alys said, stabbing her meat with her fork.

Arica brushed the dust from her clothes as she walked away from the earth casters quarter of the Ring. She had spent the last hour throwing and deflecting rocks, pulling solid earth up to act as her shield and creating holes beneath her sparring partners. Each day, she felt herself growing stronger, and more sure of herself. The simple huntress girl from Harth was slowly becoming a distant memory. She did not want to forget. Malin would be her anchor, and she thanked him for it. She rested against the wall next to the fire casters. The younger casters were practicing moving fire from one pit to another. An elderly man was calling out instructions, reminding them to breathe slowly as they focused on the flames. Arica was almost jealous of them. So young and being able to use their magic freely, even just knowing they had it. Training had become a very important part of her life. She wanted to be the greatest caster she could be.

Each and every day, she pushed herself, and as usual, caught the attention of others. At first, she noticed the whispering at the edge of the quarter and sideways glances as she walked past. While practicing throwing fireballs at clay disks in the air, she lost her footing and stumbled to the ground. An eruption of pathetically muffled laughter echoed throughout the fire quarter. Arica felt her cheeks turn red as she shuffled back onto her feet. Her mentor, Varlo, came over to help her up.

He was always so kind to her, the only fire caster that did not treat her like she was diseased. She recalled one evening after their training, they took a walk along the streets of the city. He told her that he understood what it was like to be different. That was when he lifted the skirt of his robes to reveal a metal leg. He explained that he lost it in an accident as a child and ever since then the other fire casters treated him differently. It did not matter how talented his casting was, he was different and that was excuse enough. People have a way of making those with any semblance of dissimilarity feel as though they do not belong, but she would not let them do that to her. As Varlo pulled her to her feet, she thanked him and continued her training as if nothing had happened. She would not give Bretta, or her sycophants, the satisfaction.

The night sky shimmered over Dun Ortha. The streets awash with the ethereal green glow of the lanterns' fires made it appear like an underwater city. Many people still walked along the cobbled paths and along the iridescent rivers. But the streets were much quieter than they usually were during the day which made it the perfect time for someone to wander in peace. During the day, there would always be someone stopping her or asking her questions. It was nice to be able to just walk around the city and admire its intricate beauties. Every wall was adorned with sculptures of different creatures in a range of poses. Schools of radiant coloured fish swam underneath the surface of the rivers. Everywhere the eye could see, flowers of every colour bloomed making the city a forest of its own. It really was the most beautiful place in the world. Arica marvelled at the wondrous city. *This place is unbelievable. So many things do not seem real.* She perched herself on a white marble bench, the legs of which were sculpted in the form of tree roots. With her hands laid on the seat, she leaned back and exhaled. Finally, a moment's reprieve.

'Enjoying the night air?'

She whipped her head around, drawing her hidden blade from her boot.

'Whoa, whoa! It's just me,' her brother said waving his hands in front of himself.

'My gods, Malin!' she exclaimed sheathing the blade. 'You are just asking to get stabbed creeping up on me like that.'

'I did not realise I was approaching such a dangerous warrior.'

'Ferocious some might say,' she winked.

'May I sit with you, oh ferocious one?'

'I suppose,' she said, patting the seat.

Malin propped himself next to Arica. He put his hands together and started rolling his thumbs around each other. Arica recognised this action. She saw it when he told their parents that he did not want to take part in the Trial. He did it when he told their mother that all he wanted to do was be a cook. It was always when

137

he was nervous. Always when there was something he wanted to say but did not know how.

'How are you?' she asked.

'I am well— I'm really enjoying working in Jyneera's kitchen. I am learning so much.'

'Good, I'm glad you are doing something you love,' Arica said happily.

Malin bit the corner of his lip and his eyes fell to the floor.

'Malin, you know you can talk to me,' she told him gently.

'I know— it's just, I—' he stopped himself.

'What is it?'

'I think I might burst if I don't say it,' he said fervidly.

'Then you know what to do.'

'I… I like someone.'

'Who?' Arica asked excitedly.

'Sandar.'

'That is wonderful news, Malin. Have you told him?'

'No!' he said, almost shouting. 'I do not know if he feels the same way.'

'Only one way to find out, brother.'

'I knew you would say that— it is just, I have not felt this way before. He is so kind to me, and always treats me as an equal even when he knows his own skill greatly surpasses my own.'

'Malin, you are tremendous. Anyone would be lucky to have you,' she said laying her hand on his.

'Thank you, Ari. You are forever my greatest advocate.'

'It is easy to be a supporter of someone like you, now let us go back,' she said standing and holding out her arm.

Malin stood up and linked his arm with hers and they strolled back to the Cerulean District.

Chapter 16

Sunlight poured in through the crack in the heavy curtains. They were a deep blue colour, like the ocean. It was as if a great body of water was split right down the middle. The light curved along the wooden floorboards, dividing the room in two. She watched it snake its way onto the opposite wall. A cloud of pillows covered the bed, a mountain of silk and down. It was a comfort that Arica did not want to leave each morning the sun woke her up. But alas, the usual knock on the bedroom door came signally that it was time for the day to begin. She waited for the handmaid to enter her room, but instead another knock rapped on the door. She got out of bed and put a robe on. She approached the door and opened it. Tamar stood outside wearing a tan coloured jacket and green riding pants. Her cropped hair was pushed back out of her face.

'Good morning,' she said.

'Morning, is everything all right?'

'Wanna go for a ride? I am feeling a bit stuffy in this house as of late.'

Once Arica got dressed, the two women made their way into the stables where their horses were housed. Arica hugged Sundancer's muzzle and gently caressed his strong neck. Tamar was tightening the straps of her horse, Orial's, saddle. She was already mounted and waiting at the exit when Arica finally did the same. With a flick of the reins, the two stallions kicked off the dirt and thundered through the streets and out of the city.

The valley was beautiful at this time. The dew from the night before was still fresh and glimmering on each blade of grass. Flocks of twittering songbirds filled the air and flapped passed their ears. The morning sun's reflection was mirrored on the meandering river. It was a welcome sight from the bustling city she had been living in the last few months. She missed the smell of fresh air and the feeling of the wind on her cheeks as she rode her horse. Tamar was leading her down a dirt track that went around the perimeter of the city. A wide moat separated the city from the valley in a circle. The only way in was across a drawbridge that was manned day and night by soldiers. The next thing Arica knew, they were cantering up the side of the valley towards the top. She asked where they were going but Tamar just laughed and ushered Orial to go faster. Before long they were at the top where they dismounted and sat. White daisies were scattered all around them. Arica always liked the way their white petals were sometimes tipped with pink, like that of a blushing cheek. She picked one and twisted it in her fingers. She placed the daisy tenderly into the band of her ponytail.

'Very regal,' Tamar joked.

'I thank you, dear subject,' Arica said in a grand voice as she bowed.

Tamar laughed and knocked her shoulder against Arica's. *It was nice to get away from the city for a while* Arica thought to herself. She had not realised how much the sounds of nature were important to her. It was like a feeling of home washing over her.

They sat there talking while they watched the sun slowly move across the sky. They laughed at how frantic their handmaids would be when they found their rooms empty and then to discover their horses were also missing. Their routine was something they both enjoyed, however, they both missed the freedom of being out in the world on their horses' backs. Arica was used to going where she pleased and doing the things she loved without answering to anyone, except for her parents. Now, she was at the beck and call of many more people. It was going to be a long time before she was completely used to it.

They decided to continue along the track, down the other side of the valley. Their horses' hooves thudded against the ground as they descended. The wind was blowing against them. Suddenly, a familiar smell hit her. She inhaled deeply. Her head turned from side to side trying to find the source. There amongst a grove of trees to the south was a plume of dark smoke rising like a phoenix. She whipped the reins and started speeding towards the smoke. They cut through the long grass that was brushing against the horses' knees. As they got closer the smell grew stronger. Arica watched as birds burst from the treetops and animals of all kinds bounded out of the thicket. Shouts began to fill the air. With one last push of energy, Arica drove Sundancer to run even faster. As they broke out of the trees, they found themselves in the middle of a burning village. Soldiers bearing the mark of Haella were rounding people up into cages. *Not again.* They were waving their swords at them, shouting horrible things at the crying villagers.

'Stop right now!' Arica screamed at them, jumping off Sundancer's back.

'Ebraeyens! Kill them!' a soldier wielding an axe shouted as he barrelled towards them.

Arica unsheathed the sword at her hip, brandishing it high in the air. Tamar pulled out twin blades from her boots and ran at a soldier about to shoot an arrow. She swiped her blade across the strings, before kicking the soldier into the stomach. Arica was in the heat of battle against two swordsmen. Their swords clanged as they grunted and shouted at one another. She slashed her sword across the face of one of the soldiers, sending him falling to the ground screeching in agony. She was about to plunge it into him when the other swordsman elbowed her into the ribs. Arica winced and swung the sword at him. It scraped against his iron breastplate. He landed another punch into her stomach, making the sword drop to the ground. The soldier lifted his sword into the air, readying his strike. Arica reacted quickly and slammed the earth with her fist, sending a column of rock up and thrusting the soldier into the air. She got up off the ground to see Tamar stabbing a female soldier in the neck.

'Watch your back!' Tamar screamed at her.

Arica turned quickly, but not quick enough. She was sent hurtling to the ground by a caster's gust of wind. She landed on her back hard, making her cough. Tamar threw one of her knives at the caster, but it was knocked out of the way with another burst of air. Arica felt the tingling in her hands rise and shot a ball of flame at the caster. The caster's eyes widened as she ducked out of the way just in time.

'It's her! Take her at all costs,' the caster screamed at the other Amber Lions who were now circling around Arica and Tamar like sharks.

Tamar ran to Arica's side and helped her up. They stood back-to-back, watching the encroaching soldiers. The soldiers were equipped with swords, axes, and spears. Arica's weapon was flung across the ground and Tamar only had one of her blades left. The soldiers launched at them. Tamar stomped on the ground, creating a split in the ground. Some of the soldiers tripped, while others jumped over it. Arica threw fireballs, some meeting their targets while others hurtled passed them. Soon the soldiers were upon them. Punches and kicks were met with elbows and knees. The two women were fighting like they had never fought before. They would not be defeated easily. A large soldier backhanded Tamar across the face and she tumbled to the ground. When Arica tried to help her, her arms were grabbed and clasped behind her back. She thrashed to try and be released but she was kicked in the back of her knees. She fell down, hard.

'A lot of people are looking for you,' the caster hissed in her ear. 'I do not see what all the commotion is about, you just seem like a poor— *weak*— little girl.'

Thud. Pain. Darkness. Nothing.

Chapter 17

The sounds of waves crashing woke her up. The loud thrashing was coming from outside the wall. The floor was cold and damp beneath her. The floor was stone, hard and uneven. A dull pain throbbed in her leg. Sitting up and rolling up the torn leg of her trousers, she saw a large purple bruise. She pressed it gently with her thumb and flinched. A similar pain ached at the back of her head. She pressed her hand against it to check for blood. Luckily her hand came away dry. The room was mostly dark, save for the trio of lights breaking through the bars of the window. Pushing up off the ground, she managed to stand. She walked to the window and tried to look out, but it was too high. She waved her hand to raise some earth to elevate her, but nothing happened. That was when she noticed the bracelet on her wrist. It was silver and thin yet felt heavy. Three charms hung on the bracelet, a flame, a twister, and a mountain. She wrinkled her face. *Where did this come from?* She turned it over to look at it. Her eyes widened when the realisation hit her. Fire... wind... earth. She inhaled deeply and pushed her hands forward to send a burst of wind at the wall, but nothing came. Her heart started beating quicker. She closed her eyes tightly and said a prayer. *Please work. This has to work.* She lifted her hand and focused to summon the heat into her hand. Her hand remained cold. It was like a dam blocking the flow of the river, there was nothing getting out. This bracelet was obstructing the flow of her magic. She was now just an ordinary girl again. An ordinary girl in prison. An ordinary girl in grave danger.

She sat there in the cold, dank room with only the setting and rising of the sun to indicate just how long she had been there. Arica used a small stone she found on the ground to scratch markings onto the wall. It was her way of keeping track of how long she was trapped. Five. Five lines marked the number of days she had already been here. Her stomach was growling with the ravenous hunger that filled it. She thought about calling out again, but her last attempts had been met with silence. A long, seemingly never-ending silence. Questions swirled around in her mind. *Where am I? Who did this to me? What about Tamar?* Each one pained her to think of. Her thoughts went to her friends, how must they feel? *Malin must be worried out of his mind… I know I would be.* She almost felt guilty but then berated herself for thinking that way. This was not her fault. She had tried to help those people. And Tamar. Wherever she was. She hoped that her friend was alive. All of a sudden, a rattling came from the darkness. Keys jingling. Her eyes stared at the darkness. A door swung open. Light poured in. She squinted her eyes and tried to see who her visitor was. A man… a broad man. She blinked tightly to readjust her eyes. He seemed familiar. He stepped further into the room, his boots clicked against the ground. The blurriness in her eyes subsided and she saw who it was. Standing in front of her, with icy eyes and an ugly smirk across his face was Lord Valkor.

'Arica Preandre, my elusive friend.'

'I am no *friend* of yours,' Arica retorted.

'Oh, and I thought we could be kind to one another, being fellow Harthians— it appears as though I was mistaken.'

He stepped closer to Arica. She inched closer to the wall behind her. Thoughts flashed through her mind. What did he want from her? Why did he take her? None of it made sense to her.

'I did not mean for it to happen, it was an accident,' she said quietly.

'My dear, there is no reason to apologise,' he said almost sweetly, 'what you did was— marvellous.'

Marvellous? She thought she misheard him at first. How could he be describing what happened at the starting line as marvellous? The earth split beneath her as easily as tearing a slice of bread. Fire erupted from her like an exploding volcano. He had seen this. He witnessed the terror and panic of their fellow townspeople. Yet now he was commending her for it.

'I have been so worried about you these past few months, I wanted to make sure you were safe.'

'Why would you care about me?' she asked curiously, but apprehensive.

'You are a miracle!' he said gleefully. 'There hasn't been a caster with gifts like yours born amongst us in an age.'

'You know about casters?'

'But of course, my dear. All us lords do; we must be in the know,' he said matter-of-factly.

His black, leather boots moved forward again. Arica reacted instantly and pushed herself up against the wall. There was no more room to get any further away from him now. If he tried anything she did not have her magic or sword to defend herself. It would be down to brute force, and talented as she may be, Valkor surpassed her in size.

'I am just so glad my soldiers found you, whispers of your presence in Ebraeye reached me and thankfully they were correct.'

'Whispers? You have spies looking for me?' she asked shocked.

'You are very special, Arica,' he told her, 'and from what I am told you have shown even more strength.'

Arica was beginning to feel sick to her stomach. The feeling that her every move had been tracked and reported on was unsettling. She wished there was somewhere for her to crawl away to and get away from him, but this stone cell would not allow that.

'To be perfectly honest, after your flight from Fiermor I thought I had lost you for good but after that little note your brother sent to your aunt, my prayers were answered,' he said with a smile.

'How did you know I was in Fiermor?' Arica asked slowly, afraid of what the answer might be.

Valkor let out a chuckle. It made Arica tense up. This was not the man that she was used to seeing at home. He would never smile or show any semblance of humanity.

'My informant, you may recognise her,' he said wryly.

Valkor looked over his shoulder and called. 'You may enter.'

Arica's heart sank to the floor when she saw who it was. Never in a thousand years did she think that this would be the person who would betray her. As they turned the corner and stood in the doorway Arica's face dropped. Standing in the doorway, with her hands clasped together was Ramira Preandre.

Her mother stood before her. It had been months since she last saw her mother, but she thought of her every day. She dreamed of the day when she and Malin could return home into the embrace of their parents. How they would welcome them home with open arms. How they would all sit in front of the fire, trading stories from their lives. But now Arica did not know what to think. This woman was not who she thought she was. A mother is meant to protect and love at all costs, no matter what. That is the opposite of what her mother had done. She had betrayed her trust. Put her life in danger.

Put Malin's life in danger. And for what? Arica could not understand why she did it. No tears fell, for she did not know how she felt.

'Why?' Arica managed to push out.

'He is going to help you, love,' her mother said meekly. 'He's going to fix you.'

'Fix? There is nothing to fix!' she growled.

'Don't be afraid, Arica. You are going to be normal again, I promise,' Ramira told her daughter with a concerned look on her face.

'Get out.'

'Arica—' Her mother said, stepping towards her.

'Get out!' Arica screamed, pounding the floor with her fists.

Ramira looked at her daughter. There was a sadness in her eyes. A confusion. She opened her mouth and was about to say something, but then pulled it back in. The look in her eyes spoke a thousand words. Slumping her shoulders, she turned her back and left the room. Arica sat in silence as the sound of her mother's footsteps grew further and further away until there was nothing. Her hands stung from the impact of hitting the stone floor. Her mother did this to her. She was the reason that she had been running since she left Harth. It was her fault that she was imprisoned here. All because she thought that Valkor was somehow going to erase her magical abilities. How she thought that was possible baffled Arica. She was so lost in her thoughts that she almost forgot that Valkor was still standing in front of her. He cleared his throat before speaking.

'I am sorry about that, it must hurt for one's mother to betray them— but do not worry, her betrayal is my fortune.'

'What do you want from me?'

'Your friendship, sweet Arica— I want us to work together, we can do great things together.'

'I will *never* work with you,' Arica said, disgusted, 'I've heard what you, the Amber Lions, and Solomir have done all over Divinios— you have committed dreadful crimes and you *will* answer for them.'

'And to whom might I be answering to? Jyneera? Oh, how I quake,' he said feigning fear, and then began to laugh. It made the hair on the back of her neck stand up.

'Perhaps, after some more time down here alone you'll change your mind.'

He turned on his heel and exited the cell. He slammed the door shut and the keys turned in the lock. A narrow metal slot in the door slid open. His icy blue eyes stared in through the hole. Arica glared back at him. He threw in a piece of bread. She watched it bounce on the floor.

'Eat up, that will be your only meal for a while,' he grinned.

Chapter 18

Water dripped onto the floor from the window. The wind was howling outside, and waves were thrashing. A storm was stirring and would strike in an unknown amount of time. The sound of the drops hitting the floor echoed around the room. Curled in a ball in the corner of the room on a bed of straw was a lonely girl. She held her knees against her stomach. This was what her days consisted of. Lying in different positions in the room, wondering when it would all be over. Valkor came back to her once since the last time and left much angrier than the last time. He asked the same question, and he received the same answer, much to his dismay. He bellowed at her saying the next time he came would be his last. Now, it was a waiting game for her. When was he going to return? How was he going to react when he got the same answer? She would never agree to his terms. There was no world where she would contribute to the atrocities that Solomir's soldiers committed. Pillaging, kidnapping and murder. These cruel acts were never going to be attached to her name. He could do whatever he wanted to her, she would die before bending to his will.

A scratching noise was coming from outside the door. It was like someone was running their nails back and forth against the wood. Arica sat up and stared towards the door. A shadow was moving on the other side, she could see underneath. Then came a whisper. Arica could not quite understand it. It was muffled, but it sounded like a female voice.

'Hello?' she called.

The scratching stopped. It was quiet for a moment. But then the voice spoke. It asked her to come closer. It was not a voice she recognised. She did not know what to do. The voice called out again. This time it asked if she needed help. It wanted to help her. Arica stood up slowly, her back against the wall. She thought about it for a moment and made her decision.

'The metal slit— it slides open,' she said softly.

She waited. Would the voice react the way she wanted. Who could it be? How could she help her? Arica just wanted to get out of this place. She needed to get away. She needed to make her way back to Malin, to Alys… to Ryger. Thinking of him made her heart ache. Being locked up in here had given her much time to think. It made her realise that there was more to the two of them than merely friendship. But now, she did not know if that would ever come into actuality. The scratching noise returned. It trailed up the door and stopped again. Arica's heart was pounding in her chest. She could hear rattling and then the slit opened. Arica tried to see out but her view was distorted. She inched closer and closer to the door.

'Are you there?' she asked cautiously.

The voice did not answer. Arica moved to the door and rested her hands on either side of the slit. She lowered her eyes until they were level with it. She saw the hall outside for the first time. It was narrow with torches lighting it up. She could see no other doors. And no other people. She was about to sit back down when all of a sudden a hand burst through the slit and grabbed her shoulder. She let out a shrill scream as she tried to pry the hand off of her. The hand was scaly and its fingertips were black as ash. The nail beds were empty with nothing but raw and oozing flesh in the place of nails. Arica pulled back, but the grip on her shoulder was unrelenting. She tried to scratch the hand with her nails, but nothing was working. Then she heard a ruckus from outside the door and a gurgling screech filled the air. The hand suddenly went limp and released her. Arica fell back onto the ground and held her shoulder. She looked at it, it had already started to bruise. Her breathing was heavy. Her chest was rising and falling quickly. *What was that?* Keys rattled outside the door and it was pulled open. A tall female guard stood in the doorway. She was holding a longsword. Arica noticed the gleam of the blade. It was dripping with a slimy, black liquid.

'Are you injured?' the soldier asked.

'No, I'm fine.'

'Are you sure? We have strict orders to—' She was cut off by another door slamming open from down the hall.

'What happened?' Valkor's voice boomed.

'One of the experiments, my lord— it escaped and found its way to the prison cells.'

'Escaped,' he chuckled, 'and *how* exactly did it manage to become unchained and roaming about the castle?' his voice was filled with rage.

'I do not know, I was not stationed at the labs, my lord,' the guard informed him, she was practically whimpering.

'Excuses! You all have one job, ensure the operations run smoothly— *smoothly* does not mean to allow the subjects to wander around and almost kill my prized possession!'

Prized possession. Arica could taste the bile in her throat at that phrase. She wanted to spit it at Valkor and see his disgusting face as he wiped it off. He turned and looked right at her.

'Speaking of my prize, how are you today? Do you have the answer I want? I grow very tired of waiting.'

'I would rather die.'

'Ah, well that can be arranged, if you will not help me then you are of no use,' he looked at the soldier, 'take this little girl up to the Crest.'

The Crest stood atop the tallest tower of the castle. The castle sat on a cliffside overlooking the Nelerian Sea. The water was dark, almost black. The waves

156

smashed against the serrated rocks below. The winds howled as it blew over the parapets. All that could be heard were the waves and wind. Wooden beams were bolted to the edges of the tower, with ropes attached to another beam that hung over the water. Arica was standing on the wet stone floor of the tower as the rain fell. Her clothes and hair clung to her. A sword was pointed at her back as she moved closer and closer to the beam. Her heart was beating fast and hard; she could feel the throbbing in her chest. As they approached the edge, she was instructed to kneel. The soldier pulled the ropes over to them and tied Arica's wrists together.

'Stand.'

Arica did as she was told. The soldier told her to stand on the edge of the parapet. Arica stepped up onto it and stared down at the thrashing sea. She was so high up and there was nothing between her and a watery grave. She looked from side to side and saw other beams with ropes. Wrapped in a rope to her right was an arm, only there was not much arm left. Yellowed bones with a piece of fabric blowing in the wind hung from the rope. Arica felt sick to her stomach. This was her fate. To be food for seabirds. It was a better end than becoming one of Solomir's savage soldiers.

'Enjoy the view.'

Arica was thrust off the tower. Her legs kicked as the feeling of falling took over her. But she was stopped with a snap as the ropes tugged on her wrists. Pain seared through her arms and her wrists burned. All of her weight was pulling against her, but the beam held her up. She kept moving, trying to figure out a way of escaping from this. But the more she pulled on the ropes, the tighter they became. It felt like a snake wrapping itself around her wrists and twisting and twisting until her hands turned white from lack of blood. There was no feeling in her hands; a numbness swept over them. After a while, she just stopped fighting it, letting her body dangle over the water's ebon hue.

Chapter 19

The sun had set over the watery horizon which cut the world in two. One half was a vast body of pitch-black water. The other was a matching dark blanket shimmering with a thousand stars. A wide crescent moon glowed on the sea, her reflection rippling. The sea was calm after days of wild, tumultuous storms. It was almost eerily quiet. There was not a soul upon the tower. Only a lone girl hanging above the rocks. The clothes on her back were soaked and clung to her body. The added weight had hurt her at the beginning, but now, she felt nothing. Even the cold of the night no longer bothered her. Many thoughts ran through her mind. Her family and friends. The last few months. What a journey she had been on. She did not think that her body could endure all that it had. She was stronger than she had thought. But regardless, with all of her power and strength, here she hung like a rag left out to dry.

Staring at the water below her, she noticed the water was even blacker. *Deeper water*. Arica knew this may be her way out. The rocks did not spike out of the water in this place. She would not last much longer hanging like this. She began rocking herself back and forth, trying to loosen the knot that bound her. No matter how she moved it did not budge. She tried kicking her legs upwards in order to wrap her legs around the beam above, but was unable to reach it. Arica tried again and again to reach the beam until finally hearing a crack. Her eyes widened as she tried to stop the swinging. Another crack. The sound of the beam breaking was a long, drawn-out split, that made Arica's stomach twist. She fell.

The icy water hit her like a slap across the face. The sea's bite was cruel and sharp. It buried into her skin until she felt it in her bones too. Her hands were still lashed together and the broken beam was weighing her down. It was pulling her down further and further into the depths. The salt water stung her eyes. They burned as she struggled to see in front of her. Her chest was beginning to tighten. She knew she could only hold her breath for so long. The deeper she sank, the more she panicked.

Soon she reached the bottom, where stones and sand stretched in all directions. Her eyes darted around, looking for something to cut the rope but all of the stones were round and smooth. Lying on her back, she stared up at the surface of the water. It was as though it was thousands of miles above her. Her chest was growing tighter and tighter that she thought it would burst. Finally, she could hold her breath no longer and she gasped. Water rushed into her mouth and filled her lungs. She could feel her consciousness going. She tried coughing, anything to push it back out but she knew that would not work. Her eyes began flickering. Her arms and legs went limp. Her heart rate slowed. She was going to drown at the bottom of the sea in gods know where. Her family and friends would never know what became of her. Was this to be her end? Another body lost in Farrig's depths. Forgotten. This was not what she had envisioned for herself. She looked at the bracelet clinging to her wrist. She cursed them. Her lungs were heavy with the water inside. Arica willed herself to try one last time to push out the water, a futile attempt, she thought. But as she pushed, she felt the water inside begin to move. It was like snakes crawling out of her body, but instead were gushes of water. Before she knew it, she was able to breathe. She tossed her head around to see she was still lying on the seafloor. A bubble had formed around her like a wall, protecting her from the sea. She stood up and turned around. The bubble moved with her. *How is this happening?* She put her hand against her lips, they were dry. It was like there was never any water there. She stared down at her hands, dry too. The bracelet glittered on her wrist. She grimaced at the charms that bound her like an animal in a cage. Fire… Earth… Wind… but not water. Had she done what she thought? *Did I just water cast?* She did not know what to think. There had been many occasions for her water casting to manifest. Fighting next to the Karigraine. Or while escaping Serpent's Hollow. Any one of these times could have been the time. But if she had to choose a time for water casting to manifest, now was definitely the time.

Arica looked towards the cliffside and noticed a cavern. *Why would there be a cavern underneath the castle?* Curiosity was getting the better of her. The cavern's mouth was gaping, sharp rocks like terrible fangs. Something was screaming inside not to go that way but there was also an invisible tether dragging her into its black belly. She would answer the call. Each footstep was slow and careful. Walking underwater confused her and it did not make sense. But as she progressed, she became surer of herself and continued into the cavern. She walked between its jaws and feared the rocks would burst the bubble that shielded her from a watery grave. The cavern was long and dark. Somehow, she managed to manoeuvre through it without hurting herself, as if a map of the place was laid out in her mind. Her feet knew exactly where to trod. A left. A right. A second right. The cavern seemed to go on forever. But no sooner had she thought that, she saw a spotlight ahead. A dim red-orange light appeared in front of her. Arica rushed forward to the end. When she reached the light she realised that it was a pit. She craned her neck and looked up at the still surface above her. It was like glass. Not too high above her. She would need to swim but could not do it from within the bubble. She clenched her hands and willed the bubble to burst. The waters came crashing in and she thrust up.

The room she emerged into was empty, save for lanterns lining the walls and the well in the centre. Arica clambered out and wrung what water she could from her clothes. She pushed the hair from her face, she hated leaving it loose. She scolded herself for it was not as though she had intentionally styled it that way. *Curse you, Valkor.* An old wooden door stood before her. She opened it slowly, holding her breath. Another room. This time, a rather cluttered one. Tables and crates covered the room. Bottles and jars of all shapes and sizes covered the tables. Upon observing them closer, she scowled at what filled them. All sorts of body parts floated in murky green liquid. Severed fingers. Eyeballs with the nerves still attached. A heart. She felt a sickness in her stomach. She could not believe she was seeing this again. But what did it all mean? Valkor is engaging in the same sick dissections as Lord Cothomir. They were hurting people. But for what? As undeniably awful Valkor was, he did not seem like someone who would aimlessly torture. He needed a reason. Whatever it was, it was disgusting. And deranged. This was not the collection of a person sound of mind. She remembered what the guard had said earlier, *one of the experiments escaped.* This was a part of the experiments, it had to be. A shiver went up her spine. She needed to get out of these clothes. Her eyes darted around the room, searching for somewhere clothing might be stored. She scoured through the many chests shoved into corners and underneath the tables until she found one made of mahogany. Beautiful brass clips held down the lid. She flicked them and creaked it open. She made a sigh of relief as she pulled out a light blue tunic and tan trousers. She slipped them on and was elated to get out of those wet clothes. She rummaged around for some boots or slippers, but she was not so lucky. Barefoot it was.

She left the room to end up in a short hallway lined with weapons hanging on the wall. Giant crossed battle axes. A blunt mace. Even a scythe. Not that she could see why someone would favour a scythe over arrows or blades. Valkor's personal artillery was strange. Fitting. She looked into the first room she came across and another familiar scene lay before her. A wide table with metal fixtures on the sides. There were locks attached to each. These were to hold down a person. While being dissected? Definitely. Nothing else would explain it. So, it was all of the lords of Haella engaging in this horrible practice. Plucking innocent people from around the country and experimenting on them. But for what? She needed to find out. Arica started rummaging through drawers and the pieces of paper within. Inventory. Lists of herbs and insects and animal parts. And something else was written countless times, underlined in places... nalerium. *What is that?* She had never heard of such a thing. She knew it must be kept next door in the storage room.

She continued to look through the drawers until she found a small leather-bound journal. Its yellowed pages contained more of the same. Lists of items, including the nalerium. Except this time, it also included notes. Scratchy handwriting noted how the early "subjects" were not receptive to the treatment. It resulted in collapsed organs or haemorrhaging. The subjects clawed themselves until they were raw and bleeding. They all lost their minds. Until, it claimed, nalerium was introduced. Arica's mouth hung open as she read on. Something referred to as *subject 451* was the answer to their prayers. Their experiments now began to work. They were now able to remove human parts and replace them with animal parts successfully. *This was a person.* They had chopped up some poor person and turned them into a mutant. She read on further and saw that not everything had worked out as they had hoped. *Subject 451*, while having accepted their new parts, had started to act differently. At first it was merely aggressive behaviour but as the weeks went on, they turned feral. It killed a number of the experimenters if they got too close. It was unpredictable. So, they had to euthanise it. The time and date of *Subject 451's* death was marked at the end of the page. Arica did not know whether to cry or scream. These people were being tortured to be turned into monsters. Arica thought back to her time in Cothomir's lab… and her cell in this castle. That girl… the scaly hand that grabbed her. They were like that. They were just like *Subject 451*. They did that to those people on purpose. They *wanted* to create monsters. But she still did not understand why.

Her search was interrupted by a bang. Her head shot up as she looked around in a panic. There was no sign of anyone entering the room. The room was silent again, but just for a moment. Another crash. The noise was coming from another room next to the lab. Arica grabbed a satchel that was hanging on the wall and stuffed the notebook inside. This information had to be passed on. It would be detrimental to the wellbeing of the people of Divinios. Upon reaching the door, she crept into the hallway. Her eyes searched for any guards, but it was clear. She walked up to the door to the room next door. Turning the handle slowly, she entered the room. The room was empty except for an old, beaten wooden table in the middle. And strapped to the table, was Tamar.

'Tamar!' she exclaimed.

Her friend was lying on the table with a ball of fabric stuffed into her mouth. Her muffled screams told Arica that she was conscious. Rushing at the table, Arica fumbled at the leather straps holding her Tamar down. They were tied so tightly that her hands' colour had changed. They were an off-white colour. A sickly colour like that of sour milk. She pulled and twisted them until they eventually came loose. She helped her friend sit up. That was when she realised that something had happened to her. Her eyes started to roll and blinked uncoordinatedly. Arica quickly checked Tamar's legs and arms until she found a black dot on her right shoulder. Tiny black veins were spreading out from it like a menacing spider. This blemish meant danger. This blemish meant something malevolent. After throwing Tamar's arm over her shoulders, Arica helped her walk out the door and into the hallway. *We need to get out of here.* Arica started hurrying the two of them back towards the storage room. The well was her only hope. There was no chance in the world that she would be able to escape any other way. As she turned the handle of the storage door, a shout came from behind them. A guard with their swords unsheathed was standing at the end of the hallway. He started running. Arica dragged Tamar into the room and slammed the door shut. Setting Tamar down on a crate, she quickly turned around. Using all of her strength, she pulled down a large bookshelf behind the door. Sweat trickled from her forehead as the towering bookcase cascaded to the ground. The door was blocked but it would not hold back the guard bashing from the other side. Arica turned to her friend and willed herself to lift her up again and hobbled towards the well together. She helped Tamar to stand up on the rim of the well and after saying a prayer to the sea goddess Farrig, they jumped.

Chapter 20

Two days had come and gone since fleeing from Valkor's castle. Their prayers were answered when the bubble formed around them once again. It shielded the girls from the frigid depths of the sea. Luckily, the waters had remained as calm as when she plummeted from the tower. They walked and walked before coming ashore to avoid being seen by anyone watching from the castle, or possible search parties. The last thing she wanted was to end up back inside the cold, dank cell in the pits of the castle. A shiver crept up her spine at the thought of it and the hapless scaly hand that clawed at her. It was a sight that she would never forget. The red mark had faded but the memory, she knew, would not.

Staying off the road was the key to their survival. Two young girls walking along a dirt road without any shoes or weapons would draw the wrong sort of attention. They needed to reach a town where they could seek help. Arica patted the satchel, making sure it was still there. Throbbing pain seared through their feet against the rough ground. They walked over hills, passed wild-looking thickets and through flower-filled meadows. It was unclear where they were exactly as Ebraeye and Haella's landscapes were so similar. Arica was hopeful that they had not been whisked across the Karigraine, but she could not be certain. The land seemed to be endless with not so much as a wooden hut to break it up. No one lived around here and it was unsettling to wonder why that may be.

They were forced to halt their journey when the clouds burst open and rain started to fall. Normally, rain would not be a problem but with no shoes and little clothing it was a nightmare. A tall chestnut tree became a shelter from the rain. Its long and thick boughs were bare. No leaves or nuts had started to grow. That was a game that Arica always loved playing with her brothers, chestnuts. They would draw a ring in the earth with a stick and then flick chestnuts into the middle. The aim of the game was to knock the other players' chestnuts out of the ring and for you to be the last one inside. Malin was always so good at it. A natural. Arica wondered what he was doing right now. Was he cooking with Sandar? Or sleeping? Perhaps he was out searching for them with Ryger and Alys. Dun Ortha was the goal now. They needed to get back. Tamar let out a groan from beside her. Arica looked at her and noticed her chest was rising and deflating quicker than normally. Beads of sweat were dotting her forehead. With weather like this it did not make sense. After putting her hand against her forehead, it was clear there was a fever beginning. Heat was starting to radiate from Tamar who was going in and out of consciousness. *What am I going to do?* Arica's mind was racing. Something had to be done to keep her cool.

'Tamar, can you hear me?'

Her eyes flickered open. They looked glassy. Arica could see her worried reflection looking back at her. She thought about what to do and then stopped. The rain. Arica stood up and took a deep breath. She raised her hands and closed her eyes. This was the first time she was going to try to water cast outside of the sea. Maybe it would not work. Maybe it would only work when she was in a life-or-death situation. Her hands started moving through the air and she imagined an invisible rope pulling in the drops of rain and gathering them between her hands. Soon, a sphere of sparkling water was floating over her hands. Kneeling down, she lowered the sphere of water against her friend's forehead and prayed for a miracle. The cool water brushed against Tamar as her eyes closed. Arica moved the water onto Tamar's neck, wrists, and chest. She had to cool her down before she got sicker. She stayed working the cold water against Tamar's skin for minutes that felt like hours. Time passed by slowly, but after some time her breathing slowed down to a normal rate. Life appeared back in the eyes staring up.

'Arica? Where are we?'

'Far away from that horrible castle— they will pay for what they have done to you.'

'I'm just so— so tired,' she said, closing her eyes.

'Rest, we can continue later,' Arica said rubbing Tamar's cheek.

Tamar quickly fell asleep next to Arica. Both girls had their backs against the thick trunk of the tree. Tamar's head stooped onto Arica's shoulder, who in turn, rested her own head on Tamar's. The day had been long and draining. The rain was saturating the ground. Puddles lined the dirt road. Dark, grey clouds masked the sky and hid the sun from view. It was a much different scene from the inside of the stone cell. The green grass almost seemed dreamlike. The sound of chirping came from above. A nest made from twigs and leaves housed a family of swallows. Two parents fluttered around the nest as they dropped food for their four chicks. A family of six. *Just like mine.* It was painful to think of family after the betrayal she became aware of in the castle. It was confusing. It hurt. A piercing pain in the chest. A tear fell, warm against her cheek. She wiped it away quickly. She had enough of sadness and crying to last her a lifetime. It was not a story she wanted. Her only desire right now was to get back to Dun Ortha and ensure Tamar's safety. Sleep seemed like her only option. She nestled in closer to her friend to keep warm. Together, the two girls huddled under the canopy of the tree and let their slumbering minds fill with dreams.

The rain had stopped, while the ashen clouds still hung in the sky. The muted yellow glow of the sun lingered behind the clouds. The two adult swallows had fluttered away in search of their young's next meal. A wild boar grunted as he foraged for food on the ground. His snout was burrowing into the earth, lifting it up in search of grubs and roots. Mud clung to his tusks as he pulled his head up and down. All of a sudden, he lifted his head and froze staring into the distance. The sound of thundering hooves broke the peaceful silence of the plains. Riding up the dirt road was a cart being pulled by two black draught horses. Their feathering was white with splatters of mud from the puddles. Two hooded men were sitting on top of the cart, bouncing over the bumps in the road. The noise of the approaching cart stirred Arica and her eyes flashed open. She quickly shook Tamar awake and the two of them stood up. Tamar leaned against the tree to steady herself. Arica stepped in front of her as the cart stalled on the road next to them. One of the men dismounted the cart and started to walk towards them. He stopped after a few steps, noticing the distress of the girls.

'You do not need to worry, I just wanted to see if you wanted some help,' he called.

'No, all is well,' Arica said quickly.

'I do not think your friend would agree,' he said nodding at Tamar.

Arica turned around to see she had become slack against the trunk. She grabbed her to stop her sliding down. Tamar's eyes found Arica's and she tried to say something that came out like a muffled whisper. Sweat covered her forehead again. The man approached closer to them, causing Arica to jerk back. The man held his hands up.

'I promise you, all I want is to help— your friend, she looks very ill.'

Panic was starting to overtake her. The worry for her friend and the fear of the uncertainty of these men were mixing together. It was not a combination of emotions that she particularly enjoyed. But what choice did she have? Tamar was getting sicker as time went by and they were soaked and barefoot. After holding her breath to think, she exhaled heavily.

'Please, just help her.'

The man nodded at her and proceeded to approach. He put an arm around Tamar's shoulder, as did Arica. They walked her to the cart together. The second man was standing in the cart and pulled her up and laid her down. They use a sack as a pillow for her head. One of the men pulled out a dry blanket from one of their bags and draped it over Tamar. Arica settled down next to her, never taking her eyes off the men. She needed their help, but it did not mean she trusted them. Too many times people had surprised her for the worse. She said a prayer to her favoured goddess, Merenia, to keep them safe. *May your arrow guide us. May your wolf travel at our side and protect us from harm. O Lady of the Hunt, watch over us.*

Chapter 21

The road led them miles away. The brown earth transitioned to rock. They were travelling up a rocky mountain. The rocks were flat and spread around in all directions. Tufts of grass and little purple flowers sprouted from in between the cracks. The formation of the rocks, was like that of a grand staircase; thousands of steps going up and up as far as the eye could see. The men explained that they were on Aflosi border of Ebraeye.. Shock washed over Arica upon hearing this. They were to the west of Dun Ortha, near the Wimertos Wood where they had been captured. The road was bumpy and the cart wobbled from side to side. Arica understood why they were using draught horses to draw the cart. Any smaller horses would have been slipping and sliding in all directions, especially with the added weight of the two girls. Large boulders of the same stone dotted the landscape. Moss clung to the underside of the rocks, thriving in the shadows. It was a strange place, not enough water to drown a dog, not enough wood to start a fire. It was unique. But beautiful.

A pair of wooden huts appeared around a corner. There was a makeshift stable next to the huts with a small fenced paddock with a brown cow and pig with seven suckling piglets. It was a modest home, but a home, nonetheless. It was more than Arica had right now. The cart pulled up outside the stable and the horses were unhitched. They were put into their stalls and thick blankets were thrown over their strong backs. The two men patted their muzzles and walked back towards the cart. Just as they came to the back of the cart where Arica and Tamar were sitting, the door of one of the huts slammed open. A woman with a fiery mess of red curls came barging out. An off-white apron was wrapped around her waist with flecks of flour splashed across it. Her face was covered in freckles like hundreds of stars in the night sky. Her face seemed warm, but a clear look of shock was strewn across it. The two barefoot girls in ragged and wet clothing must have had that effect.

'Goodness, boys get these girls inside faster than lightning!'

The two men lifted Tamar down and put one of her arms around each of their shoulders. The red-haired woman rushed over and wrapped Arica with her own arm and ushered her into the hut.

The smell of cooking filled the air inside. The centre of the hut was dominated by an open fire with a black pot hanging over it. The lid on top was hopping from the heat boiling inside. Beds with straw bedding were around the edge of the hut. Beside the fire, curled up, was a black and white dog with one brown eye and one blue eye. The dog's head popped up as the crowd of people entered the hut. His head tilted with confusion at

175

the appearance of the two strange girls being brought inside. The men lay Tamar down on one of the beds and Arica sat at her feet. The woman brought over a damp cloth and placed against Tamar's forehead. Arica could see that the woman was looking at the blackness that was emerging from Tamar's arm. Her hand gently touched it and as she did Tamar jerked in pain.

'This girl has been through much— she may not have much time left,' the red-haired woman said sadly without taking her eyes off Tamar.

'Not much time— there must be something I can do for her,' Arica said hopefully.

'It is spreading down her arm, soon it will appear all over her body— and seep into her organs and once that happens, she won't last much longer.'

'You— cannot mean she—' Arica felt a lump form in her throat, 'she will die.'

'My sons and I will do our best to keep her temperature down and to keep her drinking water but there is something that can help her, but we do not have it.'

Arica's eyes lit up. There was something that could help her friend. She could get it. She could save her.

Arica immediately asked the woman about this. She wanted to know how she could save her friend's life. This horrible blackness that was spreading over her body like a malevolent web needed to be erased. Whatever spider was spinning it needed to be squashed as quickly as possible.

'There is a flower that grows in the forest on the other side of the mountain,' she told Arica, 'it is white with blue thorns, when it is brewed into a tea it has properties that will help remove the toxins. We use it to extract poison from snakebites, I am hoping it will do the same for your friend.'

'I'll go, I will get that flower and bring it back here,' Arica said standing up.

'In the morning, child,' the woman said taking Arica's hand, 'she has time, and you need rest before you take this quest on.'

After much debating, Arica agreed to stay the night and to leave at first light. The sun had set and the crescent moon was glowing. The sky was a beautiful violet-navy colour. A rare colour. As she stared up at it, she could not help but smile. Just a small one, but a smile, nonetheless. A low wall made of stone became her seat. She sat there, with her legs crossed. New, dry clothes felt amazing against her now clean skin. A bath had been drawn for her and the feeling that swept over her as she felt the dirt and grime of travelling being washed away was a glorious one. Her long auburn hair was let hang loose, a rare sight as she usually had it pulled back in a ponytail. The woman, whose name she learned was Emra, gifted her the clothes and a pair of black boots that fit perfectly. Emra was the mother of the two men that brought them here to their mountain home. The mother and sons lived alone here. The land was not the most fertile, but with care and patience they were able to grow enough to feed themselves and their animals. It was a simple life, but one that they loved. The sounds of grunting piglets made a chuckle form in her throat, and she could not help but release it.

'Enjoying yourself?' a voice came from behind her.

Arica jumped and turned her head around to see one of the men, Odan, standing behind her. He walked over to the wall and sat down next to her. His shoulder length brown hair was tucked behind his ears. Seeing him up close, his freckles were clearer to her. A gift from his mother. Odan had been kind to her from the moment they met. Initially, she had been apprehensive about this kindness. The tricks of others in the past had made her wary of strangers, but thankfully, in this case luck was on her side.

'Thank you for stopping.'

'Pardon?'

'Thank you— for stopping the cart and helping us,' Arica said.

'Oh,' he seemed shocked she would thank him.

'If you had not pulled over, I fear the worst may have happened.'

'Please, do not thank me. You were in trouble, and I would never turn my back on those in need,' Odan told her.

'Even so, I do thank you with all my heart.'

Odan smiled and looked at her. Arica noticed his eyes were the colour of moss, but with flecks of brown. Even his eyes had freckles.

'What were you doing when you found us?' Arica asked curiously.

'We were buying some supplies, it's my favourite place to go,' he told her, 'what's yours?'

'Oh,' she said surprised, not expecting him to ask her, 'mine would be the forest near my hometown— I would have spent hours there, just me and my bow and arrows.'

They sat there in silence for some time then. Staring at the moon and stars. Not a single cloud was in the sky now. She could not help but be annoyed that the sky could not have been this clear during their time walking along the road. It had been so wet during their time walking; she did not know how they managed to make it as far as they did without anyone helping them. It was uncertain what she had been hoping would happen. That they would come by a village full of friendly people. Perhaps a prince from some faraway land would happen to pass them in his carriage. Or maybe she would have seen Ryger galloping towards her atop his stallion, Ebonmere. None of these had come true, but she did thank the stars above that Odan and his brother found them.

Their silence was broken by Odan hopping off the wall and holding his hand out to her. She looked at him confused at first, but his intense stare convinced her to grab it. They walked together to a small building adjoined to the stable. The wooden door was weather-beaten and cracked in multiple places. She thought it might fall off its hinges when pushed, but when Odan did push it miraculously remained hanging. The room was a storage room of some sort. Hay for the horses was gathered in one corner. Gardening tools leaned against the walls. A spare wheel for the cart was hanging on the wall like an exquisite painting might. It was an intermingling of many different objects, but what really caught her eye was what Odan held in his hand. In his hand was a beautiful bow made from a light-coloured wood. It looked as though it was never used. Sitting on a table behind him was a quiver with white tipped arrows. Arica was about to ask where they came from when Odan explained. His father had been an archer. He had trained to be a soldier in the army of Ebraeye. He had intended to go join the effort when he got ill. The illness was a short but strong one. He did not make it through that winter.

'I'm so sorry, Odan— I cannot imagine,' Arica said with sadness.

'Thank you, he was a good man and an even better archer,' he smiled, 'it is just a shame his bow never got to be used— perhaps you would consider taking it with you?'

'Really?' she exclaimed, 'it is so beautiful.'

'I would be honoured.'

A smile spread across her face as he placed the bow into her hands. It felt right. It had been too long since a bow had been in her grasp. The smooth wood felt good against her palm. It was like welcoming an old friend again. Arica ran her fingers along the curves of the bow, her eyes following. She was mesmerised. She picked up the quiver and together, they returned to the main hut. He wished her goodnight and climbed into his own bed. Arica lay down on the ground next to Tamar's bed after changing the cloth on her forehead. Emra had spread some straw there and left a blanket folded on top. She was thankful for a soft place to rest her head tonight; she had grown tired of partially soaked grass. After kicking off the boots, she settled under the blanket. Staring up at the roof, she felt the tiredness hit her. Slowly her eyes began to creep shut. Soon they were closed, and blissful sleep washed over her.

Chapter 22

The morning was cool, with a gentle breeze blowing. The fresh dew had frozen overnight and blanketed the land with a twinkling carpet of frost. With each footstep, came a crunch. The sun had just risen over the horizon and was shining down on the mountain. The rare tree cast shadows across the rocky landscape. It did not look like rain would come today, but the weather over the previous few days had been quite damp. Odan gave Arica one of his coats because he knew the day would be cold. The new clothes were dry and kept her warm as she trekked over the top of the mountain and started the descent to where the forest lay at the bottom. There was a mix of trees in the forest such as oak, birch and ash. Their thick and lush branch created a sea of green below that stretched for miles. *Where do I even begin?*

The forest was alive with many different sounds. The wind was rustling the leaves and branches squeaked with the force. Wild rabbits bounded across the grass as she walked through it. A roe deer doe pranced passed her, kicking up pieces of earth from under her. The deer snapped twigs as she walked over them. It brought back memories of the forest near Harth where she spent so much time. The plants were similar too, with the addition of ivy that encircled the tree trunks. They were like green stars swirling in the sky. Their vein-like stems connected them to form an elegant web of leaves. Beauty was all around her. Nature was a place where she always felt at home. Being around animals and plants made her feel peaceful. Today was no different, aside from the fact that she was on a mission to find the white flower with blue thorns. She had never heard of or seen any sort of plant like this. Any thorn she had seen had been green or brown, and attached to a rose. Emra knew little of the flower's location except that it grew beside water. A vague detail but it was all she had to go on. This, she knew, would not be a simple task.

The forest went on for what seemed like an eternity. Trees upon trees, bushes upon bushes. Different animals revealed themselves as she pressed on into the wood. A solitary fox poked its head out of its den. A duo of squirrels leaped from branch to branch, their tails keeping them balanced. A symphony of chirps from birds came from all around her. Her eyes scoured the forest for any sign of a white flower, but the only ones she came across were butter coloured cowslips and bluebells. Beautiful flowers, but not the one she was searching for.

Every step brought her deeper into the forest and further away from Tamar. Her mind held the image of Tamar lying on the bed with sweat across her chest and forehead. Emra was cooling her down with the cloths, but they were only doing so much. Although their friendship had been a short one, there was something special about it. Arica felt very comfortable around her, a feeling which she did not normally have around other girls. Having grown up in a house with three brothers she was used to boys and did not mingle that well with the other girls at home. But Tamar was different. She did not treat Arica like an oddity, but rather as an equal. She needed to find this snowy flower if it was the last thing she ever did.

The rows of oak, birch and ash started to spread out. More grass appeared on the ground, as opposed to the brown soil on the forest floor. Daisies and buttercups bespeckled the grass. The sound of running water hit her ears, sending delight through her heart. If luck was on her side, this could be the destination. The area opened up to reveal a small pool with water cascading down rocks at the top. Bushes and other plants clung to the rocks and settled in the cracks among them. The trees wrapped around the area and up behind the river. As she approached the pool, she noticed the reflection of the waterfall in the pellucid waters. It was so clear that everything at the bottom of the pool was visible. Her eyes rapidly hunted the area for the flower. The only white flowers on the ground were the tiny daisies that littered the grass. Her heart was about to sink when she noticed something mirrored on the glass-like surface of the pool. What looked like white stars were in fact five-petalled flowers. *Could they be?* She walked towards the rocks and looked closer at the flowers above, and much to her pleasure they had bright, blue thorns.

Arica slung her new bow over her shoulder and squeezed her hands in preparation for the climb. Her hands gripped the rugged rocks and pulled herself up. Her foot found footing and she hoisted up further. The rocks were sloped at first, making the climb easy but as she progressed it became much steeper. After some time, it became practically vertical. Her hands started to hurt from the rough edges of the rock that she was clinging to. The knee of her trousers caught on a protruding stone and cut straight across it, causing her to slip. A shriek was released. Her arms scraped against the rock side but she grasped onto a stone that was jutting out. Her legs kicked and felt around for a ridge to hold herself up. She found one and stabilised herself. Her chest rose and deflated heavily. A fall from the height she was at now could have been fatal. Arica took a deep breath and willed herself to climb up. After another few painful minutes, she reached the ledge with the flowers. She carefully pulled the flowers, thorns and all, off the rocks and put them into the hip pouch that Emra had given her. Once three flowers were safely tucked away, she buttoned it shut. She looked below her, trying to see the best way to descend when she heard a snap from above. She barely turned her head when she was met with the shrill growl of a mountain lion. It's great, big yellow eyes looked fierce but not as fearsome as the yellowed fangs. Arica let out a scream and let go of the edge.

The crash of Arica as she hit the water was painfully loud. Dizziness filled her head at first from the impact. But, the cool water made her snap back to reality quickly. Without even thinking, she water-casted the bubble around her again and clambered out of the pool. Her head turned in all directions, searching for the lion. Descending the rocks at an alarming rate was the sleek mountain lion, eyes set on Arica. She threw back a hand to grab an arrow from the quiver. *Oh no*. The arrows were gone. They had fallen out when she fell into the pool. Her bow would have to do as a blunt force weapon. The lion's paws gracefully carried it across the grass towards its prey. Arica readied herself. She slashed the bow at the mountain lion as it made its attack. It cracked against its head, causing it to push back. It roared at her. The bow would not hold up against this animal. Something else had to be used. Arica turned to the pool. She raised her arms up and commanded the wall to rise up. She sent a wave of water straight at the mountain lion. The wall of water smashed into the shrieking mountain lion and carried it across the grass, knocking it against the rocks. It howled in pain. It quickly scrambled to its feet and ran off into the forest. Arica let out a sigh of relief.

'Now, where are those arrows?' she asked aloud.

As she made her way towards the edge of the water, she could see the white tipped arrows sitting at the bottom against the smooth stones. Arica kicked off her boots. She put the bow and hip pouch down at the water's edge and prepared to dive below. When all of a sudden, another roar came from beside her. Before there was time to turn, the ferocious mountain lion was back and pounced on top of her. Arica screamed as she held the gnashing animal back. Drool dripped out of its terrible mouth and fell onto Arica's face. She tried thrusting her knee up to knock it off, but it was useless. Fear started running through her. Her arms started buckling under the force and weight of the large cat. The teeth inched closer and closer to her face. The stench of the mountain lion's breath was fetid. She did not know how much longer she could hold it up. Just as she thought her arms would give in, the mountain lion's head snapped up. It bared its teeth again. Arica turned her head to see what could possibly have startled the animal. Standing at the edge of the trees, was a big, white wolf.

The wolf's growl was low and deep. The mountain lion jumped off of Arica, allowing her to clamber away. The wolf snarled at the lion and the lion did it back. It was a standoff. Canine and feline at war. Arica did not know what to think. Her heart was racing. The wolf stepped towards them. With a roar, the mountain lion sprang at the wolf, ready to attack. The wolf ran at the mountain lion, showing all of its teeth. The animals met in a deafening collision of fang and claw. The animals bit and clawed at each other. The fury between them was immense. The mountain lion scratched at the wolf, but the wolf was too fast for it. The white wolf opened its jaws and clamped them shut on the mountain lion's neck. It let out a howl of pain as it tried to shake itself free. The look of malice in the wolf's eyes said it wanted to kill. But much to Arica's surprise, it let go of the mountain lion, who upon release, ran right into the thick undergrowth of the forest. Its roars became quieter and quieter, until it finally could no longer be heard. Arica felt some relief, but quickly lost it as she noticed the wolf treading towards her slowly.

The white wolf was larger than any dog she had seen before. Larger than any wolf she had seen before in fact. A pack of wolves lived to the south of the forest near Harth. It was known not to venture too close to their den or you would not return. However, after chasing a boar through the forest, Arica found herself overlooking the pack hunting a herd of deer. She was amazed at the unity between them. They worked as one to take down a huge stag. They had been large, but this white wolf in front of her was immense. Arica stood up but knew not to run. That would make it chase her down, like the Harth pack did that stag. The animal came closer and closer. Arica met its eyes and did not want to lose its gaze. The eyes were peaceful, and an alluring icy blue colour. Arica believed they were quite beautiful. It helped her make the decision to stand still; to allow the wolf to come to her. The wolf stood in front of her at arm's length. The girl and wolf stared at each other. It felt as though the wolf was looking into her soul. It wanted to understand her. She wanted to understand it. Arica held her breath as she held out her hand. The wolf looked at it for a moment, but then took a step forward and settled its muzzle into it. It bowed its head. It had accepted her. It was allowing her to embrace it. Arica stepped forward and stroked the wolf's head and back.

'Thank you,' she whispered.

The wolf lifted its head and looked into her eyes again. Although it did not speak, Arica felt its happiness. It wanted to help her. It wanted to protect her. After some time, the wolf bowed its head once again and turned around. Like the wind, the wolf dashed off into the forest. As fast as it appeared, it disappeared, leaving Arica alone next to the pool.

Chapter 23

The afternoon sun was shining down on the ground. Sunlight was bouncing off the rocks. Tufts of grass sprouted out from the cracks, adding colour to a monotone landscape. The green broke up the dullness of grey spread all around her. The descent of the mountain was more difficult this time. Her legs were tired from all the walking and the ordeal with the mountain lion. It came out of nowhere. That ferocity in its eyes was terrifying and having no weapon did not help. The cursed bracelet coiled around her wrist like a shackle only allowed her to water cast. Had she been able to summon fire she would have incinerated the animal without a second thought. Hate filled her heart as she thought about it. She feared what may have happened had the heroic wolf not intervened. Its alpine coat shimmered in the light. It disappeared into the forest in a flash, like a ghost. It saved her. She would never forget it.

After a while, the hut came into view. Grey-white smoke was rising from the chimney into the sky. The fire was lit, keeping them all warm inside. A lump formed in her throat as she feared the worst may have already happened. It had not been long since she left, but with a fever time was never a certainty. As quickly as it started, it could all end. Her friend, Tamar, had to be alive. She had to be all right. Fear was pulsing through her just as much as her very blood.

Arica rushed around the hut and pushed the door open with both hands. Steam was rising from a boiling pot suspended above the fire. The black and white dog was sat at the foot of the bed. His different coloured eyes were set on her friend. Emra was standing at her bedside, her hand resting on her head. She turned her head to look at the worried Arica. Arica fumbled at the hip pouch and then carefully took out the flowers. Emra immediately sped into action. She gingerly took the flowers from Arica and hurried to a table where a variety of herbs and vials of liquids sat. Emra began to work with the mortar and pestle, grinding up the white petals of the flower. A green liquid was added, and it became a paste. Next, she extracted the thorns from the stem. Emra gathered these ingredients and brought them to the boiling pot. All of them were added, and Arica watched them dissolve. They made a sizzling sound as the paste and thorns mixed with whatever assortment of things Emra had already put in. Arica really wondered about the potency of this tea Emra was brewing. Would it work? Had she ever seen a poison like this? She turned her head back towards her friend, lying helpless on the bed. The black veins had coated both of her arms and was inching its way up her neck and into the centre of her chest. Her nails were the colour of charcoal. The colour had been drained from her face, white as snow. Arica bit her lip as she approached Tamar. She sat down on the edge of the bed and gently caressed her forehead.

'All will be all right, stay strong,' Arica whispered.

After some time, Emra announced the tea was ready to be drank. She filled a bowl with the tea and carried it cautiously to the bedside. Arica went behind Tamar and raised her head to make it easier to drink. The mixture was poured slowly into her mouth. Tamar was conscious enough to swallow it, but just about. Once the last drop was drained from the bowl, her head was rested back on the cushion. Instantly, she fell asleep. A look of peace was on her face. Perhaps, she felt a reprieve from the agony of the toxin. Or perhaps, that was Arica's hope.

She did not know how long she had been sitting there beside her friend. Time crawled by. Every minute that Tamar lay there under the intoxication of the nalerium. The disgusting venom inside of her rots her. It would not be her doom, as long as Arica stood near her. She glanced out of the window and noticed that the sky had turned orange. Sunset, already. The day had come and gone as quickly as a breath. Shuffling feet and utensils being arranged on the table broke her from her thoughts. Emra was serving bowls of food, stew if she guessed the smell correctly. A growl rumbled within. Her belly was begging her to fill it. Sluggishly, she arose and shuffled to the wooden stool at the table. A fork and spoon lay either side of the bowl. Arica picked them up and started to eat. The hot food warmed her body. The sweet taste of carrots and parsnips filled her mouth. The juice of the stew was delicious. A hot meal was a wondrous thing, she would never again take one for granted.

It was then that the door swung open and Odan and his brother, Torun, entered. Their boots were muddy, and they quickly took them off after being scolded by their mother. They both sat on stools and began eating their food like ravenous hounds.

'My darlings, I believe I raised men, not wild boars,' Emra said, hitting their shoulders.

'Sorry, Mother,' they chanted between spoonsful of stew.

Arica smiled and wiped her mouth with her wrist. The bracelet caused her wince.

'A binding bracelet, how did I not see this before?' Emra said holding her hand, eyeing the bracelet intently.

'Valkor put it on, I awoke and suddenly I could no longer cast earth, wind or fire,' Arica said bitterly, 'it was only after I discovered I could also water cast.'

'All four elements— truly a marvel, not one like you in many years,' Emra said twisting one of the charms.

'Yes, centuries I believe. Not that it matters, three of the elements are now blocked.'

'Perhaps, but perhaps not,' she told Arica as she stood up and hurried to a table near her own bed.

Emra rummaged through the drawer. She tutted and hummed as she searched through the array of items inside. A small doll, a hand mirror, a polished stone. Such a variety lived inside the drawer. All so different. Each having its own purpose. An exclamation of success. Emra turned around holding a ball of white thread in her hand. It was as if it was gold. Her eyes shone with delight. Emra walked back over to the table and told her sons to go to the stable and feed the horses. After protesting that they were not finished eating, they trudged back outside. Once the door closed behind them Emra sat in front of Arica and clasped both her hands and stared into her eyes. Arica knew from the look in her eyes that she had something to say. Something that Odan and Toran did not know. Something she did not *want* them to know.

'What I tell you now must not reach the ears of my sons,' Emra told her.

'I promise.'

'I am not just a humble farmer; I am an alchemist— a sorceress.'

Arica stared blankly at Emra. A sorceress… another word that she thought held no meaning. Another word she assumed was a children's story. Another word that was as real as the earth beneath her feet.

'A sorceress— you use magic?'

'Yes, not in the same way that you do,' she explained, 'I can connect with the magic inside plants and other natural materials.'

'So, you're an earth caster?'

'No, I cannot move rock, but I can harness the energies in nature and use them.'

'All right, and why are you telling me this now?' Arica asked, her eyes looking at the thread.

'This thread,' Emra said holding it up, 'has been infused with the thorns of mountain thistle, it can cut through anything— I use it to slice my bread,' Emra laughed.

Arica did not realise at first what the thread had to do with her. Then Emra's eyes gazed at her wrist again. The bracelet.

'You can cut through this?' Arica shook the bracelet ecstatically.

'I believe so, would you allow me to try?'

She nodded her head and bit her lip. Holding her wrist out, the charms dangled above the table. She could feel a knot forming in her stomach. Would this really work? Would she finally be free? Magic had not long been in her life. It was relatively new, but she missed it. Having it taken was like having a piece of her soul being ripped away. It was a part of her. She was breathing slowly as Emra unwound the thread and held it taut. Carefully, Emra touched the thread against the silver bracelet. At first, nothing happened. Arica's heart dropped. But quickly, the bracelet started to sizzle. Arica felt a heat radiate from where the thread was cutting into the bracelet. It was like a ring of fire was set alight around her wrist. Her hand gripped the edge of the table, and she held in a scream. The bracelet was white-hot where the thread was cutting through. It was like cutting through a block of frozen butter. Slow, but making its way. It felt like her skin was being melted off her very bones. Her jaw clamp down tight, her teeth grinded against each other. The thread finally flicked through the last of the bracelet and it clinked against the table as it fell off. Arica swore the last cut almost sounded like a scream of pain. Maybe it was herself without her realising it.

The broken bracelet lay in a heap on the wooden table. A silver lump that she was glad to be rid of. Her other handheld her now naked wrist. The burning sensation had subsided, and she expected to see a wound or scorch marks, but there was nothing. The pain the bracelet had caused her was all in her head. She released a breath of solace. Freedom. She looked at Emra and thanked her. Emra smiled. Arica stood up and closed her eyes. She focused her mind and let it go blank. She formed the thought of what she wanted. It was in reach. She felt the warmth rise within herself. Holding out one hand, palm facing up, she summoned a single orange, flickering flame. She could not help but release a laugh. Sheer happiness filled her as she quenched the flame. She could do it again. Her magic was back.

'What is all the laughing about?' a voice from behind her croaked.

Chapter 24

Arica whipped her head around and saw Tamar propped up on her elbows. She rushed over to her and fell on her knees next to her.

'You're awake!'

'Could not be helped with all the cackling,' she said, cracking a smile.

'Pleased to see you haven't lost your sense of humour,' Arica told her friend.

'Where are we?' she asked, eyeing the room.

'This is Emra, she and her sons helped us,' Arica explained.

'How do you feel, dear?' Emra said as she approached the bed.

'Tired, but do not feel like I am burning up inside any more.'

As the last word left her mouth her eyes flickered. Tiredness was overcoming her. Her body had been through a lot and still needed time to heal. Arica put her hand on Tamar's shoulder and told her to get some rest. With a nod, her eyes closed and was quickly asleep. Arica felt relief wash over her, like a lightness running through her body. Her friend was safe. The tea worked. Or was it a tea? Or some sort of magical concoction.

Every day more magic presented itself. The world she thought she lived in was becoming more and more like the stories she grew up listening to. She could only imagine what her grandmother would say if she told her about everything she had seen. It only made her more curious about what else may lie beyond the horizon.

The next week passed short and quick. The days were spent carrying out chores around the house or the yard. While the night was the time for respite. Sitting around the table, eating the meals Emra prepared for them. At first, Tamar was too weak to leave her bed to eat but as the days went on, she found her strength. The stool at the table was the first goal. Getting as far as the front door was the next. Being able to go outside and stay standing was something simple that Tamar did not think she would celebrate but the sickness that befell her made her think differently. Life was a gift. The black poison that coursed through her veins made her feel weak and hot and cold all at the same time. While the pain had subsided, the memory of it was still fresh. It was like a scar, the injury had come and gone, but the aftermath remained behind to remind her of that pain. *Would it ever go away?* She thought about this every day. So did Arica. It was clear from the glossy eyes that would stare out at the rolling, rocky hills that her friend still remembered the pain and that it left a mark. Arica knew that while the toxin had been erased from her body, the trauma of it still clung. It would be a process for her to forget it. If she ever did.

Once the girls were happy that they could travel again, they sadly broke the news to Emra and her sons. Their hearts were heavy at the thought of leaving but they both knew that the time had come to return to Dun Ortha. They had been away for a long time. Gods knew what had happened since they left. Had they been looking for them? Had the city been attacked? Had Solomir invaded Ebraeye? This, Arica did not know, but she hoped all her friends were alive and well. Emra made sure they were clothed properly and packed some bread and cheese into a bag for them. Odan rolled up a spare blanket and placed that into the bag too. The journey to Dun Ortha would be about a three-day ride, everything being on their side. When the morning sun was shining high in the sky, it was time. The few belongings between them were loaded onto the cart. The big, strong horses were tied to the cart, their heavy hooves crunching the shale beneath them. Odan clambered onto the cart and held the reins; he had offered to bring them to the nearest town where they could go their separate ways. A light breeze blew the manes of the horses like flickering blades of grass in a meadow. It carried a nice coolness to combat the warm sun that was shining down on them. The days had become warmer and drier as of late. A blessing for their travels. With a tight hug from Emra, they said their goodbyes and climbed onto the cart. They settled downside by side and waved as the hut on the mountain grew smaller and soon, disappeared.

The sun sat high in the sky, its light smearing the earth with its radiance. A calmness veiled the land. Not a thing was stirring. Not a leaf on a tree or ripple in the river appeared. All was still. As if time itself had frozen, preserving the world as it was. Usually stillness insighted fear, as stillness often means lifeless. But today it felt peaceful. The sound of hooves trotting along the track was all that broke the silent tranquillity. The wooden wheels groaned as they spun around, moving further and further away from the mountain. Remnants of the mountain followed the cart as the landscape was painted with a grey blanket of stone with clumps of yellow-green grass. The stone was like a cracked pavement or wrinkles on an elderly person's face. A very unique and scenic route. But as they progressed along a dirt track less of the cracked stone became visible, and more grass covered the land. The world of stone slowly faded away to the more familiar grassland with an array of flowers and bushes. With the foliage came more wildlife. Swallows swooped past them as they hurried from tree to tree. A family of otters dipped in and out of a river, flicking the drops off their sleek coats. Startled from the approaching cart, a wild mare and her young colt cantered away before finally stopping and grazing on the viridescent vegetation. The true beauty of the continent was to be seen all around them. In moments like this it was easy to forget the troubles that were manifesting elsewhere. But for a brief reprieve, they allowed themselves to.

A small town stood at the edge of a wood. The buildings were crafted from dark wood and the roofs were thatched. Fences lined the town as if to protect the townspeople from the wilderness. Busy people moved around the town, going between the shops and homes. The town square was dominated by a large, grey statue of a familiar figure. The bearded statue of the God of Trade, Tradil, was holding up his compass that would always show the way to one's destination. The long tail of his coat had a map of Divinios on it. It was said that his coat could show the map of anywhere and guide you through anything. It appeared that this town was a hub for trade, given the many tents dotted around the square and also the grand statue of Tradil. Odan explained that this would be the perfect place to secure transport to Dun Ortha. The trouble with trying to find someone from Dun Ortha was that no one looked like they were from Dun Ortha. The city was such a diverse mix of people and cultures. It would be easy if they were trying to find passage to Telvidia, all that would have to be done was to locate people with frosty coloured hair embellished with metals hoops and beads. Or if Aflos was the goal, bright, rich-coloured clothes with golden jewellery would be the target. But in Dun Ortha people of all shapes, sizes and colours lived. The difficulty would be much greater for the two.

The cart pulled up outside a merchant's shop that had many trinkets inside the clear window. Varnished boxes, engraved drinking glasses and animals made from glistening coloured glass were among them. All beautiful and unique in their own ways. Arica and Tamar alighted from the cart, taking their few possessions with them. They stood in front of Odan, who had become a friend. It was not the fate Arica would have predicted after her first-time laying eyes upon him that day under the tree. His kindness saved Tamar's life. Without him, she would be buried beneath the earth in some strange place. The two girls hugged their friend. He pointed in the direction of a tavern where travellers often stopped on their journeys. That would be the best spot. Someone going to Dun Ortha would surely be inside. Hope clung in their minds as they waved goodbye and walked towards the tavern. The Laughing Crone. A black iron sign in the shape of a cackling woman hung above the unassuming door. Arica remembered the warning Emra had given before they left. Valkor would be after them, and they were not anonymous travellers any more. Their faces would be known. The Amber Lions would be prowling the land in search of his escaped prizes. Tugging the hoods up over their heads, they entered the bustling tavern.

Chapter 25

The dimly lit room was packed with people. A burly young man stood behind the bar passing tankards and pitchers to the serving girls, who in turn were rushing around the room passing out the drinks. Tables on tables were crowded by these people, all drinking, eating or both. It was as if a thousand conversations were being had at once. The noise was a good sign. Out of all those voices, one must be travelling to Dun Ortha. They took up residence at a small round table in the corner of the tavern. *This will be a good spot to watch from* Arica thought to herself. A duo of bards were positioned next to them, one strumming the strings of his lute while his partner sang the sweetest song about a woman fighting to return to her lover's side. It made Arica think of Ryger. She wondered what he was doing right now. It all happened so quickly, she never got to say how she felt. Or to learn how he did. Rolling her eyes, she focused on the crowd. Ryger was just a friend, not a lover. This song was not about them. There were more pressing matters at hand. To get back. Back to their friends and her brother. Without her realising it, Tamar had ordered them two cups of a deep cherry-coloured wine.

'It will take the edge off,' she said lifting her cup, 'cheers!'

They sat there for what seemed like hours searching the group of patrons in front of them. Looking for any sign of the city that they pined to return to. A group of Telvidian merchants were chortling and crashing their tankards together across from them. Celebrating some big sale Arica guessed. Their dark, leather vests clung to their bodies, revealing the thick and muscular bodies beneath them. Wherever they came from, it had been raining, for the fresh sheen of rain still remained on the vests and their white hair seemed duller from the damp.

Sitting next to them, a raven-haired woman leaned into the gaze of a blonde serving girl. They were engrossed in a hushed talk. Perhaps she was asking if they had any rooms available for the night. Or perhaps she already had one and was inviting the serving girl to join her later. Arica guessed she was from Ultarion because of the loose-fitting trousers. Those types of clothes would do nothing for you in these parts if it started to rain or snow.

A young, skinny boy stood at the counter begging the burly barkeep for a drink. He held out a single copper coin. Not even half the price of the drink. He was laughed away. His shoulders slinked and his feet shuffled to the end of a long table full of drinks and food belonging to a group of tattooed men and women. Where they came from, Arica did not know. They did not possess any of the features or clothing of any people she knew about, but then the world was much bigger than it once was. Arica wondered what lay beyond the continent that she knew, beyond the red desert of Ultarion. As a child she loved reading maps and learning about the different places but the only books that were in the Harth library were of Divinios. Nothing beyond this. Naively, she believed this was all there was. A perfect, neat little world where everyone knew of one another even though they did not travel across borders. It made sense to a child but as she aged it became obvious to her that this could not be all there was. Every now and again, some ship with an enigmatic crest or flag would dock in Harth. She would never speak to the mariners, but it was clear that they did not come from anywhere in the books or maps that she knew. All these people in one place and yet no one stood out to them yet.

Tamar sat back down beside Arica, although it was more like a crash. She had finished her third lap of the tavern with no result.

'No luck, everyone here is either tight-lipped or roaring drunk,' she said, annoyed and throwing back the last of her own drink.

'Be patient, we just have to sit here and keep our ears and eyes open.'

'My eyes will be drier than the deserts of Ultarion they've been open for so long,' Tamar remarked resting her face on a propped hand.

Arica could not help but laugh at her friend. Her humour was a blessing during all their troubles.

'I'm sure we will reach an oasis soon,' Arica smiled at her.

Tamar scrunched up her face and pushed Arica's arm playfully. They both laughed.

Night had fallen in the town. More lanterns had been lit in the tavern, but it was still ill-lit. This truly was a shadow's paradise. Tamar had completed three more laps and Arica even did one herself. Not a single mention of Dun Ortha. Not so much as a reference to the crystal rivers that ran through the city like veins. Not a whisper of the glowing lanterns that lit up the entire city in an ethereal light. It was getting late so they made the decision to rent a room for the night. They would spend the night here and hope for better luck tomorrow. Arica said a silent prayer to the gods that they would have to spend as little time as possible in this place. She longed to return to the magical city. They finished off their last drink with a final gulp and ascended the creaking staircase that led them to a narrow hallway with four doors. They entered the last on the right, as directed by the thickset man behind the bar. The room was small with a round window that looked over the town. A bed sat in the corner with a single ivory waxen candle unlit on the table next to it. Tamar put the bags in the corner while Arica clicked her fingers, sparking a flame atop her index finger that intended to use to light the candle. The flame spread a warm orange glow around the room. A gasp came from Tamar and when Arica quickly turned around she saw two hooded figures in the corner of her room.

'Who are you?' Arica said, growing the single flame into a fireball in her open palm.

The two girls stood side by side ready to defend themselves against these mysterious people. They said nothing as they took a step forward, holding up their hands in submission.

'Show yourselves,' Tamar demanded.

The figures reached for their hoods and pulled them back slowly. Another gasp left the girls' mouths when they saw the faces beneath the hoods. A tear fell down Arica's cheek as she propelled herself forward and wrapped her arms around the neck of one of them. Tamar did the same to the other. They held this position as they shook with a mixture of relief and happiness. When they finally pulled away, they stared into the eyes of their siblings.

Tamar sat on the edge of the bed with her sister and began speaking so quickly, it was like a language of their own. Arica took her brother's hands and asked so many questions his head spun. He explained the entire story to the two of them. After they did not show up for training that morning, they sent out a search party. Their tracks were easy to follow up the hill. They spotted tendrils of smoke rising from the woods below and knew they had to check it out. When they arrived at the scene there was nothing left except the charred remains of houses, hoofprints and smudged tracks. Not a single person had been left behind. They discovered their horses a little away from that smouldering clearing. The obvious signs of a fight were clear from the torn-up earth and burn marks. They had presumed that the people who attacked the village and took the people, took Arica and Tamar too. Since that day, they had all been out searching for them. They had travelled across Ebraeye, all the way to the eastern coast and now they were close to crossing into the Haellan controlled Aflosi territory. They had heard talk about a castle where the locals could hear screams from dawn to dusk so the two of them decided that would be their next destination. When they got there, they hid on the outskirts awaiting a gap to breach its walls, but they overheard about their escape then. They had scoured the surrounding villages and towns ever since, hoping they'd find them.

'We saw you buying drinks earlier but did not want to draw attention, so we hid in the room that we saw the barkeep take the key for,' Alys explained.

'I'm just so glad you found us,' Arica said happily.

'I would have spent the rest of my life searching for you,' Malin told his sister.

The siblings continued talking for hours. When the ivory candle had melted down to the candle holder it was time to sleep. The four of them climbed into the bed. With eyes heavier than stones, they fell asleep quickly. A feeling of warmth filled Arica's heart as her mind drifted into a deep sleep. Her brother had found her. She was safe once again. Tamar's illness was gone. The nightmare of their capture was long behind them now.

Chapter 26

They set off for the crystal city, Dun Ortha, at first light. The plan was to arrive before sundown. The road was a winding track that had seen hundreds of thousands of footprints travelling between Aflos and Ebraeye. Along the road the signs of the Haellan invasion were clear. Burnt villages upon villages and homesteads were scattered around the landscape. Some houses were left ransacked with notices nailed to the door, evicting the tenants, or arresting them. Aflos was an immensely wealthy region. It was known for the many miles of tunnels beneath the mountains that were filled to the brim with glistening precious stones. Rubies. Sapphires. Emeralds. A rainbow of prosperity bursting from the very earth beneath them. All of those riches were the reason Haella invaded. They wanted to secure the gold and jewels to pay for the weapons they were acquiring from gods know where. Rumours had it that they were smelting down the metals to make their own weapons too. Whatever they were doing, the Aflosi people had become shells of themselves. When they did pass a home that was still occupied, the people were skittish and cowered inside the windows. Nervous ghosts of the proud people they once were. The Amber Lions' terror had changed the way these people lived. Solomir thrived on the misfortune of those he manipulated and leached from. He was a parasite of the continent. His reign would forever be a tenebrous stain on the tapestry of its history.

The hooves of their horses thudded as they hurried back to the city. The rhythmic sound of them was carried along in the wind. Alys' dapple-grey mare, Elonwé, kept to the front. Tamar had her arms wrapped around her sister's waist to keep her balanced. Elonwé's dark mane flicked in their faces. The horse had been with Alys for many years, she was one of the few things left from their home. She was the family horse that had pulled their father's cart to and from the market where he sold the vegetables their mother grew in the garden.

Like their horse, Malin and Arica's was also from home. Malin had been using the palomino stallion who had carried them away from Harth to Fiermor to the Karigraine and to Dun Ortha. Sundancer's golden-cream body glowed in the sunshine. Light bounced off him like the surface of still water. Arica clung to her brother as they too cantered back to the city. She was glad to be back with her brother. It had been so long since they had been together. The longest since she had been born. The pair were always seen together when they were growing up. Two sides of the same coin, their grandmother used to comment as they rushed through the house playing one of their many games of pretend.

'How has everything been?' Arica asked, 'back in Dun Ortha?'

'To be honest, not good— after you were taken everyone has been up in arms,' he explained, 'but then more and more people started disappearing and villages were being pillaged by the Lions.'

'They're deranged, what they're doing to those people is disgusting.'

Malin paused. After a moment, he asked what she meant. At first Arica did not know what to say. The memory of finding her friend strapped to that table was a horrible thought that she did not like to look back on. But she knew she had to tell. It would be easier to tell Malin first before having to tell Jyneera and the others. Arica inhaled a deep breath and began to tell her brother what had happened to them after getting captured. She told him about the odious cell that held her for weeks. How she was fed scraps, slept on damp straw, and was interrogated every few days to try and break her. Malin went rigid as Arica told him about the menacing voice that called to her and scratched her arm. He released a gasp of shock upon hearing about the punishment that his sister endured from atop the castle tower. But what was even more upsetting was the sheer silence when she explained how she had found Tamar. What he said next shocked her entirely because he never uttered a bad word against anyone, let alone shout a curse. It was a few minutes of silence before she realised that her brother was crying.

'Malin, please don't cry.'

'What they di—,' he stopped, 'it's just disgusting how they could do that to anyone.'

'I know Malin, it was terrible. Those people— were wicked and it truly felt like they revelled in the torture.'

'I hate them and will hunt them down for what they did to you and Tamar.'

Arica did not know what to say. She would have said the same thing if their lives had been reversed. After a moment, she just leaned into him and hugged him.

The hill rose in front of them with the sun at their back. The warmth felt good on the nape of her neck. They had ridden through the wood that the Lions had attacked them in. The scorched earth had been washed by rainfall, but the blackened and broken buildings still remained. The fissure Tamar punched in the ground split the village in half. Arica looked at her wrist and thanked the gods for bringing them to Emra. Without her help, she would never cast again and worst of all, Tamar would be dead. The fear about what happened to her would not hold her back. She would not allow it. It was fuelling something inside of her that was creating a bubbling sensation. The destruction of Solomir's reign and the Amber Lions' terror was her goal. That thought stuck in her mind as they reached the top of the valley overlooking the beautiful city of Dun Ortha. Happiness filled her heart on sight. They did it. They made it. They drove their horses on, re-energised by the sight of the great city. Arica turned her head as a flash of white passed on their left side. As soon as it appeared, it was gone again. She kept watch on the spot as they rode further away from it. *A white deer?* Whatever the beast was, it was gone.

The familiar beauties of the city seemed to sing as they passed them on their way to the Azure House. The exquisite, shining blue tiles of the roof sparkled as the sunlight bounced off of it. It really was an outstanding building. The grey bricks that made it were so light that it was almost white. A long set of steps led up to the huge double doored entrance. Windows spread out in all directions on either side of the central entrance. The Ebraeyen crest of the horse rearing in front of the sun was nestled above the door. This building that had seemed so daunting and grand when she first arrived now seemed to have a different energy. It was almost like it was welcoming back the four friends. As they climbed off their horses, two footmen took the reins and walked them back to the stables. Arica and the other climbed up the steps, pushed open the door and headed straight for Jyneera's office.

Seated at her desk, looking like a formidable force was the stern-faced leader of the Ebraeyen people. Her palms lay flat against the desk, spread out either side of a large map. The lines and shapes sprawled across the map outlined the territories that broke up the continent of Divinios into its different parts. Ultarion's scorching deserts lay to the north. The desert was famous for its red-coloured sands that rose up in dunes. To the east were the marshlands of Telvidia where the people with hair like snow lived. The gem-filled land of Aflos was the neighbour to Ebraeye below Ultarion's ruby sands. Haella's rolling grasslands and lush forests were nestled on the peninsula of the continent. The Nelerian and Tempestuous Seas lay either side of the country. The triplet islands known as the Susrials sat on the south-western coast of Haella. All of these places made up the land Arica called home. Before this year she had never been outside of Haella but now she had been in three different nations. Her small world was growing into a much fuller place. With each passing day, she learned more about it, and she loved it. But now, she had to tell Jyneera something about the world. A darker side to it. Upon seeing them enter, Jyneera's eyes widened, and she stood at attention.

'Tamar! Arica! You're alive!'

They all sat down again once the commotion of their entrance died down. Jyneera was curious about what had happened to them. The two girls began to retell their story, detailing everything that had befallen them in the last few weeks. They spoke of the capture, the castle, the experiments, Emra and her sons, and finally, their lucky reuniting with their siblings in the tavern. Jyneera stared and listened intently and soaked up every word that left their mouths. She was taking mental notes to try and decipher what Valkor's reasons for it all is.

'This is very unsettling,' Jyneera said with a troubled look strewn across her face.

'What does it all mean? What does he want?' Malin asked.

'It appears he has a fixation with you, Arica,' Jyneera said clasping her hands together.

'He makes me sick.'

'He treats people like they are nothing,' Tamar said venomously.

'You will have your revenge in time, but before that we have to understand what it is he wants,' Jyneera told the four.

After that, Jyneera asked if she could have the room. They nodded and turned on their heels. Alys, Tamar and Malin had already stepped out of the room when Jyneera called Arica back. Arica closed the door and walked back to the desk. Jyneera stood up and walked around the desk and leaned on it, facing Arica.

'Your casting is unique, we know this— but something tells me there's more.'

'But what? I do not understand.'

'Is there anything you can think of? Anything that would make you a target?' she asked intensely.

Arica pursed her lips as she tried to think of something. She thought about her family and her background, but they were just like every other family in Harth. Her mother spent her days preparing meals, keeping the house, tending the garden, and feeding the animals while her father worked on the docks, loading and unloading cargo from ships. She and her brothers went to school and competed in the Trial like every other child in Harth. There was nothing that made her special. Not until that day on the Javelins when the fire inside her burst. *That* was it. That moment was the special thing about her. After thinking about it, Arica apologised and admitted she could not think of anything else. With a heavy sigh, Jyneera excused her. Arica bowed her head and left the room.

With a heavy heart she trudged up the flight of stairs that brought her to her bedroom. She closed the door behind her and rested her forehead against it. It felt good to be back in the safety of the four walls of her room that surrounded her. Slowly, she turned around and ambled to the comforting embrace of her bed. It had been a long journey since the last time she lay here. That morning that Tamar called for her, never could she have imagined that it would have ended like it did. She was thankful that luck had been on her side and she escaped the frightening experience she had been through. The thoughts were in her mind for a time, but soon the heavy call of slumber came and soon, she fell into a deep sleep.

Chapter 27

A small, blue bird was perched at the foot of the bed when she awoke. Its head twitched to the side and stared. The beady eyes blinked once, twice, before it fluttered away and back out the open window. The pitter-patter of raindrops rang from outside. She was glad to be indoors and out of the downpour. The poor bird was using her room as a shelter. Sitting up in the bed, she looked around the room. The familiar colours and furniture made her smile. She felt safe wrapped up in the quilt and with the soft pillows at her back. The fireplace that was directly across from her at the other side of the room was lit. A small fire crackled and popped with the heat. *The handmaid must have come in while I was asleep*, Arica thought. Arica scuttled out of the bed and draped herself in the navy robe hanging next to the bed. The light fabric felt good against her skin, smooth and soft. Her bare feet carried her to the fireplace. She stood in front of it, the warmth radiating on her body. She closed her eyes and drank in the feeling of serenity that the quiet and warm room brought her. A knock interrupted her thoughts.

'Enter,' she called.

The door swung open. Standing on the other side was a welcome sight. He wore a simple deep green tunic that left his arms bare, showing off the black lines that tattooed the whole way up. This was paired with chocolate-coloured pants and boots. His brown hair was tussled, like he just rolled out of his bed. He looked gorgeous. They stared at one another, but not for long as they rushed for each other and they embraced. They held each other and she could not help but smile. He smelled of sandalwood. Taking in a deep breath, she revelled in being wrapped in his arms. His strong arms felt tight around her, his muscles pulsing.

'I am so glad you're back,' he whispered into her ear.

'Me too,' she replied.

He pulled himself back so he could look into her eyes. Her hands wrapped around his back and his arms held her waist. Her green eyes looked into his hazel ones. *So beautiful and bright*, she thought to herself. Ryger lifted his hand and brushed back a loose strand of hair that had fallen over her face. His fingers gently swept against her forehead causing her to shiver. Their heads inched closer together and when they were a hair's distance apart a cough interrupted them. They faced the door to see Tamar standing in the doorway.

'Jyneera would like to speak with you,' she said flatly.

Arica and Ryger looked at one another once more, and then started for the door. After walking out and heading for the staircase, Tamar put an arm on the wall, blocking Ryger's movement.

'Not you, just her,' she stated.

Ryger attempted to say something, but she interrupted him again, repeating the same thing. He scrunched his face as he watched the girls descend the stairs. Arica looked back at him over her shoulder. The confused look still on his face as he turned around with his palms on the back of his head.

The two girls walked quietly to the office. The air felt icy to Arica. When she did try to say something to Tamar, she was only met with silence. Arica knew that Tamar could be capricious at times but usually there was a clear reason. But they had been friends long enough to know that she was also not one to push for an explanation. That would result in a fury that one would very much prefer to avoid. The halls were empty too, not a single person walked along the shiny floors. Tamar's heels clicked as they thudded off the floor. It was only then that Arica realised she had forgotten to put her own shoes on. Her feet were bare and cold. She squirmed as she stood in front of the office door as if that would mask her forgetfulness. Tamar turned and began to walk away.

'Where are you going?' Arica asked.

'It was you who was summoned, not I,' she replied and sauntered away.

The door swung open with ease, revealing the office full of light. The thick curtains were pulled back allowing golden rays of beautifully warm sunlight into the room. Arica closed the door behind her and went for the desk where she expected to see the Ebraeyen leader but instead was met with two familiar figures that sat on the seats in front of it.

'Grandmother! Khea!' she exclaimed, running to them.

Arica threw her arms around her aunt who stood to meet her. There was a scent of roses off her hair. She wore a simple dark green dress that reached the floor and her curly hair was tied back off her face. Arica then knelt down next to her grandmother and hugged her tightly. Tears began to stream down her cheeks. She had missed her family desperately these last few months, and seeing them now she was overcome with emotion. Her grandmother held her face and wiped her tears with her thumbs.

'It is all right my love, everything is good,' she said, her voice sounding as sweet as honey.

'I missed you so much— how are you? How is Father? Kal? Garo?'

'Your father and the boys are well, still at home— and Malin?'

'He is living his dream of being a cook right here in Jyneera's kitchen.'

Her grandmother smiled at that. It was obvious to anyone that knew the youngest Preandre brother that all he wanted to be was a cook. Any chance that he got he could have been found baking or cooking something. It was his true calling. Arica took one of their hands in each of hers and smiled up at them. Her grandmother began asking her a barrage of questions, all about life since she left Harth. She exhaled and started to inform her aunt and grandmother about her adventures until now.

It had become easier to tell her story each time. The details were clearer and she was quicker to remember them. The peaks and pits of her journey seemed as though they were etched into her mind, like the ink of the tattoos that lined Ryger's arms. Every memory glowed brightly in her mind, even the darkest ones. Her description of the cell was accurate down to the grease-like grime that coated the stone. Khea and her grandmother shivered at the thought of Arica being held against her will in such a caliginous place. With a deep sigh, she finished telling them about it all. Arica threw her arms around each of them again out of sheer joy and relief to see them again.

'I am so glad you are here, both of you— but how is it you came to be here?'

Khea's head dropped. There was a look in her eye that told a sad story. It was a look that she knew from experience for both her grandmother and father would don it when they were about to say something she would not like. The three of them all shared it, the tell-tale sign of some foreshadowing news.

'The Black Rose is gone.'

Arica could hardly believe her ears. The tavern that Khea had started almost two decades ago was just gone. How could that happen she wondered. Was it the result of an ill-placed bet? Perhaps, some drunken customer knocked a candle and set the place ablaze. But none of that seemed likely. Gambling was not a sport of her aunts who believed that the only time a person should wage a bet is when they are certain of their victory.

'The Lions came in search of you, I barely made it out alive. I rode my horse all through the night to get to Harth and once I told Mother about it, we knew we had to come warn you.'

'Well, if you had arrived here two days ago you would not have been pleased— they found me. They knew I was here.'

'Your note— the one Malin wrote. That *must* be it, nothing else would make sense,' Khea offered in a certain voice.

'But why me?' Arica cried out in frustration.

The endless hunt where she had been the prey had gone on for so long it seemed like it would be never ending. Would it continue into her final years? She imagined her life as a silver-haired woman constantly glancing over her shoulder and hiding from the Lions. It was not a life she envisioned and certainly not one she desired. It left a sour taste in her mouth that caused the corners to sag into a frown.

'I think it is time you learned something,' her grandmother said looking at Khea as if for approval. Her aunt simply nodded her head slowly and clasped her hands in her lap. Arica cast her gaze on her grandmother waiting eagerly for what she was going to say.

With all of the gifts of a master storyteller, her grandmother began. She set the scene a millennium ago on the largest of the Susrial isles — Celaen. The island was famous for its high cliffs with stone as white as bone. Atop these great cliffs was the ancient city of Rhadirim. The Rhadiri people were wise and at one with the world around them. They understood it, some say they could even commune with it, feeling the ebb and flow of the magic beneath the soil. These were the first sorcerers of Divinios, the first casters. The men and women of Rhadirim had gifts to manipulate the elements around them — earth, fire, water and wind. The casters embraced the magic with every fibre of their being, becoming one with their element. But like the casters of the present, the Rhadiri could control only one element. That is, expect for members of House Celmere, the royal family that ruled over the Susrials. The members of the family were said to have bathed in pure magic that ran in a river beneath the rocks and soil of the island and this gave them the unique ability to channel all four elements. The Celmere's believed that their purpose on the continent was to protect the people of not just the Susrials, but everywhere from the dark forces of Vuromel. Vuromel was the home of the demons of the abyss, malevolent monsters that feast on humans and destroy all in their path. The most famous of the Celmere's was Queen Lyneer who vanquished the demons using her magic, golden sword, Solas. Legend has it she was the one to finally close the entrances to Vuromel, stopping the demons from reaching the realm of humans ever again. Lyneer continued to rule in Rhadirim for the remainder of her days but as the centuries passed by the city of Rhadirim faded away and the once great House of Celmere ceased to exist.

'Grandmother, as much as I adore your stories, what does this have to do with me?' Arica asked, trying to understand the meaning behind the story.

'Impatience will get you nowhere, my love,' her grandmother chimed. 'According to history, the Celmerien dynasty ended on the island hundreds of years ago without so much as a footprint left behind, but this is not the truth.'

Arica leaned in further to her grandmother. Curiosity was building up inside of her like molten lava brimming to the top of a volcano, daring to explode at any second. This is what her grandmother always did when telling a tale, building up the suspense so much until Arica thought she may die from anticipation. Arica suspected this was on purpose to amuse her grandmother.

'The family did cease to exist on Celaen, but not from the world— they plainly set their sights elsewhere. The mainland. Haella to be exact.'

'There was nothing left for them on the island. Having fulfilled their purpose, they thought they would start anew under a new name— Preandre,' Khea informed her niece.

'But that would mean—' Arica began.

'Yes, we are descendants of the Celmeres— we are descendants of Queen Lyneer.'

Chapter 28

The family took their evening meal in Malin's room to have some private time. His room was above the kitchens so he would be closer to his workplace, but Arica suspected it was really because Sandar's room was also there. He had originally been in the same hall as his sister but made the request not long after arriving in Dun Ortha. The two had been spending a lot of time together and from what Arica could tell, Malin had revealed his feelings to him. Malin had invited Sandar to dine with them and he fit in with them perfectly. Their grandmother was giggling like a schoolgirl whenever he spoke, and Khea smiled to show her approval. Arica raised her eyebrows and smirked at her brother who replied by sticking his tongue out. It was fun to have some quality time away from the hustle and bustle of the rest of the building. Here, it was just them.

While their dinner conversations did distract her somewhat, Arica could not help but think about the news she had received this morning. A descendant of a queen. *Queen Lyneer*. The woman that she had been inspired by from a young age. It was another piece of the puzzle of her life and at least one of her many questions answered. Her casting abilities suddenly felt

227

less bizarre. There was a reason she could control them all. There was history behind it. Her grandmother told her that even though the gifts were passed down through the family, it was still rare. The female line in their family was more in tune with magic than the male and was more often seen within the women. Her own grandmother had the same gifts but did not use them outside of her home and only her family knew of them. Her grandmother never told Arica's father about this which is why he was so surprised when his own daughter's magic manifested.

That night she did not sleep well. Her thoughts were rampant with questions when she was awake and images that she did not understand swirled around her mind when she was able to sleep. A ball of golden light accompanied each one, as if guiding her through her own mind. The ball flew past a pack of white wolves, like the one that helped her in the forest. Their alabaster fur glistened as the light's rays fell on them. Suddenly, she was facing a large wall of rock. The large, jagged shapes jutted out in many directions. A voice whispered from behind them in a language Arica did not know. Somehow she knew it was calling her. The ball of light surged forward and she felt herself following with it as if tethered to one another. She stood in a dark room; wall and floor blending into one. It was unclear if she was suspended in mid-air or standing firmly on the ground. The light was ahead of her now and floating above what looked like a stone coffin. She tried to move forward but was frozen. The light grew brighter and brighter as the foreign voice whispered again. Her arms were stuck at her sides and she could not shield her eyes from the dazzling light. Propelling herself forward and finally able to cover her eyes, she realised the light was gone. Slowly pulling her hands down the familiar sight of her bedroom appeared before her.

Early the next morning Arica quickly dressed herself and tied her hair into a ponytail before rushing out and down the stairs. She did not run into another soul on her way, the house was dead silent. The street outside was the same. Her grandmother had been put up in a guest house adjacent to the Azure House. The more modest abode was used for visiting dignitaries or ambassadors. Her grandmother felt very important when Jyneera told her she could stay there. An ordinary woman who had lived a simple life was in awe at the grandeur of this extravagant place. The maroon-colour velvet armchair in the living room was the most amazing thing she had ever sat on and that was exactly where Arica found her.

'Arica, what a wonderful surprise, how are you this morning?' she chimed.

'I did not sleep well, so tired if I'm honest.'

'Let me brew you some tea, it will help,' she said, starting to get up. If there was ever any sort of problem, be it physical or emotional, a cup of tea would cure it. Arica wondered if it was just her grandmother who used this *miraculous* cure or was it every grandmother. It was true that it did help at times as it would put her at ease if she was nervous or upset. But something told her tea would not suffice this time.

'No thank you, Grandmother. I just wanted to speak to you about something.'

'Oh? Is something troubling you?'

Arica told her grandmother of her dream the previous night. She described each detail of it, making sure she did not omit a single one. Her father always said the truth was in the detail. Truthfully, she never fully understood the saying but it was crystal clear now.

Her grandmother fell silent for a moment or two. Her eyes stared at the ground while she thought on the words her granddaughter just spoke.

'It seems to me that you have heard a siren of sorts— something calling you.'

'A siren? Like those in the fishermen tales?' Arica asked. She had heard of these scaled creatures that could enchant anyone who heard them with beautiful voices. They were something of a horror story in Harth as so many of the people went on to work on the sea whether it be fishing, trade or something else. Arica thought perhaps it was a story parents told their children to stop them playing near the water's edge.

'Those sirens are but an old wives' tale— these sirens are created through magic, a call from the other side.'

'The other side of what?'

'The other side of the Veil— what separates the living from the dead, the mundane from the extraordinary. Someone is trying to tell you something.'

'But who? I do not understand.'

Her grandmother sat back in the chair, folded her arms and looked up at the ceiling. Arica stared at her, waiting for an answer. She began to play with her fingers, twisting them or scratching her nails against each other. It was abundantly clear to anyone that knew her that she was anxious. Why had this troubled her so much, she did not know.

'A wolf— and a rose, these are symbols of the Celmeres, of us,' her grandmother finally said, 'do you still have the pin I gave you?'

'Yes, it is on the table next to my bed,' Arica told her. She had kept the pin close to her since she left Harth, but thankfully in the excitement of leaving the city with Tamar, she had left it behind. She was so grateful for her forgetfulness then, as it would be lost forever otherwise.

'It bears the same symbols— the coffin had the rose. It must be the tomb of House Celmere. There is something there that you are destined to find.'

'I cannot just leave and go on a personal mission, Jyneera will not allow it.'

'And does Jyneera have you on a leash? You are a free woman; do as you wish.'

Arica was taken aback by her grandmother's words. It was not like her to be sarcastic. It was a fire that she had not seen before. But they were the words that she needed to hear. Arica had forgotten that she had not taken an oath of some sort. Yes, she was training alongside the Ebraeyen soldiers and casters but that did not mean she had sworn her life to the cause. She was still well within her rights to come and go as she pleased. However, it was one thing knowing and believing this yourself. She would still have to break this to Jyneera who she felt would not have the same opinion. Arica thanked her grandmother for her advice and kissed her on the cheek. Before she could leave she was taken by the hand.

'Now, time for the tea,' her grandmother said with a smile.

Arica left the guest house with many questions. How would she tell Jyneera? How would she get there? Would she make it alone? What would she find there? These would plague her thoughts until they were answered so she was determined to do just that. But before she did that, she needed some time away from the Azure House to be by herself. She could not face the people inside who would be full of energy and questions. Quiet is all she desired in that moment. Instead of turning left and walking up the steps to the Azure House, she continued straight on until coming to a cross street. She took the left street and followed it as it snaked its way around the back of the government buildings and ended at one of the bridges that meant the end of the Cerulean District. She quickly trotted over the bridge, admiring the gorgeous water of the river beneath. She had entered the Ochre District, a mostly residential district that got its name from the ochre colour of the slates on the roofs. They had a mesmerising golden shimmer when the sun hit them from the right angle. It was like every building had its very own crown. The thought of crowns reminded her of her royal lineage and she had to shake it out of her mind. *Peace and quiet, Arica. None of those thoughts right now.*

Arica turned another corner and found herself in a small courtyard. The courtyard floor was polished cobblestones and there were beds of pink and white flowers planted all around it. Right in the centre of the courtyard was a fountain. Clear water spouted from the middle level and flowed down to the one below. Standing atop the fountain was a statue carved from white marble, a statue of the goddess Merenia. Merenia was of course accompanied by her white wolf. Arica almost laughed when she saw her favoured goddess' companion. Was fate laughing at her too? She sat on the edge of the fountain.

'Will a ball of light appear too?' she jested aloud to herself.

'I can make a ball of water?' a voice called from behind her.

Arica let out a yelp of surprise and fright, falling back. Her arm was grasped just before she hit the water. Her heart pounded as she looked up to see Ryger's sparkling hazel eyes staring into her green ones. A single curl of his wavy brown hair was hanging over his forehead. He pulled her up straight and sat down next to her.

'You can call me your hero now,' he beamed.

'I would not have needed one if you had not crept up on me!'

'*Crept* is a strong word— walked quietly is a kinder term,' he said with a flutter of his eyelashes.

Arica could not help but laugh at him. Ryger could seem so serious around other people but around her he seemed to let this wall he had constructed down. He had a witty side that when he showed made her laugh without fail. It seemed he decided to drop it today.

'You look simply gorgeous when you do that,' Arica joked, knocking her shoulder into his gently.

'Gorgeous? Me? It means so much coming from a girl like you,' he smiled his wicked smile.

Arica felt the temperature of her cheeks rise. She was sure they were a perfect shade of beetroot. Ryger inched closer to her. His eyes met hers once more. Being this close she could see the tiny flecks of gold that encircled his pupil. She had never seen a pair of eyes like them. His hand felt cool at the touch as he placed it on top of hers.

'You know, we were interrupted yesterday,' he said softly.

Arica, unable to form words, swallowed a lump in her throat and managed to nod her head. Her heartbeat grew faster and faster as their bodies moved closer and closer together. Ryger's familiar scent of sandalwood surrounded her until she was completely enveloped in its smell. Their faces were close enough that she could smell the mint on his breath from the leaves he sometimes liked to chew and then, their lips met. Arica's mind was filled with a slew of colours, some she did not know existed. She could hear nothing, yet everything at the same time. The outside world was not a distraction; the sounds of the city had dulled until there was a sublime cadence that felt like it was written for them. The nervous feeling in her stomach began to wane. She felt at ease when she was with Ryger, especially in moments alone. Her hand found its way into his hair, her fingers wrapping around his curls. Her heart thumped in perfect symphony with his. How long they were, neither of them knew, but before long other people started to appear in the courtyard. They broke apart, eyes still locked on one another. Both of them were breathing heavily. Arica could see the rise and fall of his broad shoulders. After a moment, Ryger stood and held out his hand.

'Can I walk you home?'

Chapter 29

Dinner that night was eaten in the dining room. Arica was seated on the right side of the long, smooth dining table, closest to the high windows. The silver hue of the moon's light cast a calming glow on the table's shiny surface. The usual crowd sat along the table's edge, high ranking members of the Ebraeyen Council, the generals of the army and the select casters who were staying in the Azure House. At first, Arica had felt disjointed seated amongst the distinguished members of society, but over time she had settled. She did not participate in the conversations about the war or politics, however there were times when they spoke of more trivial matters that she felt comfortable to engage in.

On this particular evening, Jyneera decided to join them. It was an unusual occurrence as she tended to eat in her own private quarters behind her office. That was the first indication that there was something else afoot. The meal itself was uneventful, everyone speaking and discussing their training sessions that day. Alys had a particular good day in the Ring. She had managed to master a move she had been working on for a long time. By pulling the earth upwards she created a pillar of rock that carried her high into the air, while also splitting the earth around the pillar like a sunburst. Her mentor was very pleased with her, and even allowed her to finish up early. There was an aura of happiness around her as she told her friends, who in turn could not help but smile at her delight.

Once their meals were finished and were about to leave, the Chancellor stood and cleared her throat. Arica and the others all turned their heads and focused their attention on her. She wore the typical serious face when she was about to speak. The room was deathly silent for a fleeting moment before she began.

'We are launching an attack on Valkor's castle.'

Arica did not think the room could get quieter. Her own heart skipped a beat and she felt sick at the mention of that name. She was instantly back in her cell, listening to nothing but the crash of waves outside the barred window. She could only imagine how Tamar felt, but the waxen complexion on her face told the story.

'I have discussed this in private with council members Frei and Numbaso, who are in agreement with the plan,' she continued, signalling towards an elderly man and a middle-aged woman seated on either side of her. The man's wrinkled face was frozen in a frown as though his aged muscles could no longer hold up the corners of his mouth. The woman, Frei, had the appearance of a kind woman with bright eyes and rosy cheeks. Tamar, however, had warned her not to cross the council member as those who did tend to disappear.

'Chancellor, we cannot possibly strike a Haellan castle with such little notice,' one of the generals started.

'Yes, we shall need time to strategize,' another finished.

'Rest your concerns, generals, a plan has already been decided upon. Hamir?'

Jyneera's giant shadow took a step away from the wall behind her. His arms were folded across his barrel-like chest. His menacing scowl still slapped across his face. He moved closer to the table before reaching behind his back and pulling out a rolled-up piece of paper. Hamir spread it out flat on the now-clear dining table. It was a map of Divinios. But a much bigger Divinios than she knew. The maps she had seen before this stopped at Ultarion's desert, but this map was much more vast. She read names and made out mountains and rivers she had never heard of before. It was true then; the world really was much bigger and wider than she had previously thought. What struck her most was that the *continent* she had been taught to know was not a continent at all, but only a piece of an even bigger one. The jagged form of the peninsula of Divinios pointed south, surrounded by the Nelerian and Tempestuous Seas on the east and west coasts. She instantly recognised the bay that her hometown lay. Now, so far away.

'We will travel northwest and down the Aflosi side of the mountain. Once we are close to the castle, we will send the fire and water casters to the beach, beneath the castle's walls. They will create a mist to cover our approach and distract the Haellan troops. The earth casters will then begin the assault by breaking down the walls so the foot soldiers can swarm. The wind casters will bring up the rear and cover their backs by knocking any archers off the outer walls,' Hamir explained all of this with stuttering. It was a well thought out plan.

Jyneera and Hamir took turns explaining the intricacies of the plan to Arica and the others. Every word that left the Chancellor's mouth made Arica stomach churn more and more. She needed to tell her that she could not take part in this mission. She had her own path that had to be followed. The whispering voice had niggled in her head all throughout the day. The images of the wolf, rose and ball of light flashed in her mind at unexpected times causing her to lose where she was mid-conversation and mid-training. This distraction was the reason she had received the strike of a kick in her stomach and the lash of a whip of water during her sessions earlier today. The whip left a red streak on her forearm and the kick's imprint on her stomach was purple and sore. The marks of her wayward thoughts sent a clear message to her that she needed to go to Celaen. To the tomb of the Celmere family.

When the meeting concluded everyone left the room and headed for bed. It was late and their beds called for them. The other members of the council were speaking in whispers to one another as they left, surely whispers of disdain that they held no part in the formulation of the attack. While watching her friends climb the staircase, Arica held back, pretending she left something behind. When the hall became quiet, Arica slowly made her way to Jyneera's office door. A gentle knock. The invitation. Arica opened the door and clicked it shut behind her. The Chancellor was seated at her desk as she usually was with bundles of paper spread across it and stacked in various places. A map similar to the one Hamir had shown to them all was open on the desk. This one had small; iron figurines placed strategically around it. Upon closer inspection, Arica could make out that it was the layout for the assault on Valkor's castle. She felt bile rise in her throat at the mere thought of his name. Jyneera traced a finger around in circles around the figure representing the castle.

'Something on your mind?' Arica asked softly.

'This attack— it feels like the beginning of something, something greater than anything we have ever seen,' Jyneera answered without a hint of emotion in her voice. It was a strange comment for her to make. In the dining room she seemed so confident and sure of herself when describing the plan. Arica was seeing a different side to the Chancellor than she had ever been exposed to. It was odd seeing her in this light. The obvious question was about to leave her lips, but Jyneera did not give her a chance to.

'It is like a chill. An icy shivering travelling up my spine and into my fingers, biting. Like the coldest winter you have ever known, twice over.'

Arica stared at the timorous woman before her. 'Have you felt like this before?'

'I have felt shivers before something happens, often before a battle— but not like this. This is almost overwhelming,' Jyneera clenched a fist. It was evident that she was not used to this sort of display. She was the statuesque leader of a great nation, fighting for the freedom of not just their own people, but for everyone.

'Perhaps it is a sign not to go forward?' Arica suggested, knowing already that that would be out of the question. It had been made abundantly clear during the briefing in the dining room that every aspect of the attack had been planned and would go forward without protest.

'The wheels of war have already begun to turn, impossible to stop.' Arica did not know how to feel about that analogy. She did not say anything about it.

'What is it you have come to speak to me about?' Jyneera asked, finally looking up at her. Her elbows rested on the desk while her fingers put pressure on her temples. A trick she too used to alleviate the pain of a headache.

Arica thought for a moment on how she would tell her. But then, after another moment, realised nothing she was going to say was going to be taken well so better to just say it plainly.

'This attack on Valkor, I cannot take part in it.'

'Arica if this is about what he did to you in that castle, I assure you, he will suffer.'

'It's not that— there is something I must do.'

'Something more important than destroying one of Solomir's castles?' Jyneera's voice rose to a higher level. This was the voice of someone who was not used to being questioned or refused. While she was a protector of the people, she was still a human. Vain and full of pride.

'That remains to be decided,' Arica answered, proud of the strength in her own voice. She then continued to tell Jyneera about the dream she had the night before. For some reason, however, she did not inform the Chancellor about her ancient lineage. Something told her that this was knowledge best kept between blood.

'I understand your concern with this dream. They often tell us great truths before our minds fully understand them,' Jyneera's voice was flat. 'You will be a great loss to us in this fight.'

Arica left the office of the Chancellor feeling light. The anxiety of the foreboding announcement was gone and replaced with the sweet sense of relief. While vastly displeased, Jyneera accepted that when one feels magic telling them something that they should listen, no matter the repercussions. Like her own icy body, Arica's had been telling her something. She knew now that it was a call, a call to return to her ancestral home. Now that she had told Jyneera of her own plan, she decided that she would leave the next day at first light. The sooner she got to Celaen, the better. Her morning would consist of searching for transport to the largest of the Susrials. But she knew her greatest challenge would lie with her brother. He would not take kindly to her leaving again, especially alone. Before she knew it, she was standing on the other side of her bedroom door. She quickly undressed and climbed into her bed. Turning her head, she stared at the small, brass pin that sat in a bowl made from green stone on the bedside table. The wolf and rose carved into it seemed to stick out more than before. The connection between her and the pin was suddenly much more than a reminder of her grandmother. It seemed like this little piece of engraved metal held the key to her past, present, and future.

Chapter 30

The blue-green waters of the Tempestuous Sea were relatively calm as the thick, wooden hull of the ship ploughed through it. The slapping of the waves covered up any other sound onboard the *Indrinia*. Although wind casters were on board to help propel the ship forward, there was no need for their service as a strong wind was gushing from the north. A sign of good fortune the captain of the ship had called after they disembarked from the Ebraeyen shores. The sails were full and fat from the force of the gusts. Captain Roe was one of deep faith, that much was abundantly clear to Arica. Around his neck he wore a necklace fashioned from rope; the pendant resembled a spider web, but she knew it was a net with a circular piece of blue glass in the centre. A symbol of the sea goddess, Farrig. Captain Roe had been tasked with transporting Arica to the Susrials. He had volunteered, Jyneera informed her yesterday morning on the dock. The bow of the ship had a beautifully carved form of a dolphin, yet another symbol to gain Farrig's favour. The dolphin gazed out into the open sea, guiding the ship towards its destination. The clear sky stretched around them as far as the eye could see with not so much as a breaching whale to break up the scene. Arica prayed that the rest of the journey would be this straightforward.

That night, Arica settled in the stateroom below deck. It was located next to the captain's cabin. He had been so gracious as to offer a bed in the officer's quarters to her since only one of the ship's officers would be joining them on the voyage. When the officer was spoken about, Arica had presumed to meet a hulking woman with a face that could turn milk sour. But instead, was surprised upon being greeted by a young woman a foot shorter than her with large doe-like eyes and rosy cheeks. Her small frame did not strike fear into Arica's heart but she knew not to be deluded by what lay on the outside. The tales the captain told of her meant she was more than capable of handling herself in a fight on land or sea. Arica would be sure not to displease her while sharing the room.

Lying in the near darkness of the room, she stared up at the creaking boards. An orange flame flickered at her side, blobs of wax had dripped onto the table. She thought back on the morning when she bid farewell to her friends. Tamar and Ryger, of course, stated they were coming too. Arica was thankful for their offer but knew they could not. The mission on Valkor's castle needed their talents. That, and Jyneera would have them flayed if they too said they would not be joining. Alys hugged her and told her to be careful or she would have to come find her again. She smiled as she walked away facing Arica. Arica knew that she was upset but did not want to show it. For such an emotion filled person, Alys did not like to let others know if she was worried. The sisters left her as they went to the Ring where they would train for the mission. Ryger stayed behind. When they were alone, he swept her into his arms and kissed her hard on the lips.

'I had to,' was all he said. It was all he needed to.

Arica's family met her at the base of the steps leading to the Azure House. Her grandmother, having already known that she was leaving, helped with Khea and Malin. Khea openly told her niece that she was worried, but that she understood she needed to leave.

'When a Preandre woman makes a decision, no one will dissuade her.'

The aunt and niece hugged tightly, followed by a hug from the grandmother. The three women looked lovingly into each other's eyes and held hands in a circle. Her brother stood back from them with his arms crossed indignantly. The look on his face told Arica that he did not approve of this journey she was undergoing. Arica unclasped a hand and held it out. Malin's eyes stared at it at first, as if to burn a hole through it. Upon looking at his sister's face once more he shook himself and rushed to her side and hugged her close. The four family members' arms wrapped around each other. It was the goodbye Arica needed. With her family's support and well wishes there was nothing she could not do.

Arica was shaken from her thoughts when the door of the stateroom opened. It shut with a thud. The smell of salt was ever-present onboard the ship, but a particularly strong waft entered along with the officer. Her dark curls were hanging loose, slightly damp from the ocean air. A stain smeared the front of her shirt, presumably from the ale Arica saw the other sailors enjoying before going below deck.

'How fares the night?' Arica asked.

'Quiet and easy, wind's still blowing strong,' she answered, kicking off her leather boots.

Good, Arica thought to herself. If the wind kept up like this they would reach Celaen in just over a day. Two mornings and she would be there. She wondered what the island would be like. She knew that the old city would be in ruins, but others still lived there. "Good-tempered island folk" Captain Roe informed her earlier.

'You should have joined us, everyone was singing— good ale has that effect,' Naima the officer announced from her own bunk.

'I'm not much of a singer, I'm afraid.'

'None of us are!' Naima laughed, 'didn't stop the fun.'

'Perhaps the next time,' Arica told her. She liked being around others. She did not know whether she would take part in the singing or not, but an ale she could. It would help take her mind off the Celmere tomb and what might lurk within. Whatever the ball of light in her dream was leading to, she still had no idea, but she knew it was important. She did not even know how she was going to get into the tomb. The steep rocky exterior of the tomb looked impenetrable. The craggy wall did not appear to have a door in her dream. Perhaps that was deliberate. All she hoped was that this tomb was built to keep others out and not something in.

The next day the sky remained clear. The bright sun shone down on the lapping waves, causing them to sparkle like jewels. The wind, however, had died down and now the wind caster was busy thrusting his arms back and forth. Arica took over at different times during the day to give him a rest, although he protested at first. It meant she could practice her wind casting, and since she could not practice with earth or fire onboard a wooden ship, it was necessary. As well as casting, she practiced shooting her arrows along the mast of the ship. She had tied pieces of rope around it at three different heights. Thankfully, she was a talented archer, but even the adept can miss. The captain discovered this when one of the arrows lodged itself in the steering wheel, just missing his finger. That put an end to target practice. Not long after, Arica took up an offer from Naima to spar. Unlike archery, swordsmanship was not her greatest talent. This was evident with the bruises Naima left on her arm, leg and back. These were all given with the flat of the sword. Arica did also receive one cut on her forearm before finally, in a pool of sweat, decided to retire.

After cleaning herself up as best as possible in the stateroom, she went back up onto the deck. Evening had arrived; the sun close to the horizon line. The sky was a beautiful amalgamation of purple, yellow and pink. It brought a smile to Arica's face. She leaned on the railing, listening to the ocean's song. Tomorrow they would arrive in Celaen. You would not think it with their still being no sign of land or so much as a gull to signal its closeness. The sailors were beginning to wind down for the night, sitting on barrels and crates in the centre of the deck. One of them rolled a large barrel over to the group, while another carried a box of tankards. Soon everyone had a full tankard and were knocking the ale into their mouths. It did not take long for the stories and songs to begin. Arica looked on with a smile on her face. They all looked so happy and carefree. She wondered when was the last time she really felt that way. Not as of late, certainly. Worries seemed to be with her almost as much as she breathed. The constant thoughts about training, her friends, her family, or this ongoing war whirled around in her mind every day. Sometimes the thoughts were so potent that she felt like someone had tied her stomach in a knot. Slow breaths through her nose would remedy this but that took time and in moments of struggle, she usually did not have time for the breaths. She revelled in the joyful atmosphere of the ship. If only life could be this full of happiness always.

'Care to join us?' Naima appeared; her arm extended holding a pewter tankard. The cloudy, brown liquid was filled to the top. The tempting drink was almost calling to her.

'I think I might,' Arica accepted the drink and took a gulp.

'That's the spirit,' Naima chimed and clanged her cup against Arica's before taking a drink herself.

The two women walked over to the circle of sailors and sat down on two crates. Captain Roe had the floor and was singing in a glorious baritone.

O serene bewitching moon,
shine your light on me,
Your silver glow casts a spell
On all eyes who fall on thee.
To Rhadirim's shore we go,
To the city of silver,
Where biting fangs and steel
Make all enemies quiver.

Arica had never heard this song before. Its haunting melody acted as a lullaby of sorts. A sense of peace washed over her. She swayed from side to side as the captain sang it. She took another mouthful and realised it was empty. Naima snickered next to her before grabbing the tankard to refill it. Arica did not know why Naima had taken a liking to her, but it felt good to have a friend on the journey. *You never know when you will need a friend*, her father always told her and her brothers as they grew up. She always remembered to be kind to those around her. A person, even a stranger, is more likely to help someone if they are kind to them. Holding her second drink with both hands, she paused to think of each of her friends she had met since the Trial. Tamar. Alys. Ryger. Emra. Odan. Torun. All of these people had helped her in some way and for that she would be forever grateful. Arica said a silent prayer of thanks to them, putting the cool tankard to her lips.

Chapter 31

The *Indrinia*'s large hulking frame glided past the jagged rocks off the coast of Celaen's shores. The lookout atop the ship's mast had sighted the island not long after sunrise. Arica had just woken up and was still underneath the blankets when the clambering above her began. The sailors were rushing to their posts to ensure the approach would be as smooth as possible. She quickly dressed herself, ran up the steps and onto the main deck so she got the best view of the incoming island. The sand-coloured stone of the cliffs was exposed amongst the thick green blankets of trees that snaked the island's coastline. The island began flat on the left and gradually rose to a crescendo where she could make out the ruins of what was once a glorious castle. *Rhadirim*, she thought to herself. Her family's ancestral home. Right before her eyes. It was exactly like a castle out of one of her grandmother's stories. She paused. Perhaps those castles were based on this very one on the cliff, passed down through the mouths of grandparents further back than anyone could trace. Of all the towers that once overlooked the sea and protected the city from invaders, only one remained. The tower appeared to have been masoned from the very stone it sat upon. She tried to imagine it in its height of glory. *It must have been spectacular*.

The ship moored along a long dock nestled in a bay beneath the ruined city. A village with small stone buildings dotted around the land surrounded the dock. Men and women dressed in loose fitting clothes rushed about the village. It was a busy village. Arica had expected fewer people and much more of a sparse community. Many eyes stared as they disembarked the ship. These people were not used to outsiders. The old dock groaned beneath their footsteps. The soft ebb and flow of the sea bid farewell to them as they stepped onto dry land again. The captain told the sailors to rest and be ready to set sail as soon as he called. Arica, along with Naima and Roe, then set their sights on the ruined city. The trio left the boundaries of the village. Naima suggested borrowing horses from the villagers but that was waved off as Captain Roe did not deem them necessary. The officer attempted to protest but her captain's rank held her back. Arica could see the frustration in her but admired the loyalty she had.

They made their way into the forested part of the island. The gradual incline to the clifftop was felt in their muscles as they proceeded. Arica was reminded of the forest near her home by the sounds of the birds and animals all around them. Wild pigs were in abundance on this island, their spirited grunting was heard throughout the hike. She also knew that deer resided here from the cloven hoof impressions in the earth. She itched to take an arrow from her quiver and to hunt like she once did. In a time before the reality of magic and the war entered her life. Having wanted to be an Amber Lion for years, she knew that she would have to fight but not in the way she had seen. Her mission now was to fight those very soldiers she once longed to be. The people of Haella would be free from their poisonous grasp once more.

They left the forest's edge and came upon an old dirt road. Grass grew along the centre of it, but the marks of cart tracks lay either side. *Someone still uses this*, Arica speculated. The sailors and the caster pushed on, their calves starting to tighten. The winding road was not long and soon they reached what was once a gatehouse. It had been to inspect those entering and leaving the city, to decipher whether they be friend or foe. Long had it been since anyone had guarded this city. The building was not much more than broken stone. Ivy twisted its leafy limbs around it. They continued along the path, which had flattened off. Arica took a mouthful from her flask that hung at her hip. They passed more and more ruined buildings as they grew closer to the centre of the city of Rhadirim. Some were in fairly good condition considering the ages that had passed. It appeared as though the city might have been razed by looking at the collapsed towers that sat at the southern, western, and eastern corners of the city. The lone tower to the north Arica spied from the ship remained. Arica tilted her head up to look at the carvings on the ceiling of the archway that led into the central square. They depicted beautiful creatures, some of which Arica did not know the names. Beasts bigger than houses with horns emerging from their face. Horse-like forms with a serpent for a tail. Arica shuddered at the images; strange were the creatures of old.

The archway opened up to a large courtyard. She imagined what might have happened here. Was this the marketplace? Perhaps it was where the townspeople met to gossip. It could have been a training space for warriors. Naima began asking questions and making suggestions about where to look. Both she and the captain discussed where they believed the tomb could be. While they were lost in conversation, Arica walked on. She was admiring the craftsmanship of the derelict buildings and the remnants of statues and pillars. *What a marvel this place must have been*. Even the ground they walked on was made of stone cut into oblong shapes. She too wondered where the tomb could be. Her vision had shown a great stone wall. A natural wall. The cliffside she thought. The cliffs, however, were surrounded by water. There was nowhere to stand on land and observe them. The stone wall must be elsewhere. She paused. Ahead of them, at the end of a long street were steps, cracked and in disrepair. The steps rose high to a colossal ruin. The Celmerien Castle. The home of Arica's ancestors. Arica approached the steps, all the time staring up at the castle. Her feet climbed the steps, carefully avoiding the broken ones.

She went further and further until she was high above the buildings in the lower parts of Rhadirim. The forest spread out to her back while the blue water of the sea unfurled before her on the other side of the castle.

'Preandre!'

Arica turned to see Roe and Naima jogging up the steps behind her. There was a mix of worry and annoyance on their faces.

'We did not know where you went, you have to stay close,' the captain told her sternly.

'A place as old as this, no telling what could be around a corner,' Naima warned.

'Aye, girl, ancient cities hold ancient troubles,' Captain Roe said, his eyes darting around them. Arica knew this man was devout, but superstitious she did not. Did he really believe there was some sort of spell on the city?

'Ah less of that curse nonsense, captain,' Naima said rolling her eyes, 'all that surrounds us is broken rocks and weeds.'

'Do not be so blind, officer,' Roe retorted. Arica noticed the use of Naima's title. 'In a world so full of magic, there cannot only be light. Darkness lives and breathes as truly as a newborn babe.'

'Your darkness will taste my blade if it raises its head,' Naima answered, slapping her hand against her sheath.

'Where would a burial tomb be?' Arica asked, having grown tired of the bickering. She did not have time for the incessant squabbling. The call from the tomb needed to be answered.

'Hmm, a tomb would always be underground. Somewhere deep. Somewhere hidden. A royal tomb would be irresistible to a thief so it would have needed to be well concealed,' Roe explained, his chin lying between his thumb and index finger.

'Let us search the castle, the quicker we begin, the sooner we will be out,' Naima announced, already walking into the ruins.

They searched the ruins from top to bottom. They checked in every room and corner of the castle scouring for any indication of the tomb. All they were met with were crumbling walls, smashed effigies of past rulers and caved in roofs. It had been centuries since this castle had anyone live in it, and it was abundantly clear. No doors or windows remained, only vacant crevices. Fractured pillars stood with little to hold up, most of the upper floors having fallen in. What stone was left over was beautifully carved with impressions of acanthus leaves and flowers. The stonemason that built this castle must have been a master of his craft. Arica's boots clicked against the hard sand-coloured floor. She looked down and noticed that even the floor boasted elegant engravings, these ones in particular caught her eye as they depicted a wolf atop a bed of roses. The symbol. She fiddled with the pin attached to her collar. The pin that matched perfectly with the image beneath her feet.

'Nothing! Nothing but smashed rock and vegetation,' Roe scowled from behind her.

'Sorry Arica, but I didn't see anything either,' Naima appeared from around a pillar.

'This venture is for nought, you said you knew where it was,' Roe said, his eyes still searching.

'I know it's here— I can feel it. It is a wall of stone, natural.' She knew what the wall looked like. She had seen it in her mind's eye. Rough, like the sea-beaten cliffs of the very island she was on. There had to be one like that somewhere amongst all of the remaining walls of the castle. She kicked at the ground, her foot missing the head of a wolf engravement. Its graceful face was looking towards a hallway to her right. This one was different to the others surrounding it. They all looked up, while this one did not. Her eyes followed the wolf's. Arica's feet were following the wolf's gaze without realising and soon she was met by another wolf's head. This one looked down the remains of another hallway. Arica, Naima and Captain Roe all followed the wolves down hallways, up steps, around corners and finally into the throne room. The grand seats of the Celmerien dynasty were nothing more than piles of rubble. Two seats had laid on the pedestal, one for the king and another for the queen.

'This is it? More debris!' Roe spat.

'I don't understand— I was sure of it,' Arica said in disbelief. The wolves should have pointed in the right direction. She felt it in her bones. Her magic was pulling her towards the wolves. The sensation was almost electric. It was as though someone was dragging her to a pillar to the right of the pedestal.

'Waste of time,' the captain groaned, kicking a piece of broken stone.

Arica walked to the pillar where another engraving of a wolf sat on the floor. This time the wolf's face was looking towards her. *This one is like the others*, she thought. This tile was like most of the tiles, staring blankly forward. The others had guided her here. But this tile, despite seeming mundane was different. She crouched low. Her fingers brushed against the cool, ancient stone. The lines and bumps of the engraving felt smooth to the touch. She caressed the ear of the wolf.

'What are you trying to show me?' she whispered to the lupine figure.

Her magic had brought her here. To this room. There must be reason behind it. It was then that Arica noticed the collar around its neck. Nestled in the centre was a pendant, in the shape of a star. Arica's fingers reached for it before finally resting on it. *Click.* A noise like gears began from where, Arica did not know. She jumped to her feet and stood back. Naima ran to her side and put a hand across her, sword drawn. Arica turned her head in all directions, trying to follow the noise. It led her to the pedestal which had started to slide across the ground. *A space below the thrones.* As it moved further to the left, more and more of a winding staircase beneath it was revealed. The whirring of the gears stopped all of a sudden. Arica and her companions moved closer to the top of the staircase. It twisted down, deep into the rock.

'Looks like we found something other than rocks, captain,' Naima stated as she began the descent.

Chapter 32

The spiral staircase descended below the castle into a cavern-like space. The room was dark and smelled faintly of salt. The never-ending darkness spread out before them in all directions. With a flick of the wrist, Arica ignited a ball of warm fire in her palm. The soft orange glow unfurled; their shadows danced behind them. The light opened up the room to them. Thick stone arches formed into a high, vaulted ceiling keeping the weight of the castle up. Arica was amazed at the millennium old architecture that even after all this time still held up the structure. Torches hung from the walls surrounding the room. Arica pushed the fire from her hand and into each of the torches, setting them alight. The three were basking in their glow. The entire room was aglow. Arica gasped. The wall opposite the staircase was the very one from her dream.

Arica stared up at the enormous wall. The rough facade stretched from one side of the room to the other. She took a step closer, never taking her eyes off it. Her thoughts went back to her dream. *What did it show?* Her brow raised as her mind began to work, wondering how she was to open it. She needed a key. But no keyhole existed in this wall.

'How do we do this? Explosives?' Roe asked.

'We set anything off in here and the whole castle comes tumbling down!' Naima protested.

'Listen— can you hear that?' Arica held her hand up. The faintest whisper could be heard in the cavern. She wondered if it could be an echo of some sort, coming from outside. She quickly dismissed that as there was no way any human sound could travel through the thick sandstone. Closing her eyes, she listened to the whispers. A hundred voices, speaking as one. Man. Woman. Child. The voices were unclear at first. They spoke in a language that Arica did not recognise. They wanted her to know something. They were trying to tell her something.

Come…

Arica did as she was told and took a step forward. She was within an arm's reach of the wall. The magic was strong in this place. It made the blood in her veins thump like the slow, rhythmic beating of a drum.

Come…

The whispers repeated itself. Arica did the same. Now, close enough to the wall that she could smell the rock. Her fingers began to tingle, as if to tell her something. Her body was singing, screaming at her. That electric feeling came back to the tips of her fingers. Instinct took over and she raised her hand, placing it against the cold, rough sandstone. Without realising, she had held her breath. She released a heavy breath and waited.

'I'll soon be old and dead,' Roe muttered behind her.

'Patience, captain!' Naima scolded.

Arica ignored the voices behind her and waited. It felt right to be doing this. Her hand belonged there; she was sure of it. The waiting that was in reality mere seconds, felt like hours. Her heartbeat loudly in her chest.

Please, she begged. *Open.*

The whispers stopped all of a sudden. The cavern was eerily quiet. She thought she could hear the waves outside for a moment. Her hand, still against the stone, felt warm at the palm. The warmth soon spread up her arm and to the rest of her body. It was like someone poured sunshine onto her. The warmth flowed around her before, just as fast as it spread, returned to the wall. Gone. Her temperature restored to normal. Arica was taken back, but swiftly rejoiced as an archway appeared where her hand had rested. She did it. She opened the tomb.

'Aha! Well done, girl,' Roe laughed, taking a step forward. Naima stood in front of him. Her eyes were hard on his.

'No, captain. This is *her* family's tomb, only she may go.'

The captain groaned and tried to proceed but the officer held him back. She repeated herself. Only one person would enter that tomb and it was neither of them.

Arica turned to her and smiled. She promised she would not take long and hurried through the archway.

The archway turned into a corridor, wide enough for less than two people standing abreast. If she had raised her arm up, her fingers would brush the ceiling. Thankfully, the corridor was not long and soon she was standing in a room, twice the width of the corridor. Iron sconces hung from the walls, waiting to be lit. Arica sparked little flames on her fingertips and blew them to the sconces. The flames made a *whoosh* as they brightened the room. Slowly, she edged into the centre of the room. A circular shape was etched into the floor with spiky tendrils spreading out, like a sun. Her eyes followed one of the tendrils to the wall. She noticed squares lined up the wall. Upon closer inspection, she saw inscriptions. *Frederic Celmere, Born 537CE Died 610CE. Halanna Celmere, Born 422CE Died 491CE. Meltior Celmere, Born 646CE Died 692CE.* Graves. These burial chambers were where her ancestors were laid to rest. On the other side of the wall, the remains of a dynasty rested. As she moved to the end of the room, some of the squares bore no inscription.

'This must be when the last Celmere left Rhadirim, before adopting Preandre as their new name,' she whispered.

Come…

The same collection of voices spoke to her once again. They wanted her to pursue them. Arica was unsure of where to go as two archways lay before her.

Left or right. She stopped and thought about the dream. Did she go down a hall? She cursed. She could not remember. Looking intensely at the corridors she raised both of her hands. She waited, but only for a moment before her right hand grew warm. *Right*, she confirmed. Her feet carried her quickly down the corridor, getting closer to her destination.

The right-hand corridor opened up into a much bigger room with four corners. Almost a perfect square. Large, black braziers sat in each of the corners. Arica raised her head when she noticed a single stream of yellow light shooting down from the ceiling. High above the floor was an oculus that let in the concentrated beam of light from outside. She questioned where the oculus opened up to. However, it was not truly the oculus that held her attention, but what the light fell on. Awash in the beautiful light, was the stone coffin from her dream. It was elegantly carved with depictions of roses and wolves. The symbols of the Celmere family. Arica moved closer to it, climbing the three steps that led up to the coffin. The carving that lay on the cover of the coffin was the most breathtaking of all. A frame of different leaves and flowers created the border of the cover. The central carving showed a warrior on horseback wielding a sword and shooting magic from her free hand. Arica gasped and clasped her mouth. She could not believe it. If the stories she had loved growing up were true, then these carvings were of the hero she looked up to as a child. Steel and Magic. This coffin was the final resting place of the greatest warrior of all time. Queen Lyneer.

Arica's hands lay flat against the stone slab. The coffin in her dream was Queen Lyneer's. The carvings showed her fully dressed in battle armour. Her long loose hair was blowing behind her, as if a great wind was gusting. She looked so powerful, even in stone form. There was a fierceness in her eyes. Arica had to commend the sculptor to have captured the emotion. The dream had guided her here for something. Something inside the coffin, she realised. A surge of apprehension washed over Arica. *I cannot do that. To open a coffin would be vastly wrong.* But she knew that was what she was meant to do. She sighed in acceptance. As the final part of the breath left her lips her hands grew warm. The warmth radiated from her hands and slowly began to emit an aureate glow that turned the stone incandescent. Arica watched, without flexing a muscle, as the stone began to slide over revealing the contents of the coffin. Arica's hands slipped off the stone as it pulled further away. The stone stopped once it was completely off the coffin. It floated above the ground like it was held up by invisible ropes. Time appeared to stop when her eyes fell on the remains of the great queen. The skeleton was dressed in golden armour. A matching diadem with a beautiful, deep green emerald embedded in the centre had fallen to the side. The queen's arms rested on her stomach where her once strong hands held the hilt of the most marvellous sword

Arica had ever seen. The hilt, like the armour and diadem, was smelted from gold. The blade was long and sleek, as brilliant as it had ever been. Time had not aged or weathered the sword. The coffin had preserved its wonder.

'This is it,' she said aloud. She knew as soon as she saw it. This is what called to her. The dream wanted her to find this sword. Solas, the blade of legend. Those voices had ushered her to this island and into its belly so she would take the sword. Fate had spoken. The ancient sword would lie in the hands of a Celmere once again.

Arica looked at the sword. She admired the sharp lines of the long blade. The edge of the sword was as sharp as the day it was forged. The beautiful piece of weaponry looked back up at her. The longer her eyes lay on the beaten gold and steel the more she noticed the soft yet brilliant glow radiating off of it. It seemed to be pulling her towards it. The tips of her fingers reached for the ancient sword. A humming filled her ears and all around her seemed to fade away. Her hand touched the sword, her thumb caressed the cross guard. The humming faded and was replaced by the whispering voices again. Their words changed from the common tongue to the ancient one she heard before. While her hand was still on the sword, she looked up at the ceiling of the tomb. Arica blinked her eyes, hard. She believed her eyes were playing tricks on her. She wondered if she was having another dream. Floating along the ceiling like a spectral serpent were pale blue streams of light. Arica looked on, confused and afraid. The lights spread out in all directions, moving from the ceiling to the walls and floor. Their voices grew louder. Spirits. Countless spirits glided towards her. Arica let out a gasp as the lights all converged at her feet before crashing into her.

Arica opened her eyes slowly, afraid of what she might see. Her hand remained on the sword. She was still standing in the tomb of her ancestors. But the spirits were gone. The room was solely illuminated from the hole in the ceiling above her. A breath of ease was released. As she lifted her hand off the sword the braziers around the coffin burst into otherworldly blue flames. Arica let out a shriek.

'Peace Arica, all is well,' a voice like liquid-silver crooned.

Arica's eyes shot forward to the other side of the coffin. Her eyes widened at the sight before her. A tall woman with long, dark hair was staring back at her. Her golden armour shone even in the dimly lit room. Her strong face was the colour of cream with eyes like brilliant icy glaciers. Arica had never seen one but had heard about them in a place far to the north. The piercing eyes looked at her, as if into her very soul. There was a coldness to them, but Arica only felt warmth from the woman. Armour made from the sun, Arica thought.

'You have done well, granddaughter,' Queen Lyneer told her.

'It was you,' Arica realised, 'you called me here.'

Queen Lyneer nodded. 'We all did.' She waved her armoured hand, palm up, in front of her. The other spirits. They had all called her here.

'You have travelled much since the Trial, walked many roads and now crossed the sea. You were always meant to come here, to your home.'

'But what is it you called me here for?' Arica asked. She knew there had to be an important reason that the spirits of the Celmere family would call her across land and sea. What she could do for spirits a thousand years old, she did not know. Her grandmother had always taught her to be respectful of those older than her and these spirits certainly were.

'For what is rightfully yours, sweet girl. What lies in my eternal resting place shall be yours,' the queen announced, looking towards the earthly remains of herself. Arica thought how strange it must be to look upon yourself after years of decay. She did not like to think of that for herself.

'Your sword?' Arica gestured at it, 'I cannot take it.'

'You must. With it, you shall free the world from the darkness suffocating it. A black flame has raged the people of Divinios, burning and murdering. It must be quenched,' Queen Lyneer said in a formidable voice. This was the voice of a woman who did not make requests. She made orders and they were followed unquestionably. It was clear to Arica why the stories of

269

the great queen had lived on through the ages. Her power was obvious, even in her ghostly form.

'Take the sword. It will help end this godsforsaken war,' the queen told her. 'Use it to strike down the evil from the world and cleanse it once and for all.'

Arica looked back at the sword. Her hands held either side of the coffin. The power in this sword was immense. Of that, she was sure. If it would help in the fight, she had to take it. Her family heirloom would see the light of the outside world once more.

'What have you there, girl?'

Chapter 33

Arica's heart skipped a beat at the sudden appearance of another voice. Turning on her heel, she released a breath of relief.

'My goddess, captain— it's only you.' Captain Roe stood at the entrance to Queen Lyneer's tomb. She took a step forward to greet the captain, but stopped and watched in silence. Even from this distance Arica could tell his breathing was heavy, as if he had been running. Or fighting. The leather of his jacket was sliced at the shoulder, blood streaked across it. Her eyes went to his right hand where his sword was unsheathed.

'Where is Naima?' Arica asked.

'Ah, Officer Veloras grew restless, so I sent her aboveground,' he stepped forward. 'I see you opened a grave, bad luck that is.'

Arica felt uneasy. She knew the captain was lying. The blood trickling down his arm told her that. She never took her eyes off of him, save for looking at the blank space where her grandmother many times over had stood. The spirit had departed now.

'Why is your sword not in its scabbard? Have we need to be worried?' Arica said, her own hand reaching for the bow slung across her back.

'I'm afraid it grew restless too.'

The captain began to walk toward Arica. His feet seemed to glide across the floor and soon he was into a run. Arica quickly grasped her bow and pulled an arrow from the quiver. She notched an arrow quickly and let it loose at the charging captain. He knocked it aside with a swipe of the sword, continuing his assault. Arica knew she did not have time to do that again, dropped the bow and drew the sword. Before the captain was at the bottom step, Arica jumped and brought her sword down hard. The metal clanged as they struck, the sound echoed around the room. Both Arica and the captain's jaws were set tight, their teeth grinding. Arica slid her sword around, before spinning to launch another hit. Roe deflected this and sliced his own sword, cutting her thigh. Arica bared her teeth in pain. Her eyes met his.

'Why?' this attack made no sense. They were here together. He was an Ebraeyen captain. He was fighting *with* her.

'You have something the king wants,' he said in a chilling voice.

The king? Solomir? Arica's mind raced. The captain was working for the Haellan king. He was a spy. Tasked with worming his way into the Ebraeyen forces. Now, she was alone with him. Arica took her chance and thrust her sword, hoping to make a connection. The captain sidestepped and kicked Arica on the back, knocking her to her knees. Roe dropped his sword to his side, letting the tip scratch against the floor. He was taunting her. Arica gritted her teeth and threw her arm back, hoping to catch him off guard. Nothing but air met the blade. A baleful chuckle rang behind her. He was enjoying this. Arica stood up and faced him.

'What does Solomir need from me?' she asked, her voice rough.

'The king has been searching for something for many years. He finally located it to this very shamble of an island but alas, he could not find it. No matter how long he tried. Or who,' he paused. 'That is, until you.'

The tomb. The captain's impatience in the castle. And in the cavern. This explained it. He thought they were locked out again. She had been the key they longed for. She refused to give them whatever they wanted. If Solomir wanted it, it must be terrible.

'You will not have it!' she spat. The sword of Lyneer, Solas. It had to be the sword. Queen Lyneer spoke of the weapon's great importance. If it could help stop the war it posed a grave threat to Solomir.

'And are you going to stop me? With your bewildering swordsmanship?' he clutched his chest with his free hand and laughed. Anger bubbled in her. He would not disrespect her like that.

Arica pointed her sword at him and walked around him, keeping a wide berth. He copied her movement, legs crossing as he walked. Arica attacked. Her sword met his again and again as they clashed their blades. The impact rang around the room with each slash. Her hands held tightly to the hilt as it vibrated. The captain kept up the barrage of attacks, each as swift and strong as the next.

'Come on, girl. I thought you had more in you!' he mocked.

'The sword will never be yours!' she shouted.

'The sword belongs to King Solomir now, he has decreed it so. The sword that lay in a tomb for a millennium— the sword that would control and destroy all of Vuromel.'

Vuromel? Arica had heard of this place. A chill went up her spine at the mention of its name. The legendary dwelling of the demons of the abyss. She could not let this man use it. Arica knocked a shoulder into his chest, pushing him back. He grinned and swung his sword. It cut her forearm, making her wince.

'So weak! I do not understand why every soul in Divinios is so enamoured by you. All I see is a pitiful little girl afraid of her own shadow. Too frail to defend herself.'

Arica felt the heat in her rise as the words left his mouth. The anger that bubbled, now boiled. The fingers of her free hand twitched. With a scream, she unleashed the flames from her hand. The fire burst before her, scorching her opponent. He roared as the fire burnt him and ate at his jacket. He tore it off, throwing it away. The fury in his eyes was clear.

'Was that enough for you?' Arica said, her voice venomous.

Captain Roe's shoulders were rising and falling heavily. He was angry. Hungry for the kill. And he wanted to be fed. Arica watched on confused as he sheathed his sword. *What are you doing?* She watched as his hands rotated and fingers moved like snakes. He raised hands up and with all the force of a great wave he propelled them forward letting loose an almighty gale. Arica stabbed her sword into the ground, trying to anchor herself. But the wind was too strong. She was blown off her feet and skidded across the floor.

Lying on her stomach, her eyes moved between her sword, out of reach, and Roe who was walking towards her. His sword in his hands once again. Arica's whole body ached. The wind was nothing like she had seen or felt before. Roe must be a master wind caster to have conjured a gust like that. Arica pulled herself to her knees. She lifted her arm to tear the earth under him, but he was already upon her. He kicked her shoulder. She could already feel the bruise that would be there. Roe's cold grey eyes looked down on her. She was tired, her breath was staggered, but she did not break her gaze. He pointed his sword at her face.

'Do you have a message for any of the fools you left behind?' he asked her. 'Although, they will be dead too. Valkor must have appreciated my warning of the strike, I'm certain.'

No. He couldn't have. Arica's heart sank. The attack on Valkor's castle was a surprise attack. They would have walked into a trap. Their plan would be destined to fail. Her friends. Alys... Tamar... Ryger. She felt tears build up in her eyes. *It cannot be true.* She watched as Roe lifted up his sword. *No.* Arica would not allow it. He would not win. She would save her friends. She released a scream as the captain brought down his sword. Arica waited, expecting a blackness to befall her. But nothing happened. She inched open her eyes and saw Roe still standing over her, sword in hand. His eyes were wide, as if staring at a ghost. He coughed and a trail of blood flowed out of his mouth and down his chin. Arica stared at him. Her eyes went down to his chest. To the source of the blood. Like a great arrow through a stag, the resplendent sword of Lyneer, protruded from his chest.

Arica did not believe her eyes. *How?* The sword had gained a life of its own and struck Roe down. Breathing heavily, she stood up. Roe still choked on his own blood as he fell onto his chest, his nose cracking against the hard stone. The sword remained in his back. A golden glow shone before her, behind where the captain had stood. The valorous ghost of Queen Lyneer had appeared again. She had saved her. Without her, it would be her lying on the cold floor and not her assailant. The treacherous Captain Roe.

'Thank you, Queen Lyneer.'

'Speak not of it, granddaughter. Snakes are not welcome on this island.'

'You can still fight, come with me and help free Haella,' Arica said, stepping toward her ancestor.

'Leave this tomb, I cannot. To appear in human form, even, takes great strength,' the queen informed her, 'no. Here I will stay, it is you alone who shall leave.'

The queen turned her back to Arica and looked towards the entrance to her tomb. She held out a hand, as if reaching for something.

'Perhaps not alone, I still sense some life within our family's walls.'

Naima. She was still alive. Of course, Roe had not sent her aboveground, he had tried to strike her down. Naima was loyal to the Ebraeyen people. She had thought the same of Roe, however. She had to go. Naima could be hurt. She would not have let Roe enter the tomb.

'I have to go,' Arica told the queen.

'Take my sword, use it well and save our world,' Queen Lyneer told her descendent as it pulled the sword from Roe's back. Arica took it gingerly from her. She stared down at the blood-streaked blade and wiped it on her trouser leg. It was important to clean your blade; a lesson the swordmaster in Dun Ortha had told her. As she slid the golden sword into her sheath, Queen Lyneer disappeared in a blue-grey haze that rose to the ceiling before dissipating entirely.

'Thank you,' Arica said, her head towards the ceiling. She turned on her heels and ran back the way she entered, hoping to get to Naima before it was too late.

Arica emerged from the Celmere tomb at top speed. Her heart thudded in her chest as her eyes looked around the cavern. She called out Naima's name. Nothing but her own voice echoed back. She moved closer to the staircase that led up to the ruins of the castle. Blood was smeared along the railing in different places. Arica knew Naima must have been losing blood quickly and would not last much longer. Her feet carried her up the steps as quick as they could, the heels of her boots clicking on the stone. She did not know how long she had been in the tomb for but it appeared to be sometime in the evening from looking at the sun's position. It did not take long to find the officer of the *Indrinia*. She was on the floor of the castle, leaning against a time beaten pillar. She was holding her side and her breathing was unsteady.

'Naima!' Arica exclaimed, rushing to her side. She looked over her for injuries. It was clear there was the slash of a sword across the side of her stomach. Apart from that, only a few small cuts and bruises. Arica tore the sleeve from her shirt and pressed it against Naima's side, but the blood did not stop flowing. Naima's eyes flickered open before weakly smiling.

'You beat him,' she mustered.

'I did, he can't hurt us now,' Arica said, meeting her eyes. Panic started to flow in her realising the blood was not going to stop. *What am I going to do? This is my fault.* She thought back on the lessons the masters of Dun Ortha had told her during training. While most of

278

the sessions had consisted of offensive and defensive manoeuvres, she had also learned some ways of healing. A particular lesson from her fire mentor, Varlo, came to mind. *To close a wound, use your fire. The flames will knit shut and burn away any rot.* Fire when uncontrolled destroys all it touches, but the true power of fire is cleansing. Arica had not tried to use the healing properties of the element, but now she must. She lifted Naima's hand and the fabric away from the wound. It was not too deep. Good, she thought. She placed a hand gently onto the wound causing Naima to wince.

'Sorry,' she whispered, 'this will hurt, but it will help.'

Arica closed her eyes. She imagined the fire within her, flickering to life. She commanded the fire to flow down her arms and into her hand. She willed the flames to leave her body and seal the wound. Naima let out a shout of anguish. Her eyes had flashed open from the pain. Arica assured her that the pain would only be short-lived. She held her fiery hand in place until she felt the wound was finally closed. Slowly, she lifted her hand away and saw the wound was sealed again. It would leave a mark, but she would live.

Chapter 34

The sky was a deep navy-blue colour. Thousands upon thousands of gleaming stars spread across the empyrean world above the ship. The sails were full from the strong gusts of wind from the two casters working tirelessly to move across the sea. They had been working in teams of two on the return voyage as they had to warn Jyneera if there was still time. The soldiers would have already left the city and marched on Valkor. If time was on their side, they would reach the mainland and would be able to get a message to the troops before it was too late. Arica looked out on the dark waves as they grew closer to Ebraeye and further away from the Susrials. She had managed to stop Naima's bleeding back on the island, but she had passed out from the pain. A lot of blood had been lost and rest is the only cure for that. Not sure what to do on the clifftop city ruins she sent up a flare with her casting. A local farmer came by with a cart pulled by a donkey that looked like it could be older than her own grandmother. She pitied the grey-haired animal pulling the wooden cart behind her. The farmer put them both onto the cart and brought them back to the fishing village. The sailors from the *Indrinia* rushed to their aid when they saw their officer unconscious and quickly brought her on board. She was lying on her bed below deck. Arica had watched her for the first hour of the journey but went above for air. She needed time to think. What was going to happen when she got back? What was she going to see? What had happened. But worst of all, was she too late?

The sun had not fully broken the horizon when the harbour came into view. The lookout shouted as the first sign of land, the gulls screeching. As the ship sailed closer to the continent more and more of its landscape appeared before her eyes. Arica thought it interesting to see the land appear before her eyes as if it was slowly climbing up from the watery depths of the sea. The sailors rushed around the deck pulling the ropes that shifted the beams and sails. Their calls were carried on the wind, amplifying their voices to louder than they truly were. An older sailor stood at the helm in Roe's place. His fellow sailors were disgusted and outraged when Arica told them of his treachery. She feared they would not have believed if they had not seen the injured officer at her side. Soon the ship was pulling into the harbour and the heavy anchor was dropped into the water. All aboard the ship clambered about to ensure all was secure before they disembarked. A foursome of men carried Naima's sleeping body from the ship. They were bringing her to the infirmary in the Carmine District. The best doctors in the city worked there. She would be nursed back to health before long. Arica walked off the dock where she was met by a stableman holding onto the reins of her beloved Sundancer. She hugged and kissed his muzzle, as she always did. The quartermaster onboard the ship sent a message with a messenger bird that resided in a cage in the captain's room. The black-feathered creature was tasked with flying into the city to announce their return. She wasted no time, thanked the stableman and threw her leg over the stallions back.

The morning sun glittered against the different coloured roof tiles of Dun Ortha's buildings. Sundancer's hooves thudded melodically against the stone roads of the beautiful city. She missed the feeling of riding at full speed, the wind whistling passed her ears. Her horse's cream mane flicked in her face as they reached the courtyard in front of the Azure House. After leaving her horse in the stable and thanking him for his speed, she sped off into the building. She found the Chancellor in her office, not in her usual seated position, but standing, staring out the window. Her dark hair was twisted into a knot atop her head. She was wearing a fitted shirt, tucked into a pair of brown breeches. Black boots completed her outfit. Her dress was much less stately than usual. Jyneera turned to face her visitor.

'You returned quickly.'

'Jyneera, my message— have you stopped the army?' Arica did not have time for formalities. She needed to know the answer.

'Word was sent, whether it reached our people I do not know,' she answered, leaning her back against the window. Arica noticed a strange tremor in the Chancellor's voice.

'Jyneera,' she started but was cut off.

'I should have known— that feeling I had before you left. The ice in my veins. It was telling me about the trap, but I ignored it and because of me— who knows what we have lost.' Jyneera's voice cracked. She blamed herself. If anyone was hurt, she would take the blame for it. Arica knew it was not this way. No one could have known about Roe's treachery. He was a trusted captain of the Ebraeyen forces. He concealed his identity to them all. They all believed in his lie. The fault belonged to not one person. Arica felt anger. There was one person to blame. The one person who was poisoning Divinios. King Solomir of Haella.

'You cannot blame yourself— you could not have known. That feeling could have meant anything,' Arica said stepping closer to the leader.

'I sent those brave men and women into a snare— so many of our best warriors. I can only pray to the gods to show them mercy.' That was the end of the conversation. Jyneera apologised, stating she was too troubled to continue. Arica respected her wish and left the office. The door clicked shut behind her. For a moment she stood outside the door, unsure what to do. It did not take long for the answer to come.

The Azure House, as well as being the central government building, was famous for its expansive gardens. At the back of the building were rows of meticulously trimmed and pruned hedges and flowers. It was clear to anyone who walked in them that magic was alive and not just something humans had the ability to manipulate. The plants were different in this country. In Haella they were simply plants, green and mundane. But here the plants were so unique. The gardens boasted flowers as tall as Hamir. The vines that wrapped around the trees moved like snakes, slow and peaceful. At night the flowers glowed like the lanterns on the city streets. Arica wondered if the Ebraeyen people got the idea for them from the luminescent plants. It was the perfect place to go when one needed time to think. She sat on a rock that overlooked a pond. The pond's green water was home to fish with long, wisp-like tails. Council members would often bring their children here to feed the fish if they had time to spare. Rocks surrounded the perimeter of the pond, framing its contents. She sat for what seemed like hours. She thought about her friends fighting in Aflos, her father and brothers in Harth and what happened on Celaen. Much had happened in the six days since she had left on the *Indrinia*. She looked at the golden hilt of the sword that rested on her hip. She had not even gotten the chance to tell Jyneera what happened on the island. It would be a story for another time. When the fate of the Ebraeyen soldiers in Aflos was revealed. Hunger picked at her; she had not eaten yet. She stood and strolled to the apple trees that sprouted fruit all year long, no matter the weather. Another sign of the teeming magical energy in the gardens. Soon she had eaten two shiny red apples, core and all. Wiping the juice from her lips she turned to return to the rock when she heard her name being shouted. She followed the voice to see her brother running to her. They ran into each other's arms and hugged.

'I am so glad you are back safe, why did you not come to me?' he asked.

'I'm sorry, Malin— I had much to think about.' Arica sat with her brother and told him of her travels. She described their family's ancestral home carefully, not wanting to leave out any detail. She told him of the hidden tomb and the magic that pulled her within. Her brother sat and listened like a schoolboy as his sister explained how the spirit of Queen Lyneer presented herself and gifted her sword to Arica. Malin's expression changed from wonder and awe to disgust upon hearing of Roe's perfidy. When she was finished, Malin placed a hand on hers.

'I am so sorry you had to go through that, sister. The world never tires of its surprises.'

'I certainly have,' Arica declared, 'is life ever going to be simple again?'

Malin did not answer his sister's question at first. He wanted to say the right thing. He wondered if there was a right thing to say. It was true, the siblings had been confronted with many dangers since that day in Harth when they fled their home. In a matter of weeks, they had seen so many different places compared to their entire life before it. The world had grown and would continue to do so as they explored it. Simplicity seemed unthinkable.

'Truthfully, I do not believe so Arica— but with all its intricacies, we have seen some wondrous things and met so many people. Before all of this, we were ordinary townspeople seeking meaning. Now, you are a caster, and I am finally able to live my life as I wish,' he smiled, 'I would not change it for the world.'

Malin put an arm around his sister's shoulders, who in turn, rested her head on his.

Arica spent the rest of the day with her brother. They visited her grandmother and aunt who demanded the story of her journey as her brother did. They listened as intently as adorers at the temples did to a high priest or priestess. Her grandmother's eyes lit up upon hearing of the spirit of the ancient queen appearing.

'Our ancestors favour you, my love. They will watch over you.'

Arica wondered why they would favour her. She had not earned their benevolence. She was born with magic, this alone could not be cause for Lyneer showing herself. Arica did not want to think about it and stowed away in her mind. It was a thought for another time.

In the evening, Malin brought the family to his living quarters. Sandar had been busy cooking a meal for them. Once the women were seated at the table and given drinks, Malin joined Sandar. The two of them worked together to add the finishing touches to the dinner. The smell was glorious, and Arica salivated at the thought of the food. She smiled watching her brother. He seemed so happy now. Sandar was truly a gift sent by the gods. Malin was more comfortable in his own body now than ever before and Sandar was the reason. One of life's welcomed surprises. They ate the expertly cooked venison down to the last morsel. Arica mopped up the remaining juice from the meat with a piece of bread and devoured it. With full bellies, the group moved to the sofa. While the cooks' living quarters were not as lavish, they were bigger. While she had a single room with a bed, sofa and fireplace, her brother had a living area, bedroom and a small space for preparing food. They sat and spoke for hours, laughing at stories and sang a song or two. An evening like this was what Arica needed. It took her mind away from more grim thoughts. She left Malin's room that night with a full belly and a smile on her face.

Chapter 35

It had rained the night before. A silent rain. The smell of fresh rainfall wafted over the city, alerting everyone to its presence the next morning. Light splashes from footsteps could be heard throughout the streets as the people moved around. Hood drawn, the hunter from Harth rushed to the Ring where training would take place. The Ring's usual open roof was covered today with an awning, bearing the black on orange Ebraeyen crest. The few casters that remained to protect the city were already busy training when Arica walked in. Slowly making her way to the smouldering pits of the fire casters Arica pulled on her sleeves. Her eyes had fallen on the one caster she hoped had gone to Aflos. Bretta. Her long, black hair swung behind her as she threw balls of fire at scorched targets. Arica could not help rolling her eyes at the thought of having to practice with her. So few casters were left and Bretta had to be one of them. Even Arica's own mentor was a member of the attack party. With no friendly face to be seen, she approached Bretta and the short and dainty girl at her side. Arica had not seen this girl before. She could not be much older than fourteen. The two fire casters stared as Arica walked over to them.

'Hello Arica, you made it back in one piece,' Bretta announced.

'A few cuts and bruises, but I will live,' Arica answered.

Their conversations were usually like that. Short and quick to the point. Bretta had done nothing but segregate Arica from the rest of the fire casters since her first day of training. There was an animosity between them. For what, Arica did not know. Alys and Tamar thought jealousy was the reason. Arica did not like to think that way, it made her feel conceited. There must be some other reason for her aversion.

'I'm Kailani,' the girl at Bretta's side said, holding her hand out. Arica looked at it for a moment before grabbing it. They shook.

'Arica.'

'I know— I mean, I have heard of you.'

Bretta made an audible scoff.

'You are new?' Arica asked.

'Yes, my magic manifested two days ago. I thought I was an *ordinary* folk,' Kailani started, 'my sister was only seven when her own manifested.'

'A late arrival like my own, I am seventeen,' Arica smiled. Kailani smiled back. Arica knew that magic manifestation was not set to an exact time and place, but most casters knew before their tenth birthdays. It was evident to Arica that this girl had wanted to be a caster for her whole life when she said the word ordinary. Arica could see the benefits of both sides. The magic that lived inside her was not always so malleable and easy to control. Its manifestation was a testament to that.

'I have been entrusted as Kailani's mentor,' Bretta said, pushing herself in front of her mentee.

'A great honour, Bretta.'

'It is, the council knows it's greatest casters.'

'You are truly blessed to have someone with such a strong talent mentoring you,' Arica said holding back the disdain and sympathy. She thanked the gods that Bretta had not been her mentor. She feared she would not have any control over the element if she had been left in Bretta's hands.

The three of them trained together for the remainder of the session, much to the contempt of Bretta. Kailani showed she had potential to be a fine fire caster but struggled to launch fire at a target. Bretta was hard on her, berating her. The scolding was not having the desired effect as the girl was unable to even move the fire at all. She was like a tortoise, retracted into her shell. When the new mentor walked away out of frustration, Arica went to Kailani's side. She got her to stand up straight and to centre on her breathing. Breathing helped the flow of the fire. For her, it focused the raging flames into a controlled stream that she could handle. It was a volatile element that could easily overpower someone. Especially a new caster. Standing behind her, praising her movements, Arica watched as Kailani pulled fire from a pit before throwing at the target. It hit. Not in the centre, but it was a hit. Kailani jumped up and down, cheering. She turned and grasped Arica's hands in her own. She smiled and bowed her head. Their moment was broken up by Bretta bellowing for her to do it again. Arica gave the girl a look of support.

'You can do it.'

Lying on the sofa in her room was where she spent her evening. She did not feel hungry and decided to skip dinner. Her stomach was out of sorts. She was thinking of her friends. She wondered where they were. The message must have been received by now. She prayed it was not too late. The crackling fire burned before. The logs cracked as the fire ate away at its flesh. It was a comforting sound. A sense of security came with a roaring fire. A blanket was draped over her legs, adding to the comfort. She held a cup of tea to her chest, its steam washing over her face. The peace was welcome after her day of training. After the fire session, she completed her rotation of the other elements. She alone was the only earth caster in the Ring. The others were either on mission or on guard along the walls of Dun Ortha. The day crawled by with the absence of voices and her friends. She revelled in the solace of her room. She closed her eyes and leaned her head against the back of the sofa. It was a short-lived silence when a knock thudded against her door. With a displeased sigh, she stood and opened the door.

'Good evening, Arica,' the Chancellor greeted.

'Jyneera! What a surprise, please come in.' She stood back to allow her guest to enter. She closed the door and looked around her room. It was strange having Jyneera's imposing presence in her room. It was not an ordinary occurrence for her to make calls in people's rooms.

'Please, take a seat,' she gestured to the sofa, picking the blanket up off the ground.

'Thank you.' Jyneera sat and crossed a leg. She was wearing a floor-length gown made of navy-dyed silk. It looked beautiful next to her dark skin. Her hair rested on her shoulder.

'To what do I owe the pleasure of your company?' Arica asked, sitting on the armchair next to the couch.

'I realise I was not in the correct frame of mind to speak with you yesterday. When I heard you were absent from dinner, I felt I must come to you.'

'It is not your fault I was not at dinner, I was simply not hungry.'

'That is good to hear,' Jyneera said, 'nevertheless, we still need to speak about Celaen.'

Arica dove into her telling of the story. Jyneera sat and listened with care, not interrupting Arica at any point. It was amazing that her expression never changed, no matter what part of the story she heard. The brilliant mind of the Ebraeyen leader was absorbing all details. After she finished, Jyneera leaned back and held her hands together. A pose of thought.

'Are you certain Roe said *Vuromel*?' her voice said quietly.

'Yes, but it cannot be true, it is a myth.'

'Arica, have you not yet learned that this world is much more than you thought— just as magic lives and breathes on Divinios, it does so in Vuromel too.'

'Then that means— demons are real,' Arica said in disbelief. Another addition to the world she did not know existed. Magic has been a positive force in her world so far, but now she saw the darkness in it. Queen Lyneer had spoken of such a darkness, sweeping the land. Arica thought she had meant Solomir, but perhaps she knew more than she told.

'Solomir intends to open its gates,' Jyneera realised, 'he would unleash gods know what beasts from its depths. For what? They would destroy all who crossed them, regardless of the colours they bear!'

Arica stopped and thought back to what Lyneer had said.

'The sword.'

'Excuse me?'

'The sword— Queen Lyneer's sword,' Arica said, standing. She rushed to the closet nestled in the corner of the room. She pulled open one of the horizontal drawers. Her hands lifted up the tunics within to reveal the sheathed sword. She pulled it from its hiding place and showed it to the Chancellor.

'This sword is the answer, it's why Roe betrayed us. Solomir wants this sword.'

'He must not get it. From what Queen Lyneer told you in the tomb, this sword would give him unbounded power.'

'*The sword that would control and destroy all of Vuromel*,' Arica said slowly, making sure to say it as Roe had.

'If that is the case, Arica, it can never reach his grasp. It would mean the fall of Divinios.'

Jyneera left Arica's room soon after that. She thanked the Chancellor for calling on her and listening to her story. Jyneera nodded her head and left her alone in the doorway. Clicking the door shut, she turned and sat on the edge of her bed. Her eyes went to the golden-hilted sword that lay on the low table next to the fire. *The sword that would control and destroy all of Vuromel*. Queen Lyneer's sword, now hers. What power does it hold? Could it possess the power to control the demons below? Could it give its wielder power of an army of creatures? Arica shuddered as images of what the beasts could look like swirled in her mind. She imagined lizard-like monsters, the size of horses, with blood-red eyes and rows of jagged teeth. Staring out of the drawn back curtains of her balcony, she watched the silver crescent in the sky. Its bright light spread over the city. Dun Ortha's beauty was magnified by the argent glow. The sword would stay in her possession until her last breath, she would assure it.

Chapter 36

It was early morning when the harbinger of the army rode through the city gates. The thundering hooves echoed throughout the empty streets. The denizens of Dun Ortha had not yet risen. The messenger jumped from his steed at the Azure House and ran inside to inform the Chancellor of the army's approach. With no time to waste, all necessary preparations began. The healers in the Carmine District were frenetic to ensure those injured would have a place to rest their heads, and those with severe wounds would be able to be worked on immediately. Before long, the first of the returning soldiers marched through the gates. Their tired footsteps could be heard by all who they passed. Horseshoes clacked heavily against the stone pavements as the tired horses were guided to the barracks stables. The wounded were carried into the Carmine District atop carts. The people of the city were glad to see that so many of those that left had returned. Nevertheless, the cries of those being told that their loved ones had not come home rang throughout the streets. Thousands of people moved about between buildings and streets, searching and finding. The mixture of cheers and howls was deafening.

The final soldiers had entered the city and those that were well enough went back to their homes. Arica had been summoned to the great hall of the Azure House. The room was not often used. The Chancellor used this room to host guests and foreign dignitaries. Lavish parties and grand meals were held inside its walls. Arica had not been there before in all of her time in Dun Ortha, and she wished it was under different circumstances. She had been summoned there by Jyneera, much to her surprise. She had not expected to be included in the meeting. The council members were waiting in the great hall, along with the returning generals. A large table had been set up. Jyneera sat at the head of the table. Arica entered and approached, sitting on the bottom left side. She had still not heard from her friends and did not know if they had returned. While she watched from her balcony, seeing other soldiers reunited with their friends and family, she waited for her own. Trying to spot the midnight-haired twins or the tattooed water caster. But nothing.

'Firstly, I would like to welcome back our generals and thank them for their service,' Jyneera began, signalling applause for the men and women. Arica could see that some wore bandages. A sign of battle. She also noticed that there were fewer generals present than she thought there would be. She prayed that this was the correct number and not a diminished one.

'Now, I ask that you all bow your heads in prayer in honour of those who have not returned. Bastus, carry

296

them in your arms to your eternal home.' Arica did as she was told. She asked the god of death to take care of those who had passed. Afterwards, she wished for a sign that her friends were all right.

'I ask you, General Felen, would you give us detail of what occurred?' A tall woman with brown hair pulled into a knot stood. Her right forearm was wrapped in an off-white bandage. Arica could see droplets of blood soaking through.

'Yes, Chancellor.'

The general began to retell the events that led up to the attack. They thought that everything had been going according to plan. The army marched along the foot of the mountain as they left the Ebraeyen highlands and entered Aflos. The scouts ahead of them went back and forth, telling them their path was clear. There had been no sighting of Amber Lions at any point of their journey. Arica shook her head. That should have told them something. Of course, the Lions would be roaming about the country. They had overthrown its monarchy. They were reaping the benefits of the once affluent land.

'When we were within view of the castle, we set the casters to work as we planned, Chancellor. The fire and water casters reached the beach and began to spread the mist. It washed out everything below the castle's wall. All was going well— or so we thought.' Felen rested her hands on the table and dropped her head. Arica's stomach felt as though hands had gripped it and was twisting slowly. Felen inhaled deeply before continuing.

'When we sent in the foot soldiers to begin the attack it did not take long to realise that there was something unsettling afoot. A hundred Lions— that was all that protected their Aflosi stronghold. I quickly called for a retreat, but it was too late.'

Arica watched as Felen slammed a fist against the tabletop.

'I am sorry, Felen, if it pains you too much perhaps another can finish?' Council Member Frei suggested from across the table.

'No, it is my duty. Forgive me.' She inhaled again. Arica and the others gathered around the table listened as the general told them about the trap.

As the soldiers were told to retreat, they heard a screeching. A guttural pained screech. The noise was coming from inside the castle. Soon, more screams could be heard. Screams of the Ebraeyen soldiers still within the castle's walls.

'It was horrible,' another general whispered.

Those outside the walls watched as the soldiers tried to escape their fate. The men and women were being chased by something none of them had seen before. At first, they believed they were other people. But quickly they realised they were something abhorrent. People with claws and fangs were tearing the Ebraeyen soldier's limb from limb. Many tried to defend themselves, but ultimately fell. The earth casters tried to cover them by breaking the ground beneath the assailant monsters. It halted them for a moment as they judged the distance. They began throwing themselves across the fissure, whether they could reach the other side or not. The rest of the casters joined the fleeing soldiers and used their magic to protect who they could. The order was to retreat to the Ebraeyen-Aflosi border and wait.

'After that, it was all hazy— we ran for our lives. These creatures were so like us, yet, twisted,' Felen stated. 'We fled, but a great number stayed and fought.'

Arica shuddered. The creatures. They had to be like the girl she had seen in Serpent's Hollow. Her body felt cold as she remembered the chilling voice that called to her from outside her cell in the castle. Those creatures had attacked them. Valkor used them. They were the trap.

A few moments passed before anyone around the table spoke. They were all trying to absorb what General Felen had told them. It was clear that they were distressed by this new type of enemy. They were not new to Arica, however. The mark that the one in Valkor's castle had left on her arm was still visible. Jyneera cleared her throat before speaking.

'Do we know how many were lost?'

'We do not know exact numbers as of yet, Chancellor. But we believe it to be near four hundred dead with a further two hundred injured,' a general with a patch covering an eye answered.

'Near six hundred— this is a great blow,' Jyneera said as she paced away from her seat. 'Hamir?'

'Yes, Chancellor?' Hamir asked from behind her.

'See to it that all families of our lost brothers and sisters receive reparations. Their sacrifice will not be forgotten.'

Hamir bowed his head and left the room.

The meeting was adjourned. Jyneera stood and shook hands with each of the generals in the room before taking her own leave. The room emptied and soon Arica was standing outside the grand door. *Four hundred dead*, she thought. She could not bear the thought that her friends were among them. She would not rest until she knew the truth. It was swiftly decided upon that she would go to the Carmine District and search for them. The city was alive now. The residents hurried about the streets getting on with their ordinary lives despite the catastrophe that took place in Aflos. Arica wondered if they even realised what had happened. The Cerulean District appeared normal to her. There was no air of panic surrounding the streets as the people went about their day. It was strange given the meeting that had just taken place. Arica's mind was racing as she thought about the creatures running down the soldiers. Felen's retelling had given her chills. She herself had survived one such creature months ago in Cothomir's house. She recalled the sickly yellow colour of the girl's eyes and the hard, scaled hands that tried to slash her. She rubbed at her forearm where she had been scratched by the talons in Valkor's Castle. A horde of the same creatures had killed hundreds of Ebraeyen men and women. She could not help but feel pity for the poor girl in Serpent's Hollow at the time, but now it was hard to feel anything other than rage and contempt.

Before long, Arica was wandering the streets of the Carmine District in search of her friends. This part of the city looked the way that she expected it would after an army returned from an attack. People rushed through the streets, weaving their way between others to get to their destination as quickly as possible. She looked in every building she came across and asked countless questions to the healers working there. She was not the only one doing this as she noticed a number of other people asking about their loved ones who had not come home. Some had received the answer they had wished not to get. Floods of tears and cries of anguish were the usual responses. She felt sick to her stomach, hoping she would not hear the same answer. Arica recognised casters that she had trained with in the Ring and ordinary folk soldiers she had sparred with. Some had broken bones and lacerations, but others were not so lucky. Arica saw several of the returning soldiers had lost a limb. The serrated claws of the creatures, Arica presumed. The blood-soaked bandages could only do so much for them, Arica feared they would not survive. It was a blessing they had even made it back to the city without succumbing to their wounds. The healers would do everything they could to save them.

Arica walked into a red brick building with a wide door at the front. Wide enough to carry injured people inside she thought to herself. The room was busy. People were spread out on beds that lined the entire length of the room. Orbs of warm orange light hovered along the walls, casting a soothing glow on the patients. The glow, however soothing, could not block out the groans or screams of the ill-fated men and women in the beds. Her eyes fell on each bed, reading each of the faces and searching for the ones she knew. Many faces past her. A bare-chested man with a bandage wrapped around his stomach. A woman covered in scratches and bruises. A girl no older than Arica on the next bed was missing a leg below the knee. A lot of hurt and pain. There was a strong smell of herbs and incense to try and cover the smell of rot and decay. She knew that many of the people around her would not make it much longer, and a further amount would carry this attack with them forever.

Arica moved on past more beds, smiling at the soldiers who were conscious and able to see. It was difficult to see so many people in agony. Her friends had to be here. A sheet hung from an archway, dividing the room in two. Arica reached for it and tugged it gently open, revealing another room with more beds. The smell persisted here; the malodorous stench of the incense made her wrinkle her nose. A man to her right made a moan, clutching his stomach. A healer was rubbing a reddish-brown salve on a wound on the man's thigh.

Arica turned her head away and continued along the room but stopped to ask a portly man holding a bottle of ointment about her friends. He shook his head apologetically when asked about Ryger but pointed at the back of the room where a corridor veered to the left when Arica mentioned the twin earth casters. Thanking him quickly, she rushed to the corridor that led into the third and final room of the building. Her eyes darted around taking in all of the people. She could not control the tears that cascaded down her cheeks as she ran to her friend's bedside. Alys was asleep as her sister held her hand as she watched her. A thick bandage was wrapped around her head, covering one of her eyes. Other than that, she remained unscathed. Tamar turned and looked up at Arica and they flung their arms around one another. Neither of them spoke at first, holding each other and shaking from crying. Their grip was tight for fear they would lose one another if they did. When they both had stopped crying, they relinquished the embrace. Tamar sat as Arica knelt beside her.

'I am so glad you both are all right, I have checked everywhere for you— I feared th—' her voice cracked. Tamar squeezed Arica's hand.

'We are alive. Bruised and cut, but alive,' Tamar admitted, 'thank you for looking for us.'

'Her eye?' She could see that the skin around it was bruised. The blue-black colour looked painful. Arica hoped she had gotten some pain relief from the healer.

'One of the creatures scratched her, we do not know the severity as of yet— the healer thinks she may lose it.' Arica shook her head as the words left Tamar's lips. Her eyes went to the floor. 'If that is all she suffers we will be lucky, at least she is here with breath in her lungs.'

Arica nodded and gave a smile to her friend. She had to be strong for her. Whatever pain she felt on Alys' behalf, it must be felt thrice over by her sister.

'And you?'

'Nothing but a scratch along my back. I was towards the rear of the attack; Alys went ahead to make the fissure to slow down the creatures. That's how they got her— so brave.' There was a mixture of sadness and pride in Tamar's voice. Her sister was all that was left of their family and home. If she lost her, Arica did not know what would happen. They were safe. They were home. That is all that mattered.

'Good. Dorcoga was with you on the battlefield,' Arica told her as she said a prayer of thanks to the goddess of war.

'Indeed. I will leave an offering at her temple.'

Grateful for finding her friends, she felt a sense of relief. But Arica knew what she had to ask next. The fear of reality was holding her back, but she knew the question must be asked.

'Where is Ryger?'

She knew the answer the second it left her mouth. The look on Tamar's face told the tale. Her eyes went glassy and her lips curled down at the edges. Arica felt sick to her stomach. She could not believe it. The worst had become true. Ryger was gone.

Chapter 37

She did not sleep that night. The fire burning in the room had made it unbearable to sleep beneath the covers, so she had kicked them off. She stared at the ceiling above her bed for hours upon hours wondering why it had happened. The world had become darker to her. The first person who she could call a friend in Ebraeye had perished. With each breath she felt the despair deeper and deeper. She had crumbled into a thousand pieces when Tamar told her that Ryger did not rejoin the group after the attack. They had waited as long as they could but had to move on for fear that the creatures or the Lions would catch up to them. Tamar told her how she had cried as they were ordered to return to Dun Ortha. As she sat on the cart next to her sister and a group of other soldiers, she looked back and hoped to see him on the horizon. He never appeared.

Arica thought how he must have felt. Scared. Panicked. He was brave, braver than anyone she knew but he was faced with something no one had seen before. The creatures swarmed on the soldiers and mauled them. Ryger would have been below the castle on the beach with the water and fire casters. The mist they made would have blanketed the bottom of the castle and lowered the visibility. Arica knew that he would have ran to aid his fellow soldiers once the screaming began. She knew that was what he did. His very being would have been pushing him to save everyone around him. It was his greatest fault that he felt the need to help anyone in peril. He had told her so that night many months ago in the clearing. Something in his past made him this way. Arica presumed it was what brought him to Dun Ortha and into the war. Realising that she would not sleep tonight, Arica got dressed and left her room. She looked at the three doors along the hall where her three friends should be sleeping. Tamar stayed in the infirmary with her sister, as Arica would have done for her brothers if they were hurt too. She rested a hand on the wooden door of Ryger's room. She pursed her lips as her fingertips pressed harder into the wood. She made a fist and pounded lightly on it before descending the staircase. Her mind went cloudy. Sleep may not have come to her but the exhaustion from a long day of crying and worrying had caught up with her. The day had been spent sitting with Tamar and Alys until it became dark and she returned to the Azure House. Alys woke briefly and managed to speak a few words before falling asleep again.

Arica found herself standing in the gardens late into the night. The dew on the grass left splatters of water on her boots. Lifting her chin towards the night sky, she stared up at the thousands of stars. The glinting balls of light covered the purple-black plane in exquisite beauty. The winter air was cold but did not bite. No clouds in the sky meant no rain. A beautiful winter night. Arica strolled over to the stone bench that lay in the centre of the lawn, facing a sundial carved from white granite. She stared at its surface, dull on this night due to the lack of a bright full moon. Unaware of what time it was, Arica looked out into the distance. She sat there for hours, not knowing what she thought about. All she knew afterwards was that her world would be emptier from now on.

The infirmary was as busy as it had been the previous day. The healers worked from dusk to dawn, ensuring all of the injured soldiers were seen to. It was clear more of them had been lost during the night as empty beds were scattered throughout the rooms. Some had yet to be emptied with sheets drawn over the faces of the deceased. Now she understood why the strong scent of incense burned. Upon arrival she was glad to see her usually cheerful friend was seated upright and eating some bread. Alys smiled as she saw her approach and waved. Tamar spun around and smiled too.

'You look better,' Arica said sitting on the edge of the vacant bed next to Alys.

'I feel it. Can't *see* it as well as before, however.' Arica did not know how to react to that. Alys did not give her any other way to react when she herself burst out into laughter. Her sister did the same. She reached for Arica's hand. 'I'll be fine, one eye or not, I am still the greatest earth caster the city has ever seen.'

'Second greatest,' Tamar chimed.

'You are both fantastic,' Arica stated before the sisters began to squabble. 'What has the healer said? Can you come home?'

'Last we spoke, he said the wound was healing well but could still get infected if I am careless so I will be staying here for another few days,' Alys admitted.

'You will be out by week's end,' her sister said, full of assurance. 'And back in the Ring showing us all what an awe-inspiring caster you are.'

'They will be missing me, I suppose,' she laughed.

Arica adored seeing Alys in high spirits. It was as if nothing had happened to her at all. She remained to be the positive light of their small group. It was then that two familiar faces entered the infirmary and stood next to Alys' bed.

'Good morning, Alys. Happy to see you are awake,' Malin said leaning in to hug her. Sandar followed with the same action. 'Tamar,' he added, smiling at her. They did not hug her as they knew she was not as affectionate as her sister.

'Hello boys, thank you for coming,' Alys smiled. 'What is that?'

Sandar held out his hands to her so she could see better. In a small, woven basket was something covered with a blue cloth. He pulled the cloth off and revealed fresh buns. They were still warm. Alys' smile grew bigger. They knew the way to her heart.

'Oh, thank you so much!'

'We thought you would grow tired of whatever food you get in here. You deserve something sweet,' Sandar told her as he left the basket on her lap. She looked like any child staring into the bakery window. The gift was greatly appreciated.

The friends sat and spoke long into the afternoon. They told tales and joked about the many funny things that happened since the Preandres had lived in the Azure House. Tamar had tears in her eyes as she reminded them of the time when Council Member Frei fell after the tail of her cloak got caught under her shoe. Arica recalled how angry Frei had gotten when she saw them laugh. It was the first time Arica saw the fierce side of the woman.

Arica left to return to the Azure House with her brother and Sandar when Alys said she had grown tired. The friends said their goodbyes and left the Carmine District as the bells of the temples began ringing. Each day at midday the priests and priestesses would ring the bell of the temple in which they served. It was a comforting sound. Arica had not been to a temple in a long time. Since her time in Fiermor, she realised. Making a swift decision, she changed her route waving to the men. They continued towards the Azure House while Arica headed for the Viridian District, home of the gods. It was the smallest district as it only held the

310

temples to each of the deities as well as a home for the priests and another for the priestesses. As she crossed the bridge that led to the district, she instantly saw the signs of the gods and Goddesses' presence. Sacred white flowers grew all over in flower beds and hanging baskets. The priest and priestesses were nowhere to be seen. No citizens of Dun Ortha were visiting at this time either. *Strange.* Arica presumed the priests and priestesses were in their living quarters. The temples lined the border of the island, all facing into a central courtyard where a beautiful fountain trickled. Each of the gods were represented on the fountain; A spear for Dorcoga, an owl for Rhialgir, a net for Farrig, a staff with a skull on one end and a flower on the other for Bastus, among many others. It was marvellous craftsmanship. Arica admired it as she walked towards a tall temple made from cream-coloured stone. A large archway led into a bright room lit by the light pouring in through the glass windows above her head. A space in the middle of the room lay bare for when the high priestess would speak to the acolytes or worshippers. Carvings of oxen, rabbits and deer being hunted by packs of wolves coated the walls. The predators ran after their prey and worked as a group to take down bigger animals. They never took more than they needed. It was the way of nature. Arica brushed her fingers along the grooves of the carvings as they guided her into another, smaller room. This room was big enough for one person to pray alone and the tall statue carved from a pale pink stone of the goddess Merenia. The goddess was accompanied by her wolf as usual. The statue's eyes stared out into the bigger room as if to watch over her flock. Arica knelt in front of the statue and bowed to the goddess before resting her hands, palms down, on her lap.

'Merenia, Lady of the Hunt, Protector of the Wilds, I beseech you. I adore you. I worship you,' Arica began with the traditional prayer to call the goddess. It was the same prayer she used each time she visited her temple in Harth. Her grandmother had taught it to her at a young age. They both shared the reverence towards her.

'Much has happened since I visited your home last. I have discovered magic. I am a caster. A different kind of one, although I do not know why I was chosen to have this gift. It has opened a whole new world for me. This world is filled with danger, but also many wondrous things. I have learned much and met so many wonderful people. Somehow, I cannot help but think you guided me here by some intervention. I thank you— but, I must ask you one thing. Please, watch over Ryger's spirit. Protect him in the afterlife, as you have done so for me in this world.'

Arica bowed again and paused for a time. She stood again, kissed two of her fingers and touched the heart of the statue. She turned on her heel and set out to return to the Azure House. She left the temple and entered the courtyard again. She had barely reached the fountain when a breeze blew strands of hair against her cheek.

Arica turned around and saw a beautiful woman with a waterfall of golden hair flowing behind her. A soft white light radiated from her as if hundreds of stars were at her back. A sleek, curved bow made of white oak hung across her back next to a quiver of gold-tipped arrows. Her eyes were a warm brown that almost appeared golden. Arica's eyes fell to the woman's side where a great white wolf strode next to her. The wolf's icy eyes stared into her green ones. They knew each other.

'You were the wolf in the forest.'

The wolf dipped his head in answer. The woman next to him brushed her hand along his head. They approached Arica and stopped before her. Arica was mesmerised by the woman she had looked up to for so long.

'Merenia?'

The goddess gave a kind smile before she answered in a voice like silver. Each word she spoke held great power. Arica was in shock and awe.

'I have been watching you, child,' the goddess said.

'Watching me?' Arica asked.

'Yes. I watch over all of my pack as if they were my own children,' she answered. Arica noticed the use of the word "pack". A sign of her affinity with the animal at her side.

'My goddess, why have you come here? Have I wronged you?' Arica asked, worried that somehow an action of hers had offended the goddess before her.

'Be still, Arica. Do not fret,' Merenia said as she cupped Arica's face in her soft hand. Her thumb caressed her cheek. Arica felt relief wash over her. 'I thought it was time we met. Makteera has told me of your bravery.' Merenia gestured at the wolf.

So that is your name.

It is.

Arica's eyes shot wide. The wolf could hear her thoughts. He could answer them with his own. His mouth did not move. He only watched her with his frosty eyes. She wondered if the wonders of magic would ever cease.

'Magic is all around us, Arica. In the earth, in the sea— It is in you. You have been granted great power,' Merenia told her.

'Why was I granted this magic, my goddess?' Arica asked, realising that the goddess could also hear her thoughts.

'For centuries we have waited. We waited and watched for someone who would protect this world from a darkness that would ensnare it. That darkness is coming. From the moment you were born, you were destined for greatness.'

'How am I to protect the world? Queen Lyneer gave me her sword and I have my magic, but— I cannot save the world.'

'Save it, you can. Your gods given magic merged with the ferocity of the golden sword will eradicate the blight of the world.'

'How?' Arica was concerned. She still did not understand how she could do it. Her ancestor and the goddess expected much of her. She did not believe that she was the answer to their prayers.

'Arica, you are the daughter of fire, water, earth, and air. Kissed by each element. You have great skill after such little time, why do you think that is?'

Arica did not answer. She did not know. She did not think she would ever know. Every time she asked, she was met with more riddles and questions. Her greatest desire was to know the reason she had been granted the magic and why had Lyneer chosen her.

Think, girl.

Arica looked at the wolf, Makteera. His eyes were on hers. *Think? I do not know what to think.*

'I do not know, goddess.'

'You are blessed by the gods. You are the chosen one. Your magic manifested when it was meant to. Not late as you have been told. If your magic awakened any sooner your path would have changed drastically. The magic has lived inside you, waiting to be set free. The longer you possess the magic, the stronger it will be. It was my duty to watch you grow and to help you when the time was right.'

Arica was speechless. The chosen one. Her mind swirled with thoughts about the divine providence that had watched over her since birth. She finally understood why she had always felt an affinity with Merenia. The goddess had taken care of her for her entire life. Perhaps

315

her grandmother knew, and this is why she would bring her to the temple.

'Know this, my child. Great adversity lies ahead. The journey will be arduous, but you will prevail if you are true and believe. Trust those close to you. Trust in the sword. Trust in your magic. Together you shall destroy the darkness and illuminate Divinios.'

As the final word left her lips, Merenia took a step back and before Arica could say another word she vanished in a haze of fog. As the fog dissipated the sounds of the city returned. Arica had not noticed their absence. They seemed overwhelmingly loud at first, but soon her ears adjusted. She looked around for any sign of the goddess and her wolf but they were gone. All of a sudden, the courtyard was crowded with people. Arica watched as priests and priestesses moved from their living quarters to the temples, their white robes flowing behind them. They all looked the same apart from the different coloured stoles around their shoulders. She spied the pale pink that signified Merenia. The priestess that wore it was young with the same blonde hair of the goddess. Arica wondered where the people suddenly came from before thinking that maybe the goddess had something to do with it. She took one last look around the Veridian District for some sign of the goddess before turning on her heel, crossing over the bridge and headed for home.

Chapter 38

The waning gibbous moon was obscured by thick clouds. Snow had fallen the last two days, leaving a serene white blanket across the city and its surroundings. Caretakers were assigned to clear the streets for the people, horses, and wagons to be able to move freely. The city had settled back to normality following the attack. The soldiers who could return to training did so, whether it be in the training grounds for weaponry or the Ring for casting. The numbers in the infirmaries had dropped to only a small number remaining for observation to ensure their wounds healed correctly. There was a gathering in the square outside of the Azure House to honour those who had not returned. The acolytes of Bastus lit a huge pyre atop the steps where the high priest recited the funeral rites for the deceased. Many tears fell that night. Arica was wrapped up in a thick, fur cloak next to Malin, Sandar, Khea and her grandmother watching the pyre. The family huddled close together, protecting each other from the cold as well as the sadness. She was glad Malin had Sandar. He deserved to be happy. However, as well as being a funeral, it was a celebration of their brave sacrifice. Jyneera spoke to the masses after the high priest finished. She was an excellent public speaker, her strong voice carried across the square on magical winds blown by a wind caster. She commended each and every one of the lost soldiers by name, including Ryger Alfarion. His name would live on forever.

Alys was allowed to return to the Azure House on the condition she did not return to training for another month. She joked that she almost regretted leaving the infirmary because of the fussing from the handmaids. Her sister was worse than the handmaids, never leaving Alys' side. Arica visited her each evening after dinner before going to her own room. It was her favourite time of the day. Malin and Sandar would join them on the days they could get away from the kitchen or convince someone to clean up for them. The group of five would talk until late but soon night's spell of sleep would fall on them and carry them to their rooms. On that night, Arica waved goodbye to her friends and went into her room. The fire, already burning, had warmed the room. Arica kicked off her boots and walked barefoot to the door leading to the balcony. She pulled it open and stepped out. She watched the glowing orbs lighting of the streets of the city. It was truly an alluring sight. The city glowed. It was the only sign of warmth on that winter night. The snow appeared a pale green from the light cast on it. It matched the green capped towers and buildings of the city. Even now, after so many months living here, her breath was taken away by it. She inhaled deeply and breathed out. She squeezed the railing of the balcony once before turning around and going back inside. The door clicked as it closed. Arica undressed, leaving the clothes draped over a chair. She stood at the fire, her back to it, to warm herself up. After some time, she crept into the bed that faced the fire. She wondered if she would sleep tonight as her mind was busy with thought. But no sooner had her head touched the pillow her eyes began to become heavy and drowsy. Arica fell into a deep sleep.

She awoke in a room she did not recognise. It was dark and tight. Feeling around for something to anchor her she found something hard and smooth. A table, she thought. Her hands guided her forward along the endlessly appearing room. A bright flash filled the space around her and she found herself standing outside in a large field of green grass. Tall oak trees dotted the area around her. Thick branches held many bright, green leaves. *Green leaves? In winter?* Arica was confused as it had just been snowing a moment ago. She took a step forward, the grass brushing against her ankles. The day was bright but upon looking she realised there was no sun in the sky. *What is this place?* She moved forward, stopping to stand in the shade of a great oak. The tree sat atop a hill that overlooked the entire plain. Her eyes surveyed the area. Nothing. Nothing but more grass and more hills. Snap. she turned quickly and saw a wolf. A white wolf. Blue eyes stared up at her.

'Hello Makteera.'

Arica.

'Where am I?'

Follow me. The wolf turned around and began running away. Arica did not have time to think and took off after him. It was difficult to keep up with an adult wolf but she did her best. There had been nothing as far as her eye could see on the hill but soon they reached a lake. The lake was large and shaped like an egg. Makteera turned and sat on the shore.

'Why are we here?'

Water reveals secrets. It knows all. The wolf turned his neck and looked at the rippling water. His black nose pointed to where Arica must go. She did not question what the wolf said. She understood. She stepped to the water's edge and looked in. The ripples moved like serpents, slow and steady. Her eyes followed one ripple from the centre. It grew from a small circle into a bigger one until it broke and disappeared. After the ripple broke the water grew still, like a mirror. Her reflection looked back at her. She blinked. The water began to shimmer until she no longer saw herself. She was looking into the bedchamber of a stone building. *Whose room is this?* A huge four poster bed dominated the room with red satin sheets and a dark canopy drooped over the top. The furniture was made from dark wood. The large, hulking door opened with a slam. A man dressed in black with a cloak of rich crimson draped over his shoulders entered the room. Arica had never seen this man before but she knew him. She had heard about him her entire life. The tales of his bravery in war, that she now knew were lies, were known by every man, woman and child in Haella. She was looking at King Solomir.

'Solomir?' she exclaimed, looking at Makteera.

Focus. Listen. Learn.

Arica turned back to the water. Solomir had moved to the desk next to his bed and was reading a letter. His eyes darted from side to side as he went through its content. Upon finishing he made a sound of satisfaction.

'Excellent,' he mumbled to himself, unaware of Arica. 'The experiments have worked marvellously. The trap in Aflos went off well. The Ebraeyens will think twice before launching an attack on me!'

Arica grimaced. The smugness of the king was sickening. She knew it had been a trap but to hear it come from his mouth made her angrier. He had ended the lives of so many people. *You would not be so brave to face them yourself, king.* The title of king was usually used with reverence, but when she used it she meant the opposite. Solomir sat at the desk and grabbed hold of the white-tipped quill. He dipped it into a pot of deep red ink. The quill scratched against the parchment. *What are you writing?* Solomir finished and blew on the ink to dry. He folded it and grabbed his wax before melting some. He allowed three drops to fall on the parchment. He pressed his seal into and stood. He pulled a rope that rang a bell, summoning a skinny servant boy. He took the letter gingerly from Solomir.

'Ensure this gets to Lord Valkor immediately. He must know to move on Ebraeye's borders.'

'Yes, Your Highness.'

Solomir paced back.

'Now to return to my guest,' he smirked. Solomir slowly turned his head towards Arica. He looked straight into her eyes and turned to face her. His smirk grew into a grin and he bellowed loudly. Arica jerked back and fell onto the shore. When she stood the water returned to normal. *He knew. He knew I was watching him.* Arica grinded her teeth. *What did that message say?* She still felt a seething rage when she heard Valkor's name. The very mention of it turned her stomach. She hated him. *What did he mean by* guest?

In time you will understand. Arica looked at Makteera. The wolf was standing up.

'Do you know? Tell me.' She demanded.

It is not for me to reveal the future. Use this knowledge.

'Help me to understand.'

You will in time. Farewell, Arica.

Before she could protest the wolf was gone. He vanished before her very eyes. She was alone. She turned to look at the water where Solomir had been a moment before. *Experiments? What guest?*

Arica awoke the next morning feeling heavy. She had slept through the night but felt as though she woke up many times. Her head hurt; she pressed her hand against her forehead. Sitting up, she saw the extinguished remains of the fire. It was early, the handmaid had not yet reignited it. Her mind went to her dream the previous night. Solomir was planning something. She got out of her bed and quickly pulled on trousers and a shirt. She hurried from her room and knocked on the door next to her room. She did not wait for someone to open it. Alys shot up on the bed, while Tamar rolled off of the sofa. She did not appreciate being woken so early if Arica could judge by the look on her face.

'Arica! I doubt even the cooks have begun breakfast,' Tamar chided.

Arica told the Olfaris twins about her dream. She discussed the wolf and the vision in the lake. Tamar and Alys appeared unsettled by the idea that Solomir had seen Arica watching him. They worried that perhaps he could do it again.

'I have to go there,' Arica stated.

'No. It is too dangerous,' Tamar exclaimed.

'It could be a trap. What if he intended on you seeing him?' Alys suggested.

Arica had not thought of that. What if the wolf was not the messenger of Merenia? He could have been an apparition of Solomir.

'And the Lions are moving on us! We must stay here to fortify the borders,' Tamar said with confidence.

'You're right. If they think they can come here and win, we will teach them otherwise.'

Arica left her friends to return to sleep. She closed her door and sat on the bed. The dream was clear. An attack was being prepared. Valkor's castle was just the beginning. An invasion was coming, she just did not know when. She would tell Jyneera later in the morning at an acceptable time. Waking her friends was one thing, she did not intend on seeing Jyneera's wrath at being woken up. Arica would be prepared for this attack. She would train harder than ever before. Her eyes went to the golden sword of Lyneer leaning against the wall. With sword and magic she would avenge those lost. She would avenge Ryger. She would set Divinios free.